BEYOND
INNOCENCE

Praise for LAMBDA Literary Award Finalist Carsen Taite

"Law professor Morgan Bradley and her student Parker Casey are potential love interests, but throw in a high-profile murder trial, and you've got an entertaining book that can be read in one sitting. Taite also practices criminal law and she weaves her insider knowledge of the criminal justice system into the love story seamlessly and with excellent timing. I find romances lacking when the characters change completely upon falling in love, but this was not the case here. As Morgan and Parker grow closer, their relationship is portrayed faithfully and their personalities do not change dramatically. I look forward to reading more from Taite."—*Curve Magazine*

"Taite is a real-life attorney so the prose jumps off the page with authority and authenticity. [*It Should be a Crime*] is just Taite's second novel...but it's as if she has bookshelves full of bestsellers under her belt. In fact, she manages to make the courtroom more exciting than Judge Judy bursting into flames while delivering a verdict. Like this book, that's something we'd pay to see."—*Gay List Daily*

"Taite, a criminal defense attorney herself, has given her readers a behind the scenes look at what goes on during the days before a trial. Her descriptions of lawyer/client talks, investigations, police procedures, etc. are fascinating. Taite keeps the action moving, her characters clear, and never allows her story to get bogged down in paperwork. *It Should be a Crime* has a fast-moving plot and some extraordinarily hot sex."—*Just About Write*

"Taite's tale of sexual tension is entertaining in itself, but a number of secondary characters...add substantial color to romantic inevitability."—Richard Labonté, *Bookmarks*

In Nothing but the Truth..."Author Taite is really a Dallas defense attorney herself, and it's obvious her viewpoint adds considerable realism to her story, making it especially riveting as a mystery. ...I give it four stars out of five."—Bob Lind, *Echo Magazine*

Visit us at www.boldstrokesbooks.com

By the Author

Truelesbianlove.com

It Should be a Crime

Do Not Disturb

Nothing but the Truth

The Best Defense

Slingshot

Beyond Innocence

BEYOND INNOCENCE

by
Carsen Taite

2012

BEYOND INNOCENCE

ISBN 10: 1-60282-757-5
ISBN 13: 978-1-60282-757-8

THIS TRADE PAPERBACK ORIGINAL IS PUBLISHED BY
BOLD STROKES BOOKS, INC.
P.O. BOX 249
VALLEY FALLS, NY 12185

FIRST EDITION: NOVEMBER 2012

CREDITS
EDITOR: CINDY CRESAP
PRODUCTION DESIGN: SUSAN RAMUNDO
COVER DESIGN BY SHERI (GRAPHICARTIST2020@HOTMAIL.COM)

Acknowledgments

All novels start with an idea that rocks around in the writer's brain for a while until it's ready to become a full-fledged story. The idea for this story came from D. Jackson Leigh, a generous friend and an awesome storyteller.

I believe in our system of justice, but I also realize it isn't perfect. When a system isn't foolproof, the only way to keep it from breaking down is to keep a close and watchful eye on the process and intervene when necessary. The attorneys and staff of the Innocence Project work tirelessly, and for not a lot of money, every day to provide assistance to those individuals for whom the justice system has failed. Thank you to the men and women whose efforts help keep the scales in balance.

Thanks to Len Barot, who despite being in charge of an enormously successful publishing company and being an amazingly prolific writer, still takes the time to give individual attention to all the authors who are lucky enough to be associated with Bold Strokes Books.

VK "Vic" Powell, once again you worked with me up until the very last moments before deadline to fine-tune this manuscript. Thank you. I cherish our friendship.

Cindy, your editorial touches always make me look good. Thanks for your insights and your humor.

Sheri, will you ever run out of wonderful cover ideas? I hope not!

To everyone at BSB—thanks for all the things you do behind the scenes do to make me and BSB look good.

A big shout out to the women of the Jewel Lesfic Book Club. You always make me feel like a rock star and I value the friendships I've made within the group.

Lainey, your support for my dreams makes me feel like anything is possible.

And finally, to all the readers who read my books, watch my vlogs, and take the time to let me know you'd like me to keep writing, I thank you.

Dedication

To Lainey. Our life, our love is beyond anything
I could have ever imagined.

Chapter One

Cory Lance didn't spend a lot of time at the back of the courtroom. When she was at work, the well of the courtroom was her showplace.

But today she wasn't working. She wasn't sure if she'd ever be working as a trial attorney again. Dressed in slacks and an open-necked shirt instead of her usual tailored suit, she stood as far away from the TV cameras and as close to the double-door exit as possible.

Lots of folks had showed up to see justice in action. More than had shown up for the original trial. Typical. The dead man hadn't had as many friends as the guy now standing in front of the judge. Cory hoped Ray Nelson knew his growing circle of friends was more about the headlines his release would generate than genuine concern for his well-being.

Despite Cory's attempts to melt into the background, Julie managed to catch her eye and offered a slight nod. Cory resisted smiling in response to the tiny acknowledgment. Frankly, she hadn't expected any acknowledgment at all. Julie Dalmar looked like she always did. Beautiful, confident, distant. She stood behind the state's counsel table, ready to bless the agreement that would release Ray Nelson back into the community that had banished him years ago.

Not for the first time, Cory wondered why she'd felt the need to witness this event. Maybe like loved ones who had to see the dead body before burial, she had to see her own destruction to believe it was real. She didn't have long to dwell on her reasons. Judge Yost took the bench and the cameras started rolling.

"Counsel for the state?"

"Ready, Your Honor."

"Counsel for the appellee?"

"Ready, Judge."

Yost shuffled through the papers in her hand, glancing at the pages, more for show than real purpose. This event had been carefully choreographed days in advance. After a few minutes of pretend consideration, the judge set the documents aside and faced Nelson.

"Mr. Nelson, I have in front of me a motion from your lawyers and an accompanying order signed by your attorneys and the attorneys for the state of Texas. Have you had a chance to review the documents that have been filed on your behalf?"

Nelson shot a quick glance at the young male attorney at his side before strangling out his confirmation. The attorney was one of a larger group who'd flown in for this event. Cory wondered if they'd drawn straws to decide which one got to take center stage.

"The parties have asked me to dismiss the case against you and commute your sentence. Do you understand what that means?"

Nelson met her intense gaze and said, "I'll be a free man as soon as you smack that gavel." The courtroom erupted in laughter. Even Julie, who never laughed except at her own jokes, faked a chuckle. Wouldn't want to stand out, Julie, would you? Cory inched closer to the exit. Almost time to go.

Judge Yost continued. "I don't make a habit of smacking my gavel, but I think today I will make an exception." She paused and waited until the room grew silent. "Mr. Nelson, the judicial system upon which our country was founded has failed you. I still believe in that system. I am a part of it, and I will work hard as long as I am on the bench to ensure that the system works, that it is fair, that it is just. The system failed you in the past, but today, we shall right this wrong. Today, we recognize the misconduct that placed you behind bars and kept you a prisoner for the past seven years." Cory edged closer to the door. "I may not have the power to punish the people who are responsible for your fate, but I do have the power to rectify what happened to you. I hereby accept the agreed order filed by your attorneys and the state of Texas, dismiss the case against you, and order the sheriff of Dallas County to release you from custody. Immediately." She struck her gavel hard against the bench and the courtroom burst into pandemonium.

Cory felt the tide of excitement course through the crowd, and she almost became caught up in the frenzy. Until she heard a man on the row in front of her ask his seatmate, "Isn't that Cory Lance?" She slipped out the door before he could turn his head. This show was over for her.

❖

Serena Washington summoned all her dignity as the uniformed man thrust a plastic dog food bowl in her direction and barked, "Empty the contents of your purse into this tray."

She endured this, the third such search in the last half hour, without comment. She'd planned ahead, sorting necessities into the smallest handbag she owned before she'd begun the three-hour drive from the Dallas airport to this godforsaken place. She didn't bother watching the guard as he rummaged through her belongings. Not much there. Her Florida driver's license, a car key, and two rolls of quarters. The guards at the previous two gates had viewed the sparse contents with suspicion, but she was prepared to explain. She'd combed through the instructions on the website meticulously. The long list of contraband included paper money. She'd decided to be overly cautious and she'd left her wallet in the rental car. Lord knows with the security surrounding this place, it should be safe there.

At the man's direction, she strode through the metal detector and winced at the loud beep. She stepped to the side and waited while he swept a wand over her entire body almost close enough to touch.

"You wearing any jewelry I can't see?" he asked with a disinterested tone.

She shook her head. Her simple gold chain and locket were tucked away in her suitcase. She felt naked without the usual accessories to accompany her favorite blue suit, but she'd concentrated hard on getting through this day unnoticed. The plain, professional dress had already caused her to be mistaken for an attorney. He ran the wand across her chest again, and she immediately knew the source of the offending beep. She glanced around, but none of the guards were female. Summoning all the dignity she could muster, she leaned in close to the man and whispered, "It's my bra."

He looked puzzled and she wondered if he was new. Surely she couldn't be the first woman to step through these doors wearing an underwire bra? She tried again. "Underwire. In the bra. I don't have any other metal on me."

He nodded, but stepped quickly away from her as if she were an alien. She watched while he conferred with the man monitoring the X-ray machine. They put their heads together and engaged in a lively, whispered discussion for a few seconds before the man with the wand finally waved her through. Apparently, they decided she wouldn't be able to fashion a weapon out of the tiny piece of wire giving her lift.

She followed the herd of other visitors into a large room. One end was lined with Plexiglas stalls, the other with vending machines. A different guard directed them to sit and then shouted out rules. No knocking on the glass, no attempts at direct contact. "Hold your quarters. We'll let you know when it's time to use them."

She sat at a corner stall and waited. She watched while others met with their loved ones. The prisoners uniformly asked about quarters before launching into questions about life on the outside. Diversity filled the room. Whites, blacks, Hispanics, Asians. Texas didn't discriminate when it came to killing. She found the realization oddly comforting.

Twenty minutes passed before Eric arrived. She'd run out of distractions in the sterile environment, and her entire focus took in his entrance. Wrist cuffs ran through a belt around his waist, which was linked to a chain that ran down to his ankles. Cuffs around his ankles kept his steps short, but the real motivation to move slowly probably came from the three men who surrounded him. Each of them carried a long instrument. It took her a few seconds to get past the shock before she realized they sported cattle prods, the tips inches away from Eric's skin.

They shoved him onto a seat identical to the one on which she was seated, small, steel, round. He wore a white T-shirt and khaki pants. He looked old. He wasn't. He was only two years older than her thirty-three years. She leaned closer, stopping just short of the glass, but she didn't speak. The guards hadn't left yet. Finally, they stepped away and she sighed as she considered her first words.

Eric beat her to the punch. "Thank you." Tears coursed down his cheeks, the restraints on his hands too tight to allow him the dignity of wiping them away. And just like that, she pushed aside her fiercely held resolve to cut ties with her troubled brother for the second time in her life. Blood runs strong.

She bit back a "you're welcome." Platitudes had no place here. Time was short. There was so much she didn't know. Why he was here. What he wanted from her. Why she'd come when she'd sworn she wouldn't be in this position ever again.

"I got your letter. I had to come. Tell me what you need."

"I didn't do it."

She'd heard the words before. Believed them once. He didn't steal the car, he'd only borrowed it for longer than the owner had originally allowed. He didn't deal drugs, he was only in the wrong place at the wrong time. He didn't break in the house, he'd been housesitting and the police didn't believe him. She had vowed she would never believe them again.

Blood runs strong.

Never mind the fact she hadn't spoken with him in three years. She'd spent the first few months of silence resisting the urge to check in, struggling against the draw to violate her vow of letting go. Finally, her urges had settled into forgetting her past and all the baggage it carried. She went on with her life, enjoyed her successes, and drowned her guilt in activity.

Until the letter. She'd read it a dozen times in the week since it had arrived in a plain white envelope, nestled among bills and credit card offers. It was wrinkled with wear. It scared her. It drew her into a past she'd rather forget. It was family, and the concept was foreign to her.

She'd left the letter at home. She didn't need to keep it with her—she'd memorized every line.

I'm in real trouble this time. A jury sentenced me to death. Said I raped and killed a girl. They're going to kill me, Serena. Make me pay for what they think I did. This is Texas. Folks don't sit on death row long here. They got a hankering for blood on this case, and I don't know how much time I have. I should've told you sooner, but after last time, I wasn't sure. I'm tired of disappointing you, but I don't have anywhere else to turn. You don't have to help me, but could you at least come and visit? I don't want to go to my maker without a chance to tell you I'm sorry. Face-to-face. Sorry for all the pain I've caused

*you. Sorry for not being what you wanted me to be. Just once. Please
come see me just once.*

She'd immediately picked up the phone and dialed the number
of the attorney who'd forwarded the letter to her. She'd asked pointed
questions and made copious notes. She hadn't heard from Eric in
three years, since the last time he'd gotten in trouble and took a trip to
the penitentiary. She'd sworn then she was done. Done trying to help
someone who obviously didn't want her help. Eric was on his own,
sink or swim.

Until this letter, she had kept her vow. The promise of death
made her break it now. She'd learned to doubt Eric's protestations in
the past, but she knew in her heart he wasn't lying now. Didn't matter
if he was. He was her flesh and blood, and he didn't deserve to die,
no matter what he did. Blood still ran strong between them, and she
would fight to keep the connection alive.

"If you have quarters, you can use them now."

The guard's loud voice startled Serena, but Eric seemed
nonplussed. Serena pulled a roll from her purse and showed them to
Eric. "Not sure what I'm supposed to do with these."

"You can go with the guard to buy stuff out of the vending
machine. He'll give it to me. How did you know?"

She mock huffed. "I do my research. I may be the little sister, but
I've got skills."

He smiled, not the tentative expression he'd offered when she
first showed up, but a genuine, little boy grin. She grinned back. "You
still like Hershey's with almonds?"

"And a Coke. Thanks, sis."

"My pleasure."

A few minutes later, she returned to the booth and watched Eric
devour the three candy bars she'd purchased. When he finished, she
broached the unpleasant subject that hung between them. "Talk to
me, but don't tell me anything confidential." She'd read about how
these visits were taped, and she didn't want him to tell her anything
that could snip the last strings of hope he had to appeal his case. "I
want to know where things stand as you understand it. I talked to your
attorney, and I have his version."

"Then you know I'm at the end. We lost our direct appeal. He
said I may have a chance at a writ, but he can't do it for free."

She already knew that, but she wanted to hear him say it. Ian Taylor had told her that all the direct appeals had already been exhausted. She could hire an attorney or find someone to take the case pro bono, but the only shot Eric had now was a writ of habeus corpus. She didn't really understand the difference, but from what she'd been able to gather, Eric had been entitled to have a court paid attorney for the appeal, but any extra shots at overturning the verdict would have to be on his own dime. Ian had been clear about the slim chances ahead. She was both relieved and disappointed to hear Eric admit the truth. With the reality in the open, they could move past it.

"I talked to Mr. Taylor. He said he did his best, but you're right, there isn't much for him to work with. Seems the lawyers who handled your case from the start bungled things up beyond repair." She didn't ask the question that was foremost in her mind, but Eric answered without being asked.

"I couldn't afford a free-world lawyer. The court appointed those guys to my case. Said they were qualified. I figure they know plenty, but they didn't talk to me much, so I guess they didn't know much about this case."

His even tone didn't convey a lick of chastisement, but she silently berated herself. If she hadn't cut all ties, he would have come to her for help, and she would've hired him a lawyer. A good one. Sitting here on death row shouldn't be about uncertainty or lack of money. She would have exhausted every avenue to make sure he was well defended. If she hadn't cut all ties.

As if he read her thoughts, he said, "You were right to cut me off. Last you saw me, I was headed down a path of destruction. I know it. When I got out of the pen, I promised myself I'd get my act together before I looked you up." He ducked under her intense gaze. "I wasn't out long before I got picked up for this. No way was I going to call you then."

She understood. She had a million questions to ask about his case, but without privacy, she didn't want to risk too many details. Problem was, if they didn't talk about why he was here, there really wasn't much else to discuss. The only thing they had in common was family, and they were the only two family members left. She risked a couple of questions. Things she had to know.

"Did you know her?"

His face fell. He knew who she was talking about. Ian had said Eric's acquaintance with the victim was the final pin in the coffin of his case. She could understand why. Harder to say you were the random black man, selected to take the fall if you actually knew the victim of the crime.

"I did. We worked together. We were friends, kind of. I'd been to her house, helped her move in. She was always nice to me."

Serena struggled not to react, instead formulating her next question. "Why didn't you testify? Tell the jury you didn't do it?" Two questions, but really only one. She needed him to tell her he didn't do this thing. That no matter how far he had fallen, he hadn't sunk to the depths of inhumanity, hadn't raped and killed an innocent girl who'd never done harm to anyone.

"Lawyers told me not to. Said if I did, the jury would find out my whole record. I guess I shouldn't have listened to them." He shook his head. "I don't know." He met her eyes. "I didn't hurt her. I didn't touch a hair on her head. I swear it to you."

His eyes begged for a response from her. She sifted through her doubts, searching for the truth. A memory surfaced. Her eighth birthday. The woman who'd given birth to them was nowhere to be found. Instead, Eric had met her after school and walked her to the shady convenience store near their dilapidated building. "Wait here," he'd said. He was inside only a moment, then he emerged in a flash, grabbed her hand, and took off running. "Hurry, let's get home. I have a surprise for your birthday." When they were safely inside and all three locks were bolted, he presented a handful of candy bars, with a flourish.

Even her eight-year-old brain knew he didn't have the money to buy her anything, but she hadn't cared. He loved her enough to be there, to try to make her birthday something special. Her adult self would be revolted at the thought of taking stolen property, however trivial. She'd been disgusted by Eric's behavior many times throughout the years. He lied, he cheated, he stole. But murder? Rape? She couldn't fathom either. Not from the boy who had stolen candy so his sister could have a special day.

She locked eyes with him. "I believe you."

CHAPTER TWO

Late that evening, Serena waited for the red-eye back to Florida. She hated airports. The first time in her life she'd flown on a plane she'd been leaving a tragic past to head to an uncertain future. The whole gravity thing didn't help matters.

She'd been thirteen years old. Not only had she never been on a plane, no one in her circle of influence ever had. Of course, that circle was small. After the court declared her junkie mother unfit, she and Eric had spent several years in foster care. Sometimes together, sometimes apart.

When the folks from the agency came to visit, they took pictures. She stood still and listened while they made comments to the foster parents about how attractive her mocha skin was, how acceptable. How it would make it so much easier to find her a permanent home. She wondered why they didn't know she could hear them. She wasn't stupid, but in her young brain, that permanent home would always include her older brother. Her protector.

When the time came to seal the deal, Eric wasn't part of it. Platitudes like, "He'll be happier in a place that's more for boys," and, "You'll both be able to visit and share your experiences," didn't soothe the pain. Serena had grown to love Don and Marion Clark, the couple who'd adopted her. They were Mom and Dad, but she'd never gotten over the pain of losing the only real family she'd ever had.

Years had passed before she'd seen Eric again. She'd almost learned to forget her past when it came roaring back in the form of a late night phone call.

"Honey, sorry to wake you, but I think it's important."

The urgency in Marion's voice had been a cold blast of wake up. Serena shook herself awake and waited with panic for the only kind of news that comes in the middle of the night.

"It's your brother, Eric. He's in trouble."

That was the first time. Two months post graduation from the local community college, she was only one week into her job at the bank, but she didn't hesitate. She had walked into her boss's office the next morning and, in vague terms, explained she had a family emergency that required her to travel out of state. She said she'd only be gone a few days, but she really had no idea what to expect. She purchased her flight, leaving the return trip open. Marion drove her to the airport.

"Do you want me to come with you?"

Serena almost said yes. She hadn't been back to Dallas since she'd first stepped on a plane, a week after her thirteenth birthday. As reluctant as she was to leave her life behind on that day, she was just as scared to return to it now. Although she'd resisted making connections here, she'd managed to weave her way into the lives of the couple who'd adopted her. But one thread remained unraveled, back in Texas. Eric. For a few months after she'd been whisked away to Florida, they'd written letters back and forth. Hers, timid descriptions of her new life in a distant place. His, thinly veiled missives of resentment. Eventually, one or both of them realized that no matter how they tried, they weren't connecting. The letters stopped. If the Clarks had ever moved, Eric wouldn't have been able to reach her that first time. He'd explained on the phone how he'd kept her last letter. How tenuous their family tie must be, reliant on a simple fact of geography.

The gate attendant called her boarding group. She rose to join the cattle call, wishing she'd purchased a book to distract her from thoughts of Eric during the flight home. As if he could read her mind, the gentleman who'd been sitting next to her offered her his newspaper. "I'm about to toss this. Would you like it?"

She smiled and accepted the paper. Within moments after boarding, she was completely immersed in an article about a recent conviction that had been overturned because of prosecutorial misconduct and the organization that had won the appeal. Hope renewed, she started making notes and planning a strategy to help Eric. She would not give up without a fight.

Cory opened the door a crack, but only because she couldn't figure out how to disable the doorbell. The Nelson hearing had been five days ago, and she hadn't spoken to a soul since she'd been placed on indefinite leave. Melinda Stone, hands on her hips, dripping wet from the rain, said, "Thank God, I was about to melt. And I was almost certain I could smell your rotting corpse. What's for dinner?"

Melinda has always made her dizzy, from the first moment they met as 1Ls in law school. The last thing she needed right now was an infusion of her energy. Needed or wanted—Cory wasn't sure of the difference. Didn't matter. She'd get rid of her quickly. What the hell was she doing here anyway? Cory didn't open the door any wider. "I'm alive, but I'm really busy."

Melinda pushed her way in. "You're barely alive and you're not busy at all. You're about to have your license suspended, and word on the street is that you're letting it happen. Where's the tiger I remember? She wouldn't go down without a fight." She rubbed Corey's chin. "Where's my tiger? Where is she?"

Cory pushed her away. "Not funny. I think you have me mistaken for someone else. Some other victim who might actually desire your house calls. Seriously, Mel, I have stuff to do."

Melinda shook her head, conveying her opinion that Cory was pathetic, and walked into the kitchen. "You look like shit. When's the last time you washed your hair?"

"I washed my hair this morning," Cory protested. She hadn't felt like combing it though, and the dark strands hung like thick ropes around her face. She looked down at her usually lanky frame. Her sweats hung in loose folds. She'd definitely lost a few pounds. She was a tall, skinny, shaggy, former lawyer. Dressed like a homeless person. Appropriate.

As Cory watched, Melinda riffled through a few drawers, finally uttering an "ah ha" when she located the plastic folder housing a variety of takeout menus. She thrust her find toward Cory. "Pick one. It's on me."

Cory gave up. When Mel was in one of these moods, nothing would dissuade her. "Pizza. I Fratelli's."

"I'm thinking Thai." Melinda pulled a phone out of her purse.

She knew better than to fight. "You can use my phone." Cory handed her the cordless handset.

"It doesn't work."

"Yes, it does."

"I've been calling you for three days. You don't answer. Either it doesn't work or you're ignoring me. You pick. You want soup with your Pad Kee Mow?"

"Why don't you tell me what I want?" Cory pretended to grouse.

Melinda waved her off. "Don't be a pissant. I'll tell you plenty before we're done, but I'll let you pick your dinner. Chicken or beef?"

Cory shrugged. She wouldn't win this fight. She may as well save her energy for the real reason behind Melinda's visit. "Chicken. Extra spicy." She waited until Melinda phoned in the order, then started her own round of questions.

"Who told you?"

"No one had to tell me."

"Oh, I see. Now you're going to add psychic to your long list of talents."

Melinda reached into her enormous handbag and pulled out a rolled up newspaper. She spread it out on the kitchen table, and Cory could tell it was actually various sections of four newspapers, different dates. Each one contained a headline, decreasing in size and placement about the Nelson case. The first one, the one with the front-page headline, contained a feature story that spanned several pages. *Innocent Man Freed After DA's Office Admits Wrongdoing.*

She didn't need to read further. She knew her name would be splashed throughout the pages. Cory Lance—lead prosecutor at Nelson's trial. Cory Lance—her arguments convinced a jury to put Nelson away for life. Cory Lance—the prosecutor who kept valuable, exculpatory evidence from the defense team. Cory Lance—the reason the case was overturned.

The article wouldn't contain a single statement from her about the appeal and subsequent dismissal of charges. Not for lack of trying on the part of the press. For days following the entry of the

Innocence Project team, reporters had dogged her every move from her house to the courthouse. She'd finally stopped repeating the officially sanctioned two-word response, "no comment," and maintained a stoic façade, when all she'd really wanted to do was shout, "You don't know anything about how the justice system works." Ray Nelson was a danger to society. She knew it, the cops knew it, the judge and jury had known it. Now, because of what was perceived as prosecutorial misconduct, he'd be walking the streets of Dallas again. Free to offend again. She for one wouldn't be sleeping until he got himself locked up again.

She tossed the paper aside. The stories in the media sensationalized everything. "Ray Nelson may be a lot of things, but innocent isn't one of them."

Melinda shoved her toward a chair at the kitchen table. "That's better, Tiger. Talk it out. If it makes you feel any better, I did see at least one story about the case that didn't mention your name." She looked around. "You have wine?"

Cory sighed and pointed to a rack on the counter. "The Pinot is the best. Corkscrew in the drawer."

Melinda poured two glasses and settled in at the table. "Drink and spill."

Cory took a sip of the wine to delay the inevitable interrogation. The Nelson case was the last thing she wanted to talk about, especially with Melinda. She wouldn't be satisfied with cursory answers. "Nothing to it. We had him, dead to rights. Judge knew it. Jury took less than an hour to find him guilty."

"And?"

"And an appellate lawyer got him off on a technicality."

"Technicality?"

"The police had a suspect prior to arresting Nelson. They liked the other guy. A lot. We didn't give that information to the defense." Cory had gotten used to the "we" word. Melinda called her on it.

"Didn't Julie try that case with you?"

Cory hesitated as she considered how to answer. "She did, but the case was mine." She silently willed Melinda to drop the subject. No such luck.

"Uh huh. So you didn't tell the other side the cops were on to someone else?"

"Sounds worse when you say it."

"Sounds like a little more than a technicality to me."

"I've worked dozens of these cases. I've seen cops chase their tails more often than not."

"Ever heard of Brady?"

Every lawyer knew about the seminal U.S. Supreme Court case, *Brady v. Maryland*, which required the prosecution to turn over exculpatory evidence to the defense. The fact the police had pursued other suspects qualified as Brady information, but this case had been different. She wasn't ready or willing to explain why.

"Trust me." She hoped Melinda wouldn't dwell on the irony of her request. "Nelson did the crime. That he's walking the street today is a travesty. He beat his wife on a regular basis, and she wasn't strong enough to fight back, with her fists or in the courtroom. It was a miracle we ever got an assault conviction on him before he killed her. Was the evidence against him circumstantial? Yes, but so was the evidence they say proves he's innocent." Even though she was riled, she carefully worded her next statement. "The defense may not have been given some of the evidence, but I'm still not convinced the guy is innocent."

"Tell me why you think you got tagged as the bad guy in this mess?"

Cory shook her head. She had no intention of getting into the exact details with Melinda or anyone else. All she cared about was minimizing the damage. She didn't have any hope of making the situation go away. "My case, my consequences. Doesn't matter now. All I care about is putting this behind me and getting back to work."

"Okay. Got it. The question now, is how are we going to accomplish that?" Melinda's response signaled she'd caught Cory's "this subject is closed tone."

Cory purposefully ignored the "we." "I don't have many choices. I got a letter from the state bar requesting my response slash explanation. Pretty sure it's for show. They can't wait to hang me out to dry so the press will die down."

"And that's where I come in. I've got a letter here for you to sign stating I represent you. I'll fax that in tomorrow, but we should start planning for your hearing right away. I have some ideas, but I'll want you to be totally involved in your own representation."

"Whoa, wait a minute. I thought you were here to drink my wine, not hustle a new client. Besides, I can't afford you." Melinda had carved out a specialty over the years, representing lawyers and other professionals in administrative hearings. Her success rate was unparalleled, and Cory imagined her fees were as well.

"You'll be my pro bono case this month." Although Cory had barely sipped her wine, Melinda topped off her glass. "Seriously, let me help you. Pay me what you can, when you can. Say yes, or I'll bail and leave you on the hook to pay the delivery guy."

Cory hadn't given the state bar procedure much thought. In the back of her mind, she supposed she thought she'd represent herself. Fall on her sword and hope for the best. Probably not a great idea, but she didn't want Melinda or anyone else witnessing her disintegration. She had another reason for going it alone, but she wasn't ready to reveal it now. Or ever. She knew she was supposed to try to avoid a hearing, but no one had offered any guidance about how to make that work with her personal goal of keeping her license. She was only just beginning to realize how adrift she was. Maybe Melinda, who knew the system better than anyone, could be valuable after all.

"I'll say yes, under one condition."

"Name it."

"Negotiate the best possible outcome short of a full-blown hearing. I don't want this to drag on. I want to put it behind me as quickly as possible. I'll do whatever it takes, as long as there's no permanent suspension."

Melinda opened her mouth, but Cory held up a hand, palm out. "Say yes. I mean it." Melinda lifted her wine glass and touched it to Cory's. "Fine. You're the client. But promise me you'll keep an open mind."

"Deal." Easier to say what she wanted to hear than argue the point. Quick and easy. The faster this was over, the faster she could resume her life. Right now, all she wanted was a big plate of Thai food and something stronger than the glass of wine in front of her.

As if on cue, the doorbell rang. Melinda reached for her purse, and then shoved a couple of twenties into Cory's hand. "Tip him big. Someone should have fun tonight."

Cory headed for the door, wondering if she'd ever have fun again.

CHAPTER THREE

Serena had spent the last several weeks trying her best to contain the seething mix of emotions she'd brought back from Texas. She'd worked hard to defy the odds of her past and become the first of her blood relatives to graduate from college, hold a steady job. Her achievements were a credit to her ability to compartmentalize her life. No one at the credit union where she worked knew more about her than she cared to show. One simple, framed photo on her desk was the only allusion to her personal life. Don and Marion Clark hugged their adopted daughter on the day she graduated from college, the pride on their faces beamed off the page. Serena loved the photo for the journey it represented. From the projects to the middle class. From a junkie mother and no known father to the care of two individuals who'd sacrifice anything for her happiness. The framed picture was an anchor that kept her from drifting back to her roots.

But her roots still had pull. Her birth mother was long dead. She'd never known any of her other blood relatives. Eric was the single thread connecting what she'd become to what she'd been. And his days were numbered.

Serena reached into her purse and pulled out a small notebook. On one of the pages were the copious notes she'd taken when she met with Ian Taylor, the attorney who'd been appointed by the court to represent Eric on his direct appeal. That part of the appeal process had been exhausted, but armed with the information she'd gleaned from him and the newspaper article about the Innocence Project that she'd devoured on the plane, she had plenty of ideas. She spent the time since she'd returned from Texas working hard to put a plan in motion. She knew it was a bad time to take off work again, but she needed to make another trip to Dallas.

She touched the intercom button on her phone. "Nancy, would you see if Mr. Rutgers is available? I need a few minutes of his time."

As she left her tiny, neat office, she glanced at the space where she spent so much time. As head teller, she'd achieved stability, which is all she thought she'd ever wanted. Over the years, she'd been offered various promotions, but she'd politely declined positions further up the ladder, content to trade security for what others perceived as success. This space and her small apartment down the street were all the success she thought she wanted.

Rutgers's office was the polar opposite of hers. The bank president's desk was cluttered with pictures of family and children's clay artwork. Whatever couldn't be identified as an ashtray or pencil holder, served as a paperweight. The desk was full of paperweights. Serena looked around the room and swiftly calculated that, unlike her, it would take him hours to vacate his office. Of course, he wouldn't ever need to. Time to get to the point of her visit.

"Mr. Rutgers, I need a favor."

"Have a seat, Serena. And please, call me Jerry. There're no customers here."

"Thank you, Mr. Rutgers." She did sit, but perched on the edge of her chair.

"You want some coffee, water?" He smiled. "Something stronger?"

She smiled back, because she knew he expected it. "No, thanks. I'm fine."

"You don't look fine. You look like you're here to deliver bad news."

"Depends. I need another few days off. I realize this isn't a good time, and I know I just took time off a few weeks ago, but it can't wait." She had plenty of vacation time accrued, since she rarely took time off, but they were short-handed and she knew he depended on her to take up the slack. She didn't expect his reaction.

"Why don't you tell me what's going on? Maybe I can help."

"I appreciate the offer. Really, I do, but this is something personal. Private. I hope you understand I need to take care of it on my own."

The organization she'd contacted, an offshoot of the Innocence Project, had explained the process, and they'd come to an agreement about Eric's case. She would hire an investigator to do the groundwork on Eric's case, and the clinic would handle the legal work, pro bono. The clinic director suggested she come to Dallas, meet with the staff, and they would help her locate an experienced investigator. She had a flight reserved for first thing in the morning, and she hoped the process would only take a couple of days, but even if it took longer, she was committed to making sure Eric received every last chance she could make available to him.

"Are you okay?"

The question caught her off guard, partly because her sudden departure wasn't about her. "It's a family thing," she said. And it was. Eric was her family. First, last, always. She hadn't been there for him when he needed her most, but she would make up for her absence with every ounce of determination she possessed.

As if he could hear her thoughts, Rutgers echoed. "Family is important." He crossed his hands and scrunched his brow. "I respect your desire for privacy. Go. Do what you need to do. We'll miss you desperately, but family comes first. Your commitment to your family reflects the commitment for your job. We need people like you, and we'll still need you when you return."

Serena endured a few more minutes of small talk before she was able to gracefully exit. She was grateful for his compassion, but uncomfortable sharing details about her personal life. She supposed she'd have to get over that if she was going to do Eric any good.

❖

Cory held a suit in each hand, uncharacteristically unsure about her wardrobe. She'd spent the last month in sweats and jeans, rarely leaving the house for anything except groceries.

Melinda had called the night before and told her to dress for court and be ready to go at eight a.m. sharp. She hadn't slept, and being awake all night hadn't improved her decision-making ability. Part of the problem was not knowing what to expect. She and Mel had spoken a few times over the past couple of weeks, and she'd made a point of emphasizing her desire to conclude the disciplinary matter without the need for a full-blown hearing. Each time, Melinda muttered a vague response, but when pressed, assured her she would respect her wishes. Telling her to be dressed for court didn't sound like avoidance, but Cory held out hope. Maybe they were going to a preliminary meeting with the hearing examiner. That could be short and sweet, she hoped. Cory wasn't in the mood to rehash. She only wanted to take her licks and move forward.

The doorbell rang. She glanced at the clock on her bedside table. Quarter to eight and she still wasn't dressed. Melinda would have some explaining to do while she waited.

Cory swung the front door wide and announced, "Come on in and occupy yourself. While I'm figuring out what to wear, you can explain what you have planned."

"I think you look great in what you have on."

Cory blinked. Julie, not Melinda stood in her doorway. Cory looked down at her tattered University of Texas T-shirt and faded jeans, as a way to avoid the glint in Julie's eyes. "What are you doing here? You shouldn't be here." Both the question and the statement were delivered with a whisper. She hadn't seen Julie since that morning in the courtroom. Seeing her now released all the feelings she'd managed to box away. "Come in." She grabbed Julie's arm and pulled her into the foyer.

Julie pulled her close, hugging her tight, her hands roaming. "I've missed you. You haven't called. I've been worried. I haven't seen you since the hearing and even then you were gone so fast I didn't get to talk to you."

Cory didn't trust the words, but she wanted to. She'd purposefully avoided any contact, didn't want to open the connection and risk all that came with that. For sure she didn't want to risk it now. Still, Julie had noticed her at the hearing, noticed she'd made a quick exit. The revelation gave her cautious hope. She kept her answer simple. "I'm fine."

"Sure you are, but still, I worried." Julie pushed gently away and examined her from head to toe before pulling her back into a tight embrace. "You look great. Comfortable. Don't get too used to casual. You'll be back in no time. We need you."

Again with the "we." *Do you need me, Julie?* Cory wouldn't ever ask the question out loud. Wasn't sure she wanted to know the answer. *She's here. That means something, doesn't it?* "I don't know when it will be. Things aren't settled yet." Cory glanced at the clock again. "In fact, I have to get dressed. My attorney will be here any minute. She's picking me up for a meeting."

"A meeting? With who? And she's picking you up? Pretty personal service, don't you think?"

Cory took on the last question because it was the simplest to answer. "My car's in the shop." Thank goodness. Otherwise, she'd be forced to make up some lie to respond to the "with who" and details about the "meeting." She didn't have a clue what Melinda had planned for the morning, but no way did she want to let Julie know how far she'd fallen from taking personal responsibility for her life. She'd stopped doing that the moment she'd fallen under Julie's spell.

"Bummer. Hate not having wheels. Well, I'm sure you're paying her out the nose, so the least she can do is pick you up." Not a trace of sympathy that Cory had to hire an attorney in the first place. Cory filed the observation away for future examination. The ring of the doorbell interrupted any further conversation. "Damn. That's her and I'm not even dressed yet."

Julie looked around, a hint of panic in her eyes.

"You can go out the back door, but if you parked in front, she's still going to see you. Don't worry. She's not going to rat you out."

"Don't be silly. I'm just a colleague, dropping by to check on another colleague."

We were never colleagues. Cory stepped to the door. "Thanks for stopping by. To check on your colleague. She's fine."

Julie walked to the door, kissing her cheek as she passed. "I really can't wait until you're back. Things will be better for both of us. I promise."

Maybe they would. Cory tried not to think about how much energy she'd expended thinking that over the course of their relationship. She swung the door open and held a finger to her lips when she saw Melinda about to burst into a fit of scolding. "Melinda Stone, Julie Dalmar. Julie was just leaving and I'm going to get dressed. Coffee's in the kitchen." She strode away quickly before either woman could ask her any more questions.

Ten minutes later, outfitted in a sharp black suit, she walked into the kitchen.

Melinda looked up from her steaming cup of coffee. "Black, huh?"

"Considering that we're probably headed to my funeral, I thought it was appropriate."

"Oh ye of little faith." She set the coffee cup down and grabbed her purse from the counter. "Come on, we're late. I'll explain in the car, but first you're going to have to explain what Julie Dalmar was doing at your house first thing in the morning."

Cory read the real question in Melinda's eyes. "She didn't spend the night if that's what you're asking."

"I was. But she has before, am I right?"

Technically, no. Julie always left before dawn. She could only sleep in her own bed, always had an early morning, didn't want to keep Cory awake by tossing and turning. None of her excuses explained why she never invited Cory to her place. As always, Cory ignored her desire to push for answers. She spent her professional life asking questions, but in her personal life she found it was fairly easy to gloss over personal curiosities.

Melinda, on the other hand, never let up until she got answers. Cory hoped she could get away with being thin on detail. "We've slept together, if that's what you're asking."

"That's exactly what I was asking. Don't you think that complicates things? Didn't she work with you on the Nelson case?"

"Don't go there."

"I will go wherever I think I need to. She's your boss, right?"

"She was my boss. She's not my boss now." Cory knew she was mincing words again, but the distinction was important for a number of reasons.

"I need to know everything in order to properly defend you."

"I don't need defending. What I need is to put this whole affair," Cory winced at her own poor word choice, "behind me. Tell me what you have planned for this morning and I'll let you know if I'm up for it. Last I remember, the client gets to call the shots. Right?" She fixed her face into a neutral expression and waited out Melinda's scrutiny. Finally, Melinda shook her head and acquiesced to the change in subject.

"Sure. Whatever you want. I've worked out an arrangement with the hearing examiner. You'll perform some community service restitution and the case will be dismissed. You'll have a note about the sanction on your record until the restitution is complete and then it will come off and you'll be free to resume your regularly scheduled programming—putting bad guys away."

Could it really be as simple as that? Cory jumped on the plan. "Sounds great. I'll take it."

"You sure about that? You don't get to pick your own community service. The bar does—take it or leave it. If you've got some good defenses to raise at a hearing, you should consider that route, but I can't help you make that decision unless you talk to me about exactly what happened with the Nelson case."

"There's nothing to talk about." Cory wasn't going to fall into the trap of discussing her personal life. Melinda was one of her best friends, but she didn't trust her to put aside her lawyer role in favor of friendship. Someday they'd share the story over cocktails. When this whole ordeal was way behind her. "So if there's no hearing, where are you taking me?"

"Call it incredible service, but I'm escorting you to your first day of community service." Melinda turned into a parking lot and gestured at the building ahead.

Cory couldn't tell anything about the place from the outside, but she was anxious to get inside and get started. The sooner she could put this behind her, the sooner she could find her way back to normal. Whatever that was.

CHAPTER FOUR

A re you sure you have everything you need?"
Serena shook her head. Her adoptive parents had been asking that question her entire life and had taken whatever steps were necessary to make sure all her needs were met. In the fifteen minutes they'd stood at the ticket counter, Marion had offered her chewing gum, Kleenex, spending money—everything a mother could offer her child short of taking on the task herself. Yesterday, at lunch, she'd come close to offering that. Today, she renewed the offer. "I can still go with you, if you want."

"Thank you, but no. This is something I need to do on my own." She softened the rejection with a smile. "Besides, who knows how long I'll be gone? Dad would be lost without you for more than a couple of days." She closed her eyes as they hugged her tight. She knew they would do anything for her, but Eric wasn't their problem. Handling Eric's troubles was something she had to do on her own. "I'll keep you updated." The promise was all she could offer.

As she drew back, Don pressed a small envelope into her hand and waved off her immediate protest. "Take it, or we're boarding that plane with you. We insist."

Serena didn't need to open the envelope to know the cash contents would be generous. She'd come to expect, but never take for granted, the Clarks' generosity. They'd been in their late thirties when they'd gotten the news they would finally have a child. When she stepped off the plane at the Orlando airport with the advocate from the adoption agency, she'd been overwhelmed at all the sensations and didn't even notice the anxious couple whose arms were laden with stuffed toys. It was months before she felt comfortable enough to accept anything they offered over and above food, clothing, and shelter. They'd quickly learned to respect her boundaries, but she'd never wanted for anything during the years she'd lived under their roof. Her life with them was not extravagant by any means, but it was a stark contrast to her early childhood when she wore the same two dresses to school, day after day, and dinner was often a watery version of the soup she and her brother had shared the night before.

"Thanks. I better get going. I'll call you when I get settled. And I promise I'll keep you posted." Serena started to move toward security, but the expectant looks on their faces prompted her to give them each a quick hug. Marion's eyes got misty, and Serena took off before their quick good-bye dissolved into an emotional display.

She devoted her time on the plane to rereading all the materials she gathered about the Innocence Project, the organization she'd read about in the paper the day she'd left Dallas to head back to Florida. The organization she'd contacted, the Justice Clinic, was an offshoot of the project, working in conjunction with Richards College, a university law school in Dallas. The information online billed the clinic as being fully staffed with experienced counsel and it provided an opportunity for third year law students to gain exposure to the criminal justice system. Unlike the Innocence Project, which only accepted cases where DNA evidence was available that might exonerate a defendant, the Justice Clinic accepted cases where guilt was at issue based on various types of erroneous evidence, like unreliability of eyewitness testimony. Similar to the national program of the Innocence Project, the clinic had become inundated with requests for assistance, and the waiting list for case review was long. However, death penalty cases rose to the top of the list, and Eric's appellate lawyer, Ian Taylor, had paved the way for Serena to speak to the clinic's director about her situation. Together, they'd worked out an arrangement she'd reached for the clinic to take Eric's case without a fee.

She'd asked Ian about hiring a lawyer to work on the writ, but he'd encouraged her to take this route. After a few dozen phone calls to top Texas firms, she decided to follow his advice. The other lawyers she'd spoken with either didn't work on death penalty cases or they wanted more than the value of her parents' home to take on the case. Even with the latter, she'd learned the most experienced death penalty attorneys were the ones who worked in group environments like the clinic at Richards. The synergy of working together as a collective unit, especially in a teaching environment, seemed to make for the best representation. She'd meet with them and make a decision about whether to go with them or figure out a way to find the money to fund her brother's defense. She'd already turned down her parents' offer of assistance. They'd both just retired. She would not consider taking a risk with the nest egg they'd worked so carefully to build. The whole situation was a disturbing throwback to her past. She and Eric, left to their own devices to take on the world.

By the time the three-hour flight ended, Serena had put the finishing touches on an exhaustive list of questions for the team at the Justice Clinic. She picked up her luggage and then phoned Ian to let him know she'd landed. After she arranged to meet him at the clinic, she rented a car at the airport and plugged the address into the GPS.

Driving in Dallas was a lot like navigating around Orlando—sprawling highways, lots of suburbs. She had plenty of time, so she took an easy pace, memorizing the details along the way. She'd made a reservation at an extended stay motel, but she'd need to find a regular place to buy groceries, get gas. When she'd lived here before, her only concern was finding her way to and from school on her own, hoping there would be food in the apartment at the end of the day.

The clinic wasn't located at the college. It was housed in a nondescript building a few blocks from campus. She parked in the ample lot and walked over to Ian who was waiting by the front door. He locked arms with her in an affectionate embrace that obviously came very easily to him. She resisted the impulse to pull away, half wishing she could enjoy closeness instead of avoiding it.

"Good to see you again, Serena. I delivered Eric's case files to the clinic last week so I imagine they've had a chance to get up to speed. I'll sit in on today's meeting to help with the transition, and I can provide you with some names of private investigators." He drew back and gave her a long look. "You made the right choice. These are good people, and some of the best lawyers in the nation work with them."

She nodded, but saved her words until after she'd had a chance to assess them for herself. Ian led the way into the building, narrating all the way. The off campus location was the result of a generous donation from a group of prominent defense lawyers. A major benefit was free parking, a scarce commodity at the college, hence the off-site location.

Serena barely listened to his rambling tour. A long list of questions occupied her thoughts, and she was anxious about meeting the attorneys who would head up Eric's case. Ian rapped on an office door, but barely waited a second before sticking his head in. "Paul, Serena Washington's here to see you." He gestured for her to follow him into the large, but modestly furnished office.

A burly, bearded man stood to greet her. He wore khakis, a white oxford shirt, and a tweed blazer, and he looked more professor than lawyer. His weathered face told her he'd seen his share of more than a classroom. His handshake was strong and firm. "Ms. Washington, I'm Paul Guthrie. Pleasure to meet you."

He held her hand long enough to convey his sincerity. She read kind resolve in his eyes and instantly trusted him—a rare occurrence. When he let go, he pointed across the room. Serena followed the direction of his gesture. He spoke, but she didn't hear a word he said. The tall brunette standing across the room wore a hint of a smile, but her silent welcome wasn't enough to explain why Serena felt warmth course through her belly. As she took in the woman's chiseled features and sea-green eyes, she recognized the feeling she'd spent years struggling against. She was no stranger to the pull of attractive women, but a fierce determination to never be like her mother—dependent on others—had always given her the strength to keep her distance. Casual dates, playful touching, but never passion, fervor, or craving. Captivated by the contrast between this woman's kind eyes and gentle smile and her commanding presence, she couldn't remember the last time attraction had paralyzed her, threatened to consume her. She wasn't sure it ever had. No one had ever made her feel so unsettled. That the person to rouse these undeniable feelings was here, in this place where she'd come to find help for her brother, meant she would have to be more vigilant than ever.

❖

Cory had followed Melinda into the building. She whispered, "What is this place?"

"This place , is you, avoiding a hearing. Your wish is my command." She pulled Cory aside. "It's the Alfred T. Linney Justice Clinic. Surely you've heard of it?"

Cory's back stiffened. "Is this some kind of joke?" Like most attorneys at the DA's office, she was familiar with the Linney clinic since they worked like rabid dogs to undo all the hard work she and all the other prosecutors did on behalf of the citizens of Dallas County. The clinic was funded primarily by a generous endowment and operated with assistance from the law school at Richards University, a local college.

"I can't do this. Seriously, Mel, what am I supposed to do here? I'll be conflicted out of half the cases they have."

"Take a deep breath, girl. They'll erect a Chinese wall for any cases out of Dallas County." Melinda referred to provisions taken within a law firm or office to shield communications about a particular case from attorneys who might represent clients in conflicting matters. She mimicked gentle breathing as if she could coax Cory into relaxation. It wasn't working. Cory was only just beginning to get ramped up.

"I'm not kidding. Schedule the hearing. I'll go down in flames quicker that way."

Melinda grabbed her arm and squeezed hard, apparently giving up all pretense of being soothing. "I'm all for a hearing, but if we have one, I'm not prepared to lose. That means that I'll be a rabid bulldog hell-bent on showing the hearing examiner the Cory Lance I know wouldn't withhold evidence in a first-degree felony trial. Are you prepared for battle?"

Cory sagged. Doing battle in the courtroom was what she did best. A state bar examiner's hearing, being judged by her peers, wasn't familiar and wasn't home turf. Too many variables she couldn't control, and she knew Melinda well enough to know she wouldn't rest until she got to the bottom of what had happened with the Nelson case. Those details could and should remain buried. Maybe she could handle this penance for a little while.

"How long?"

"Two months."

"That's practically forever."

"It is not. It'd take longer to get a hearing."

"Why this place?"

"Paul Guthrie, the senior staff attorney, is an old friend of mine, and he agreed to take you on. And I figured a little work for the other side would help your reputation. The state bar folks ate it up.

"Look, you can sit at home wondering what's going to happen to you or you can work here and get on with your life. Your choice." Melinda tapped her fingers on Cory's shoulder, waiting.

Cory did a quick mental inventory. Not a choice really. Hell, she was here already. May as well at least check it out. Two months wasn't enough time to get too involved.

Paul Guthrie, the clinic director, greeted her like a long-lost friend. Cory struggled not to let suspicion about his motives color their first meeting. Melinda made sure she was settled in before abandoning her to her adversaries. Cory looked around the room, but there was only the one escape route. Paul grinned at her as if he knew what she was thinking, and then motioned her into a chair and launched into a brief orientation.

"Lucky you could be here this morning. We have a new client coming in, and I'd like you to sit in to see how we conduct intake. My understanding is that this one's on a short timeline so we'll have to jump on it if we're going to take it on."

"Where did the case originate?"

"Don't worry. I've already screened the cases you'll be working on. None from Dallas. This one's from Rinson County."

Cory sighed. She knew a lot of the prosecutors in the neighboring county, but other than what she read in the paper, didn't keep up with their case load. Rinson was a primarily rural county and a well-known bastion of conservatism. No surprise when juries handed out death sentences. "How about a thumbnail sketch?"

"In five words or less: bad eyewitness testimony, racial profiling."

"No DNA?"

"This isn't a very old case, so normally they would've done testing, but the DA's office says there were no usable samples."

"Happens sometimes."

"I know, but it's not the norm."

"You think they're withholding evidence." Cory didn't even try to hide the rising defensive tone in her voice.

Paul shrugged. "I don't have any reason to believe they are or they aren't. They convicted him on kidnapping and murder, but not rape. They only used the allegation of rape as an issue during punishment. If they'd had DNA evidence he was the rapist, they would've added sexual assault to the list of charges. So I don't know what the deal was, but we'll need to review their whole file if we're going to have a shot at a writ of habeas corpus."

And that was the problem. Getting access to a prosecutor's complete file was a battle, pre and post trial. The law may require that exculpatory evidence be turned over to the defense, but the frontline decision about what was exculpatory was one made by the prosecutor, which made for a chicken and egg dilemma. Better not engage until necessary. Instead, Cory asked a safer question. "If the defendant's in prison, who are we meeting with?"

"His sister. She flew in from Florida this morning." He glanced at the doorway to his office. "I think this is her now." Paul stood and waved at the man entering his office. "Come in. Sorry, our receptionist only works part time, and today's her day of freedom."

Cory stood and shook hands with the tall, thin man that she recognized as Ian Taylor, an appellate attorney with a solid reputation. He stepped away and motioned toward the door at a tall African-American woman whose bearing suggested a healthy mixture of pride and humility. And she was gorgeous. So beautiful Cory had to force her gaze away when she realized she'd been staring. She pushed away the confusing sensations and appraised her with a keen sense of intuition, well honed during years of searching for the truth.

She wore a skirt suit with straight lines, not very expensive, but well cared for. Mid-level heels, a medium sized simple handbag, and plain gold accessories. Nothing she had on appeared to be new, and she wore her outfit with the ease of someone who dresses up on a regular basis, not just for visits to an attorney's office. A professional. A strikingly beautiful professional whose modest attire couldn't hide her attributes. Cory remembered Paul's words: "racial profiling."

This woman must be the client's sister. How could this attractive, put together woman be associated with a killer waiting for his execution date?

"Serena Washington, meet Cory Lance. I asked Cory to sit in on our discussion because she may be doing some work on your brother's case."

She shook Serena's offered hand and held it a beat longer than she intended, but her warm, firm grasp begged to be savored. At least that's how she felt. Serena seemed frozen in place, her gaze fixed firmly on Cory's hand in hers, her expression unreadable. When she finally let go, Serena moved back a few steps. The distance immediately chilled the air between them. Paul started talking, but all Cory could think about was how to reconnect with Serena.

"Have a seat, everyone." Paul picked up a file from his desk. "I've read the summary Ian prepared. Looks like there may have been a few issues we can explore that might be ripe for a writ." He directed his attention to Serena. "Have you hired an investigator yet?"

Ian spoke for her. "We plan to work on that today. Ms. Washington came here directly from the airport."

"Cory, I bet you have some good contacts."

Paul's voice startled her out of her staring. "Contacts?"

"For a private investigator?"

"Sure. No problem." She lied. She didn't work with private investigators. She worked with cops and the finest investigators the DA's office had on staff. Not a likely pool of candidates to try to clear a death row inmate. Still, something kept her from expressing her disdain in Serena's presence. She barely knew her and she couldn't stand the thought of disappointing her. Well, that would have to change. She didn't plan to be around long enough to get involved in this woman's or her brother's lives and she didn't plan on getting too involved in any of the cases the clinic handled. She'd do simple tasks, bide her time, and get back to the life she knew, the one she was passionate about.

Passion. Didn't the punch in the gut attraction she'd felt when Serena walked in the door foretell passion? She squelched the thought before it could take hold. No good came of feelings reeling out of control.

Paul stood. The meeting was apparently over. "Let me know who you hire. I'll want to meet them, but Cory will be primary liaison. Cory, why don't you huddle with Ian and Ms. Washington and we can talk later about our next steps?"

Cory shot a look at Serena. Her expression of displeasure surprised her. She didn't necessarily want to huddle with the sister of a clinic client, but she hadn't expected a reciprocal reaction. Especially not after the sparks she'd felt during their handshake. Could she have imagined a mutual attraction? Didn't matter. She had work to do if she was going to find her way back to the job she loved, and she wasn't about to let anything get in the way.

❖

Something about Cory Lance was familiar in an unsettling way. Serena watched her closely during the meeting with Paul. By the time the meeting ended, she was convinced she had never met Cory. She'd remember if she had. She'd taken every opportunity to study her, and while she pretended her interest was purely professional, it wasn't. Attraction fueled her close inspection. Distracting attraction, obsession almost. Cory was a forceful magnet, and her steely resolve was no match for her pull. It would have to be. She'd risked everything to come here, to work on Eric's case. She had to remain focused.

When Paul suggested she "huddle" with Cory, she opened her mouth to protest, but shut it again when she realized she didn't have a clue what to say. *I can't possibly work with someone who makes my insides melt? Don't you have any other attorneys who aren't so attractive? Can I work with a man?* She listened to her internal litany and gave in to Paul's request. She'd managed all these years; surely she could keep it together for a bit longer.

As they walked out of Paul's office, Cory spoke to Ian. "How about lunch? We can talk while we eat." She reached into her suit pocket. "Oh shit. I just realized I don't have my car with me."

Ian jingled a set of keys. "I've got plenty of room. Is Hillstone all right with you?"

"Perfect."

"I'll bring my notes and we can discuss the points of error."

Serena watched the exchange, immediately feeling like an outsider. *Lawyers*. She wondered if this was how Eric had felt during his trial, watching his life play out with no control about the direction it was headed. The people managing it speaking in code. Determined to wrest back some control, she pulled out the keys to the rental car. "I'll drive. I need to learn my way around. You two can navigate."

Ian and Cory exchanged glances. "Sounds good," Ian said. Serena led the way to her car. Ian was on her heels, but Cory hung back for a second before following. Cory caught her eye before she could look away, and in the moment she saw a flash of uncertainty. Funny, she'd thought she was the only one experiencing that particular emotion.

Cory took the backseat without asking. Ian chatted affably during the entire ride to the restaurant, gesturing to points of interest along the way. Serena snuck a few looks in the rearview mirror but never caught Cory's glance since she spent the entire drive studying every aspect of the rear floorboard. Ian seemed not to notice Cory had nothing to contribute to the conversation.

They were early arrivals at the restaurant, and the hostess escorted them to a booth right away. Ian stood beside the booth, waiting for them to take a seat. Serena slid into the booth first, relieved when Cory slid in across from her until she realized now she couldn't avoid her gaze.

After the waitress took their drink orders, Ian excused himself to the restroom. Serena searched for something innocuous to discuss. "How long have you worked for the clinic?"

Apparently, the simple question was anything but. Cory squirmed in her seat. "I don't really work there. I'm volunteering my time."

"That's nice of you. For how long? What's your background?" Serena was used to directness and she would've thought Cory, a lawyer, was too. Apparently not. Cory's head moved back and forth, and it was immediately apparent she was looking for a way out. Serena decided to let her off the hook and swiftly changed the subject. "Never mind. I didn't mean to get personal." She held up the menu. "What's good?"

Cory flashed a wide smile. "Everything. Try the French dip. The fries alone are to die for, but the sandwich is perfection."

Serena closed her menu. "French dip it is. Though I have no idea why I'm trusting food advice from a skinny white girl." She grinned to soften the faux insult.

Cory's retort was cut short when Ian slid into the booth. "I see you two are becoming acquainted."

Serena looked back and forth between them. Maybe she could find out about Cory in a roundabout way. "Have you two known each other long?"

"Years," Ian replied. "Though this will be the first time we've ever worked on the same side." He fiddled with his silverware and napkin, completely missing the killer stare Cory leveled in his direction. The reappearance of the waitress saved him from Cory's wrath. When she left with their food orders, Ian launched the conversation in a different direction.

"Your brother's case was mishandled from the start, but the problem is that once he's been found guilty, the burden is on us to show he is actually innocent or should at least be entitled to a new trial."

Serena crossed her arms and leaned in close. "Okay. How do we go about doing that?"

"Cory and the team at the clinic will worry about the legal stuff, but we need an investigator to follow up on all the unturned leads the trial team overlooked."

"Didn't they have an investigator working on the case?" Cory asked.

"Well, they filed a motion to have one appointed, but I can't for the life of me tell what he did. It was George Patton. He's a popular investigator, retired cop, and very old-school. Didn't keep notes or write anything down."

"Guess we should start by having whoever we hire interview George and determine what he was able to find out." Cory realized she'd said "we." Too late to bite back the words. She wasn't officially assigned to this case and she wouldn't be. She'd do what she promised and move on. "I have an idea about who you can hire. Her name is Skye Keaton and she used to be a homicide detective for the Dallas Police Department."

Ian flashed her a questioning look and she answered his silent query. "She's a private investigator now, doing a lot of work for the Bradley and Casey law firm. She's good, better than a lot of the top investigators with the DA's office."

Serena piped in. "Is she expensive?"

"Good question. I've never had to hire a PI, so I don't have any idea about her fees or investigator fees in general." As she spoke the words, she realized with every response she seemed more and more inept. Good thing she wasn't trying to impress anyone.

Serena cocked her head at Cory's response, but didn't pursue the query. "Do you think we could meet with her this afternoon?"

Ian glanced at his iPhone. "I have an appointment this afternoon, but perhaps Cory could set up a meeting. I'll give you my notes to help her get started."

Serena caught Cory's eye. "Are you in?"

"Sure." Cory spoke the word, knowing she was anything but.

Chapter Five

Cory pointed out the route, only half paying attention, focusing more on her situation than where they were going. A week ago, she'd worked for one of the most powerful law enforcement agencies in this part of the country. Now she was helping represent a loser on death row, on her way to meet with a turncoat private eye. As if that weren't enough to give her an identity crisis, the driver on her trip to hell was the sister of the killer whose life she was supposed to be trying to help save.

Serena didn't look like the next of kin of a rapist slash murderer. No, she looked like a gentle soul, a working woman. Maybe a teacher or an accountant. They were in a rental car, so she wasn't from around here. Cory looked at her hands, gripping the steering wheel. No ring. Not that unusual for a woman in her early thirties, but still…She should just ask all her questions, but she didn't. Cory couldn't put her finger on it, but she sensed strong walls around Serena, boundaries long in place. She respected a healthy desire for privacy, but at the same time the attraction she'd felt when she'd met her urged her to push through, find a way inside. What would she find? Did she have more in common with her brother than she'd like the world to believe? Was her professional appearance a front? And the question that topped her wave of curiosity: was the attraction she felt mutual? What if it was? What if it wasn't? Fear of both the known and unknown kept her silent. She remained quiet during the ride except when her navigation skills were necessary.

"Turn into that driveway, up ahead on the right."

Serena's head followed Cory's hand. "Doesn't look like office space."

"It's not. Well, not conventional office space, anyway. Most good private investigators I know work out of their cars. Not a convenient place to meet, especially since I think Skye probably still rides a Harley." Cory kept talking in an attempt to hold off any more questions from Serena. When Skye had suggested Sue Ellen's as a meeting place, she'd balked, but Skye was in the neighborhood, and a Wednesday afternoon at a lesbian bar would give them as much privacy as they'd be likely to get from any stuffy office setting. She directed Serena to a parking place and practically jumped out of the car to avoid further discussion.

Serena walked fast for a woman in heels. She paused in front of the door. "Sue Ellen's?"

"It's a local hangout. J.R.'s is just around the corner. You know, from the show, *Dallas*?"

Serena shook her head. "I don't watch a lot of TV."

"It's old." Cory felt lame, because both the reference fell flat and because she watched way more TV than she should. She pushed open the door of the bar, spotted Skye, and waved. She held open the door for Serena, but she grabbed her arm instead of walking into the bar.

"Tell me something."

"Sure." Cory waited patiently for the question.

Serena shot a look at Skye, before fixing Cory with a hard stare. "Whose idea was it to come here?"

"Here? Right here?"

Serena nodded.

Uh-oh. Didn't take a genius to discern Serena was displeased. Maybe she didn't like bars. There were only a few other women in the place, but one couple in the corner was treating the quiet bar like a good place for an afternoon delight. Probably the source of Serena's obvious discomfort. "It was Skye's idea. She was in the neighborhood. Thought it would be a quiet place to meet. Coffee shops get too crowded this time of day, what with everyone looking for an afternoon coffee fix. Bars? They tend to be pretty empty until happy hour starts." Too late, Cory realized she was rambling. "Come on. She's waiting."

Serena had known from the moment they drove into the neighborhood exactly what kind of bar this was. She wasn't blind. Couples wandering out of nearby restaurants, hands intertwined, were her first clue. Each set the same, women with women, men with men. What she didn't get was why Cory had thought it was okay to bring her to a bar for a business meeting. And not just any bar, but a lesbian one. Did she have some hidden agenda? Surely, the chemistry she felt wasn't mutual. Not likely since Cory had barely paid any attention to her all through lunch, directing her questions to Ian and avoiding eye contact. Odd. Especially since Ian mentioned they'd never worked together before. She filed away the exchange for when she could catch Cory alone.

Skye stood as they approached. Cory shook her hand and then made the introductions. "Skye Keaton, meet Serena Washington."

Serena held out her hand and Skye gave it a firm shake. Skye was drop-dead gorgeous and Serena was fairly positive she was a lesbian, but unlike when she'd shaken Cory's hand for the first time, she felt nothing. Except relief. Good to know every good-looking woman in Dallas wasn't going to ring her bell. She'd worked so hard to keep herself in check.

Skye interrupted her musings. "Can I get you something to drink?"

Serena looked at the half-full glass on the table. "What're you having?"

"A double. Club soda with lime." Skye's grin was infectious.

"I'll have the same."

"Cory?"

"I'm good."

Serena watched Cory watching Skye walk to the bar. "How long have you known her?"

"Years." Cory didn't take her eyes off Skye. "We haven't worked together in a long time though."

Again with the vague reference. The way Cory stared at Skye seemed detached, but Serena wondered what she wasn't seeing. She started to form a question, but Skye returned before she could ask. She'd have to try a different tack if she wanted real information. "Skye, I was just asking Cory how long you two have known each other."

Skye gave Cory a careful look before answering. "Wow, it's been years. We haven't had the pleasure of working together for a few years though."

Still vague. Serena decided she wasn't going to pierce their united front. She gave up. For now. "Where do we start?"

Skye answered. "You tell me what you need me to do and I quote you a fee."

Cory took the reins. "Short story. Serena's brother, Eric, is on death row. I'm helping her find an investigator to look into evidence for a writ. This morning is the first opportunity I had to hear about the case, so I don't have much detail other than what his appellate attorney shared with us over lunch."

Cory's summary didn't jibe with how Serena saw her role, so she filed it away with the rest of the pieces of Cory Lance that itched along the edges of her awareness. She didn't have time to consider the issue before Skye began peppering her with questions.

"Tell me the basic facts of the case."

Serena had studied the case file and could recite most of the relevant details from memory. "Eric was arrested by the Rinson police after a woman he once worked with, Nancy McGowan, was raped and murdered. In my view, the evidence was slim. No one witnessed the incident, but a customer of the bar where they worked had seen a black man standing next to Ms. McGowan by her car on the night she died. He picked Eric by his photograph—a mug shot the police showed him. There were a few other details that connected Eric to Nancy, but nothing that pointed to him as a killer."

Cory interjected. "Someone gave the cops a picture of the two of them that a witness testified was taken at her birthday celebration at the bar about a week before the murder. Running theory was Eric had a thing for McGowan and, when she rejected him, he took matters into his own hands."

"Any other suspects?"

"Doesn't appear that they investigated anyone else. Once they had Eric in their sights, they were done."

"DNA?"

"No."

"They didn't test for it or it just wasn't there?"

Serena quoted what she'd been told. "'Tests were inconclusive for DNA other than the victim's, and it doesn't appear that a rape kit was done.'"

Skye shook her head, muttered "small-town cops," and made some notes. Serena relaxed. The fact they were in a lesbian bar and Cory's sudden distancing of herself from the case, had her on edge, but Skye's sharp, no-nonsense style of questioning bolstered her confidence.

"Give me your impression of the trial attorneys."

And bam. Just like that, a question she couldn't answer and for an embarrassing reason. Serena took a deep breath and plunged in. "I don't have an impression other than what I've read in the legal papers. I wasn't at the trial." She looked back and forth between Skye and Cory. Neither was particularly good at hiding their surprise at her statement. She didn't blame them. How many defendants went on trial for their lives without a single family member to see them through the process? She could imagine what they thought of Eric. So unredeemable that even his sister couldn't stand to be in the courtroom.

"Surely, you were in court for the punishment phase of the trial?"

This from Cory. She had some nerve, pressing the point. Serena rewarded her candor with a string of answers. "I wasn't. I didn't know Eric had been arrested and charged with this awful crime. I didn't know he was convicted. I didn't know he'd been sentenced to die. I didn't know he'd exhausted his appeals. I didn't know anything about this case until a few weeks ago when he wrote to tell me he was scheduled to die. We don't have a lot of time. If you're going to work on the case, I need you to get started right away."

She leaned back in the booth, waiting for their shocked responses to her confession. Neither of them spoke for a few minutes, and Serena absorbed the surreal atmosphere of exposing her vulnerability accompanied by a light disco beat. She pondered how she could escape without them noticing. Return to her safe, secure life back in Florida, the comfort of family, and the security of her job. No crime, no questions, no recrimination.

Cory's hand on hers stopped her thoughts cold. Warm, accepting, and not completely unwelcome. Seconds passed. She couldn't bring herself to meet Cory's eyes, but she couldn't avoid Skye who looked between them with the hint of a smile playing at the corners of her lips. She gently withdrew her hand and placed it in her lap. The entire exchange likely only lasted a couple of seconds, but the effect lingered. Would she have pulled her hand away if Skye hadn't been right there? Didn't matter. She was here on a mission and she would not be distracted. She focused her attention on the reason for this meeting.

"What do you need to get started?"

Skye leaned back and stared at the ceiling. Serena watched and waited, resisting the desire to shake an answer out of her. She'd started out this meeting relaxed, but after speaking out loud about Eric's plight, anxiety now had a firm grip. Action. She craved action. Eric had waited long enough.

Thankfully, Skye spoke before she exploded. "I need to make a couple of phone calls. I'm in business for myself, but I need to make sure I can clear my schedule with the attorneys who rely on my services on a regular basis. And my wife will need a little notice that I'm going to be out of pocket."

"Married, huh?" Cory asked. "Never would've pegged you for the marrying kind."

Skye's grin lit up the room. "Not only married, but starting a family. Aimee's in her third trimester. You should know that a phone call from her is going to trump anything else for the next ten weeks."

Cory's smile was genuine. "Congratulations! You should definitely talk to her since there could be some out of town travel involved. Some of the trial witnesses have scattered to the wind and, of course, you'll need to visit Eric at Huntsville." Cory made a note on the pad in front of her. "The clinic has all the current contact info for the witnesses in their file, and we'll get you a copy of all the police reports."

Serena watched their easy exchange with a mixture of envy. Marriage, pregnancy, relationships. The ease with which they discussed these topics stung. She'd never pictured herself in their place, blithely discussing happily ever afters. She asked a question to bring things back to reality. "What's your rate and how much of a retainer do you need?"

Skye drummed her fingers on the table and cocked her head, as if considering the question. "I usually charge a hundred dollars an hour for in-town work and extra for travel. As for the retainer, it's hard to tell at this point. I'll need to review what your attorneys have compiled and work out a game plan. Why don't I make those calls I mentioned, get with Cory to review the evidence you have, and I'll put together a strategy that will include an estimate of the work that needs to be done? That should take about half a day and you can pay me in advance for that."

Skye sounded professional, thorough, and more than competent. Cory obviously trusted her and, despite a nagging sense she didn't have enough information to draw this conclusion, Serena trusted Cory. She pulled a checkbook from her purse and scrawled out a check for five hundred dollars. She stood and handed the check to Skye. "I guess you better start making those calls." She turned to Cory. "Ready?"

Cory answered her loaded question with a loaded answer. "If you are."

She nodded, knowing she was agreeing to way more than leaving the bar.

Cory assumed the role of GPS and directed Serena through the crowded Dallas streets. Melinda had left a voice message on her cell to say she was stuck in a deposition. If she went back to the clinic now, she'd have to find a ride home, a situation Melinda clearly hadn't contemplated when she'd dropped her off this morning. She could take a cab, but the cross-town ride would cost a fortune. Who was she kidding? Saving money wasn't the reason she was pointing out the route to her house. She'd hardly had a moment alone with Serena and she craved the connection that coursed between them during the few short seconds in the bar.

Madness. She spent her entire career as a prosecutor vigilantly guarding all aspects of her personal life. Unlisted phone number, stellar security system. She didn't participate in the frenzy of social media that had overtaken the rest of mankind. And her employer supported her desire for privacy. The DA's office had an agreement with the local papers—no photos would accompany news articles about current cases. The very last thing she would have done as a prosecutor would be to invite a defendant over to her house.

But Serena wasn't a defendant, and Cory was hard-pressed to even see her as the family of a defendant. Fragile, yet steeled. Intelligent, yet naive. Serena was a victim in her own right. If her brother was a killer, she was burdened with his evil deeds. If he wasn't, she was burdened with guilt for his mislaid penance. Either way, Cory cared. Cared that Serena hurt, admired the courage it took to ask for help, and she longed to coax a smile from her weary, stress-filled eyes.

She almost cared enough to ignore reality. Eric's execution date might come and go with hopeful, last-minute bursts of legal brilliance, but in the end, justice would mete out an unforgiving dose of poison. Once on death row, the path to life was nearly impossible to navigate. Very few dodged the executioner's needle.

"Up here, on the right." She'd let the entire drive to her house pass with only directional terms exchanged between them. So much for the moment alone. She'd wasted the time, unsure how to broach more personal topics in a way that wouldn't cause Serena to shut down completely. As they pulled up to her house, she made a snap decision. "You can park in the drive."

Serena's eyes signaled surprise, but nothing else in her expression showed anything but the cool, calm composure Cory knew had to be a mask. She wore her own mask often enough to see through others. Cynical instead of compassionate. Objective rather than outraged. Her job as a prosecutor demanded the façade. What motive did Serena have for hiding her feelings?

The car idled in the drive. Serena obviously had no intention of assuming any hospitality on Cory's part. Time for clarity. "Why don't you come in for a few minutes? We haven't really had a chance to talk, one-on-one."

Serena stared at the front of Cory's house for a few seconds before turning to face her. "Okay."

Cory took more encouragement from the one-word answer than it probably merited, but she didn't care. She waited until Serena shut the car down before opening her own door just to be sure she wouldn't drive off the minute she exited the vehicle.

Once they were both out of the car, she considered her impulsive invitation and wondered if her house was clean. She'd been squirreled away there for several weeks, waiting to hear the outcome of her suspension. She'd lived on whatever could be delivered to her door and lived in every pair of sweats she owned. The only other person who'd gotten beyond the foyer was Melinda, and, since they'd lived together in college, she'd never given a second thought to what Melinda thought of her housekeeping skills. As she turned a key in the front door, she tossed a just-in-case apology over her shoulder. "I was in a hurry when I left this morning. The place might be a bit of a mess."

It wasn't too bad. She moved quickly to grab a few random takeout boxes. She pointed Serena in the direction of the formal dining room she never used, and snuck to the kitchen where she stacked the boxes in the pantry. "I have water, Diet Coke, and wine. Can I get you something to drink?" She called out the question, feeling woefully inadequate for her lack of selection.

"A glass of water would be great."

Cory loaded the last clean glass with ice and water and met Serena in the dining room. She'd emptied the contents of her bag onto the table and had various files spread about. Serena was focused on the case. Not what Cory had in mind when she'd invited her in. Serena looked up when she entered, took the water glass, and drank half of it down. "I guess I was thirsty."

"Looks like you've accumulated a lot of paperwork about your brother's case."

"I've tried. I think there is more paperwork associated with the appeal than there was for the whole trial."

Cory considered her next question carefully before wading in. "Were you living in Florida at the time of the trial?"

"I was, but what I really think you want to ask me is why I didn't attend my brother's life or death trial."

"Yes, that's exactly what I'm asking." Maybe a truthful answer would garner an honest response.

"The short answer is, I didn't know about it. The long answer is, well…it's long."

Cory pointed at her glass. "I have something stronger if it would help the telling."

Serena cracked a mirthless smile. "Something with caffeine would be great."

"I can make a pot of coffee." She may not have a well-stocked fridge and pantry, but coffee was one staple she'd never be without.

Serena's smile was real this time. "I'd love some."

"Join me in the kitchen?"

"That would be nice." Serena lifted the water glass and followed Cory into the massive room. "What a wonderful kitchen. You must be an accomplished cook."

Cory followed her gaze to the bright copper pots and pans dangling from the ceiling. The room was pretty impressive. And clean. Very clean, since she never used it. "Actually, I can barely boil water." She gestured to the large oak table. "I copied the kitchen of my childhood. I have tons of good memories from being a kid, sitting around the kitchen table, watching my mom craft amazing meals, not to mention cookies and cakes. I never got the chef gene, but re-creating the atmosphere is the next best thing. Sometimes I burn one of those cake-scented candles for ambiance. Do you think I'm a total dork?"

Serena mumbled something and looked away. Cory was torn between pressing for affirmation and accepting that her banal conversation wasn't endearing her to Serena. The dork comment was already out, she may as well go for broke. "Now I'm sure you think I'm a dork."

Serena turned to face her and Cory saw tears in her eyes. "I don't think that at all."

"Good. Most people get to know me a little better before they draw that conclusion." Cory reached for a napkin and handed it to Serena. "I didn't mean to make you cry with my ramblings."

"You didn't."

"Okaaaay," Cory drew the word out. Better than calling Serena a liar. She'd clearly hit a nerve, but she couldn't imagine how. She reviewed her words. She'd been talking about the kitchen, her mother, cooking..."Was it the mention of cookies? Because I might have a box of store-bought ones somewhere in here." She grinned as she kidded. Anything to get the smile back on Serena's face.

Serena's smile didn't reach her eyes, but it was something. "Thanks, but I'll pass on the cookies," she said.

Cory gave it a last shot. "How about a good ear while you tell me what's wrong?"

Serena half stood, and for a minute, Cory thought she'd chased her off. Instead, Serena walked over to the coffee pot. "I don't trust a woman who can't boil water to make my coffee." She reached into the coffee canister and started scooping grounds. "But I guess if you're going to be my brother's lawyer, I better trust you enough to tell you our story."

Chapter Six

E ric raised me." Serena had never spoken those words before, but she knew with all her heart they were true. "We shared a mother, and neither of us knew who our fathers were. Didn't matter. We may as well not have had any parents at all. The woman who gave birth to us didn't care about anything other than where she'd get her next fix or fuck." Serena met Cory's eyes and was pleased she didn't flinch at the profanity. Instead, she looked interested in hearing more. Serena wasn't used to telling her story, but the interest and instant compassion reflected in Cory's eyes compelled her to keep talking.

"Our mother was a junkie. She slept with whoever would buy her drugs. Sometimes she was home, but most of the time she was at the local convenience store, begging a smoke from everyone who walked in, scoping the customers out until she found the one who would make her night.

"I don't remember how old I was when I figured out she wasn't going to take care of me. The food on the table was there because Eric put it there. I never wondered how my brother, only a few years older than me, provided for us. We never had much, but we always had something to eat, at least once a day.

"We moved a lot. I remember angry words when the landlords would come by, looking for the rent. Eric would pull them aside, and after the visits we usually got to stay a bit longer. When we moved, it was in the middle of the night, and we took only what we could carry in one trip. Didn't matter much since we didn't own much more than that." She paused for breath. She'd blurted the details out fast, scared they wouldn't come if she didn't hurry them along.

"I'm glad you had Eric to take care of you."

Serena was surprised by the insight. Those who knew the story—the agency worker and her adoptive parents—focused on what she didn't have—parents, rather than what she did have—a brother who loved her without conditions. Their focus was likely the reason they minimized her loss once they were separated. "He was my world."

"What happened?"

A simple question. Serena cast about for a simple response. She took a sip of her coffee as she gathered strength for the hardest part of the telling. "We finally managed to stay in one place long enough to feel like it was home, but as a result, Child Protective Services finally got wind of our mother's antics. They made several home visits and removed us and filed papers to terminate our mother's parental rights. I was ten. They placed us in a foster home, together at first."

Cory nodded her head. "They always try to keep siblings together."

Serena wondered if Cory had personal experience with the agency, and she wondered how much. "They don't try hard enough." She didn't bother trying to keep the anger out of her voice. She reached for her coffee, but Cory's hand met hers midway. She didn't pull away, enjoying the light touch, the gentle comfort. Cory had the singular ability to still her mind from the whirling guilt, misgiving, and stress. In the calm, she was able to access the truth.

"I should be honest. Eric didn't handle the environment very well. We were in three different homes together before the agency decided he was the source of the problem. After years of being in charge of himself and me, he didn't take too well to being told what to do."

"How old was he?"

"Fourteen."

"It's hard for kids to adjust at that age."

"Do you have kids?"

Cory abruptly pulled her hand away and leaned as far back in her chair as possible. "Uh, no. None." Cory seemed taken aback by the question. Another fact Serena filed away for later inspection. Her thoughts wandered to Skye, weeks away from having her first child, a child born on purpose, not by accident like she and Eric had surely been. Skye was clearly excited about the prospect of parenthood. Did

Cory want children of her own, or did she share Serena's fears about re-creating mistakes? The question seemed too personal. She ignored the irony in not asking and changed the subject.

"You just seem pretty familiar with CPS policies."

"I am. Part of the job."

"Of course."

"So what happened when Eric could no longer get along in foster care?" Cory seemed to relax as the questions moved away from her and back to the original subject. Again, Serena noted the vague answers Cory gave when any subject turned personal, but let it go. She could ask Paul more about Cory's background. After all, she had a right to know more about the attorney who would be working on her brother's case, didn't she?

"We gradually slipped apart. Eric was arrested several times. Petty thefts, but enough to wind him up in juvenile court. No foster family would take him after that, so he went to a boys' home, which wasn't a home at all; it was really a last stop on the state dime."

"It's hard to find permanent placement for older kids."

"I know. The agency didn't even post his profile on their adoption site."

"But yours?"

"Mine was up for only two weeks."

"I suppose you were beautiful even then?"

Serena felt the heat of the blush. Funny, Cory was blushing too. She glossed over the remark. She couldn't afford to do anything but. No way was she going to confront Cory about what she considered mild flirtation. By calling attention to it, she'd have to discuss it. What would she say? Are you a lesbian? Is that why you took me to a lesbian bar for a business meeting? Are you attracted to me? Is that why you keep touching me, with your hand, with your smile?

What if Cory thought her questions were crazy? Even she thought her questions were crazy. Better to ignore these subtle actions than make a fool of herself. Still…

"I was cute. Cute dress, cute bow in hair. Besides, little girls are less trouble. At least that's the prevailing theory."

"Good one. So you were adopted and Eric wasn't."

"I was not only adopted, but I was adopted by a family in Florida. Eric was still in the boys' home when it happened. We never even got to say good-bye before I got on a plane for the very first time in my life and flew away from everything that I knew."

"But you kept in touch."

"Letters, an occasional phone call. I saved every letter. The phone calls were usually laced with anger. Eric became hostile. I was living the privileged white life with my white parents in white America."

"Hardly fair. It wasn't like you had a choice. You were too young."

"And he was too young to realize he wasn't being fair. He softened up later. When he started getting into more serious trouble." Serena considered her next words. She'd only discussed Eric's past with the Clarks, and then only what was necessary to disclose. She considered his past private, like her own, and kept shared details to a minimum. But Cory would have to know everything if she was going to represent him. She may already know the outcome of Eric's transgressions, but she didn't know the details behind his wayward path, and that was why Serena was here in Dallas, instead of dispassionately phoning in her help from Florida.

"He was seventeen the first time he was arrested as an adult. He burglarized someone's home. With his juvenile record, the public defender gave up without trying. Eric took his first trip to the pen."

"I don't think that a pen time plea recommendation was out of line. Probation is usually reserved for first time offenders."

"Don't you tell me that there aren't tons of seventeen-year-olds offered probation, no matter what they did as children. Shoot, a seventeen-year-old is still a child in my book." Serena folded her arms. "Here's what I think. I think the system wrote Eric off—aged out of foster care, problems with authority. That court appointed lawyer told Eric he didn't have a choice. He didn't even bother to fight for him."

Serena shuddered at the memory. She'd received a letter from Eric, return address one of the state correctional facilities. She was only thirteen when she received it, but smarter about the system than any teenager should be. Eric explained what had happened. He'd aged out of foster care. Homeless and jobless, he got in with the wrong crowd. He'd been the lookout for a couple of other guys who'd broken into a house and stolen whatever they could carry out in one trip. Instead of his past mitigating his culpability, the court system viewed him as a lost cause. He got the minimum, but the minimum was two years in the penitentiary. He did a year before he was released on parole. At thirteen, she'd been angry about the sentence, at thirty-three, she was indignant.

"That began the downward spiral. A felon on parole can't find a job, so he either steals to earn a living or he does drugs to forget his troubles. Since he can't afford to buy drugs without a job, he steals. Either way, he's doomed. Seventeen is awful young to realize you've hit a dead end."

"There are alternatives."

Serena heard the trace of judgment in Cory's otherwise gentle tone. She knew Cory was right and she'd ultimately come to that conclusion herself, but she didn't need a stranger to tell her how she should view her brother's cause. She started to tell Cory exactly what she could do with her uninformed opinion, but stopped short when Cory added, "I get that he couldn't see his way through to them."

She reined in her anger. "I made excuses for him for years. It wore on me. Wore on everyone around me." The late night phone calls—she'd braced herself with every ring. Was he arrested or was he dead? Either was dreaded. Either could be a relief. How could she explain the roller coaster of emotions to a total stranger, especially one who'd probably never experienced what she and Eric had?

"It sounds like you've had a really hard time. But look at you." Cory paused to do just that. "You started out with nothing, and you've obviously done well for yourself. And you're here now to help your brother. And you're not alone. You have lots of smart, capable people working on his case."

Did Cory include herself among the smart and capable? Did she really care about her, about Eric? The doorbell interrupted her thoughts.

Cory stood, her expression puzzled. "Wait here. I'll be right back."

Serena waited a few seconds, but discomfort settled in. She paced the kitchen while she waited. She'd spent the day with Cory, but hardly knew a thing about her. And she wanted to. She wanted to know all about her. Severe restraint kept her from glancing through the stack of mail scattered across the kitchen counter. The return address on the top envelope read "State Bar of Texas." Of course. Cory was a lawyer. That much she knew. But she was also a woman with a big kitchen, and seemingly a big heart, even if she kept sections of it closed off. Probably to keep herself from being hurt. Now that was something she could relate to. She would do well to keep a cooler head, guard her emotions. Eric's case was going to sorely test her abilities. She should start by leaving her, or his, lawyer's home. As much as she enjoyed the connection between them, she had no business in Cory's personal space.

Serena grabbed her purse and left the kitchen. She found Cory standing in the entryway with a wallet in her hand. An enormous vase loaded with red roses rested precariously on her hip. Cory looked up and Serena read chagrin in her expression.

"Hey. Sorry to keep you waiting. I was trying to find a tip. For the guy. He just left. The flower guy." Cory stopped talking, but the fluster didn't leave her face. Roses, fluster. Serena couldn't help a quick glance at the card perched on a plastic fork in the forest of roses. Of course it was in an envelope. Didn't matter what the card said, only one kind of relationship merited red roses. Wasn't any of her business anyway. Time to leave.

"Let me set these down and then we can talk some more."

"You put those in a vase. I'm going back to my hotel."

"I'm sorry; you must have had an exhausting day. I forgot you flew in this morning."

"Long day." Serena kept the words short so she wouldn't say what she really felt. She preferred Cory's home to the drab motel, Cory's company to the solitude she normally enjoyed. Her changing preferences confused her. As long as she was in Cory's presence, she didn't need to examine them. So why was she leaving? She shelved the introspection and opened the door. "Thanks for the coffee. For everything. I appreciate your kindness."

She didn't wait for Cory's response before she shut the door behind her and walked to the car. As she drove away, the image foremost in her mind was the huge bouquet of deep red roses and Cory's reaction to them. There were layers to Cory she may never see.

But she wanted to.

CHAPTER SEVEN

C ory called a cab the next morning. She'd be glad when her car was out of the shop and she had more freedom. Dallas wasn't a city designed for those without wheels.

While she waited for the cab she filled a travel mug with a third cup of coffee. She needed at least that much to get through the first half of the day. No sleep. All she wanted was to crawl back in bed, but bed hadn't been her friend the night before. She'd tossed and turned most of the night. Thoughts of her future, feelings about Serena— both had conspired to rob her of sleep.

Julie had left two messages on her phone, both stating she was lonely and urging her to call. She'd ignored the pleas. The massive arrangement of roses sat on her dining room table. Cory passed it on her way out the door and fingered the card. She'd read it several times yesterday, after Serena had left. "You deserve the best. Always." It wasn't signed.

No matter how hard she tried, she couldn't decipher a secret message in the sparse phrase. How like Julie, to be guarded even when expressing affection.

When she arrived at the clinic, she felt out of sorts. Other than foisting her off on Serena the day before, Paul hadn't really discussed what her role would be while she lived out her sentence here at the clinic. The receptionist wasn't at her desk, so Cory wandered the halls of the office in search of Paul. She found him in a makeshift library, hunched over what looked like several volumes of trial transcripts.

"Hi, Cory. Glad to see you back for another day." Paul's smile was infectious, and Cory couldn't help but smile back. He tapped the shoulder of the man next to him and motioned for him to turn around. "Greg Levin, meet Cory Lance. Cory, Greg's our senior writ counsel and he's going to take the lead on the Eric Washington case."

Greg offered his hand and Cory shook it. Would she be working with Greg? What would Serena think about him? Senior writ counsel. He certainly sounded experienced. Serena would want the best working on her brother's case. She should be happy for her.

"Nice to meet you, Greg. I introduced Serena to an investigator yesterday, and I'm ready to get started. Just let me know what you'd like me to do."

Greg shot a puzzled look at Paul who intervened. "Cory, I thought we'd have you work in our intake division. We have a few interns who could use guidance from a pro about evaluating whether a case fits our services. I'm sure Greg will let you know if he needs help on the Washington case, but why don't you come with me now and I can introduce you to the rest of the staff."

They were halfway down the hall before it hit her. She wasn't going to be working on cases. She'd be pushing paper to serve her time. Paper about strangers. Not Eric. Not Serena.

She went through the motions as Paul introduced her around the office. She could barely remember anyone's names, but then again, it didn't seem important since she wouldn't be sticking around. She did notice that Paul used delicate phrasing to describe her experience. She was by turns a "veteran trial attorney" and a "seasoned litigator." Did the clinic employees know who she really was? Her name had been splashed all over the papers for a few weeks. Kind of hard to imagine they wouldn't have a clue that the enemy was in their midst. Yet, Paul treated her like an equal, no judgment, no animus.

"Here's where we have the students set up." He motioned her into a small room, sparsely furnished with three folding tables and a scattering of mismatched chairs. "The interns usually don't show up until after their morning classes, around ten. I'll stick around until then and help you get started." He pointed to a brass coat stand in the corner. "Make yourself comfortable. I realize it's not the kind of space you're used to, but we use most of the donations we receive for legal talent, not for furnishings."

"No problem. I'm used to county digs. Not much plush about the offices at the courthouse." Cory hung up her coat and settled in at one of the tables. Paul pulled over a box and sat beside her. He reached in and pulled out a rubber-banded stack of mail.

"We get literally hundreds of requests for help every month. The first step is weeding through the letters to figure out if there might be a viable claim. Next, we identify which cases need immediate attention. You might say intake is a bit like triage."

"Except I won't be doing any actual treatment."

Paul folded his hands on the table and fixed her with a stare. "No, you won't. It's not because of where you come from; it's mostly because I don't know how long you'll be with us." He stopped and appeared to consider his next words carefully. "I'm not going to lie. I know all about the Nelson case. We didn't work on it, but the indigent defense community is small. Word gets around. But here's the deal: I believe in the inherent good of people. I believe that someone can make a mistake and live to redeem themselves another day. Maybe that's why I don't believe in the death penalty. It forecloses all possibilities." He sighed. "Sorry, I get on a tear sometimes. All I meant to say is, here you start fresh. You're a lawyer and you're here to help us out. I don't care where you came from and where you're going. While you're here, work hard, work smart, and keep an open mind. That's all I ask."

Cory had spent her entire professional career prosecuting criminals of all shapes and sizes. She'd stared evil in the face and raised many a glass of whisky in celebration of guilty verdicts, long prison sentences, and capital punishment. She believed in the death penalty, even considered it necessary. She didn't agree with Paul's ideology, but his request was fair. She could do this. It wasn't forever.

Paul spent the next hour explaining the process they'd set up for reviewing and prioritizing the requests for assistance. By the time he left, Cory felt overwhelmed by the volume of correspondence and the level of care required to evaluate each cry for help. Most of the cases were hopeless, and had been so from the start. Once a defendant was convicted at trial, the burden to overcome the jury's guilty verdict rested entirely on his or her shoulders. And it was a heavy burden. The cases Cory had to review had already wound their way through several sets of appeals, from the trial judge who had originally heard the case to the two layers of appeals courts in Texas. Some had gone even further, all the way to the United States Supreme Court before seeking their last chance with the Justice Clinic.

The appeals for help generally recognized they were running out of hope, and they were heart wrenching. Cory was deep into an emotional letter from the mother of an inmate when she heard a familiar voice.

"Working hard, as usual." Skye Keaton stood in the doorway. Except for the day before at the bar, Cory hadn't seen her in over a year. Skye had been a regular lead witness in many of the cases she prosecuted until her abrupt departure from the Dallas Police Department. Cory knew the official story. Skye had decided to pursue other interests, but she also knew the scuttlebutt. Skye had been asked to resign after she disclosed mishandling of evidence to a defense attorney on a prominent case. Cory figured the truth fell somewhere in between. She wondered what the gossips were saying about her own sudden departure from the side of law and order.

"Come on in. I could use a break." Cory gestured at the boxes on the floor beside her. "Lots of bleeding heart pleas for justice."

Skye slid into one of the chairs and crossed her legs. "You so sure some don't deserve a second look?"

She wasn't, but she didn't feel like admitting it. Hell, if she couldn't trust a former cop, who could she trust? "To tell you the truth, I don't know what to think about most of these letters. I guess I figure if someone's sitting on death row or spending the rest of their life in prison, they'll probably say anything to get someone to take a second look."

"Would you?"

"Excuse me?"

"Would you say anything if it meant you could get your case a second look?"

The knowing expression on Skye's face urged Cory to tread cautiously with her response. "I don't have a case. Not sure what I'd do, but I'd like to think I'd have a fair perspective."

"We all would, but when you're in the middle of a case, it's hard to be objective. Doesn't mean what you see isn't right."

"I guess that's true."

Skye leaned across her chair and shut the door. "How about you? I'm willing to bet you got a bum deal. How long are you out for?"

"I don't want to talk about it." And she didn't.

"Doesn't do any good to keep it to yourself." Skye's stare was intense, and Cory did her best not to flinch under the scrutiny. Keeping it to herself was working just fine. She was biding her time here, with these files, with these pseudo victims. Soon, she'd be back doing what she did best. Back in a courtroom, seated at the prosecution table.

She thought about the roses. Julie would keep her promise. She had to believe that or she'd never make it through. "I don't know what you've heard, but I just did my job."

Skye stood. "The line between job and justice gets blurry sometimes. Take it from someone who knows. I let things get blurry. Nowadays, I can see clearly. You want to know what I learned?"

Cory wanted the uncomfortable conversation to be over, but Skye wasn't going to let it be until she'd said her piece. She didn't have to act interested though. She projected as much apathy as she could into her tone. "Sure, Skye, what have you learned?"

"We're working in a blurry business. You may think everything can be defined as right and wrong, good and evil. It's not that simple and things aren't always what they appear. I was asked to resign after what I did on the Burke case. At first, I was angry. I lost everything, and the people who took it from me were convinced they were justified, that I was wrong. I don't blame them. I'd thought just like they did until my moment of clarity. I did the right thing, even if I had to go against everything I'd believed in to find my way there."

Skye's confession moved her, but not enough to confide her own secrets. Skye had cut all ties to the life she'd led. Cory hadn't. She wasn't about to burn the bridge that would lead her back to the career she'd dedicated her whole life to. No matter how many bleeding hearts crossed her path. Not even if they intrigued her as much as Serena Washington did.

❖

Serena pulled into the parking lot of the clinic and glanced at the cars already there. Did one of them belong to Cory? Her hope was mixed with apprehension. What did Cory think of her after she'd bared her soul the night before? Or would Cory be too preoccupied thinking about whoever had sent the beautiful flowers to give her and her problems a second thought?

Paul met her at the receptionist's desk. "Serena, good to see you again. I understand you've hired Skye Keaton to work on your brother's case."

"Yes, I hope you don't mind that I didn't run it by you first. Cory recommended her, and we met with her yesterday. She seems very competent, and since she and Cory have worked together in the past, I thought she'd be a good fit." Skye had intrigued her, but Cory's recommendation was what sealed the deal. She barely knew Cory, but she trusted her. Completely at odds with her usual mode of operation. She didn't make a habit of trusting folks, especially not ones she barely knew. Yet Cory had invited her into her house. Treated her like a real person, despite the fact she knew her brother was a convicted felon, a death row inmate.

Eric's fate would be in good hands, and she realized she'd done all she could at this point. She hadn't expected to hire an investigator so quickly, but now that she had, she should go home and let the professionals do their work, let her personal feelings go. But she needed to see Cory one more time before she left. "Is Cory here?"

"Yes. She showed up early this morning. Let me take you back to meet the attorney who'll be working on your brother's case and then you can stop in and see her."

Serena followed Paul, slowly digesting his words. By the time he introduced her to Greg Levin, she'd figured it out. Cory wasn't going to be working on Eric's case. Was it a sudden change? Had her outpouring of personal information the night before sent Cory packing? She knew she'd shared too much. Now she'd have to relate the whole story of her and Eric's childhood to another stranger. This time she'd give the short version, with none of the emotion she'd shared with Cory.

Cory. She'd counted on seeing her this morning. Even worn the navy wool suit and green silk blouse everyone said looked good against her mocha skin. She hoped the outfit would be comfortable later on the plane since she'd already checked out of the hotel. She risked a question. "I'm sure Greg's a great attorney, but I thought Cory would be working on Eric's case."

Paul looked surprised. "Cory Lance?" At Serena's nod, he added, "Cory's just helping us out temporarily. I apologize if I gave you the impression she'd be taking the lead on Eric's case."

"You didn't. My misunderstanding. I'm sure whoever you assign will be perfect." She wasn't sure of any such thing, but it seemed like the right thing to say. She wanted Cory, but she wasn't sure if that desire had anything to do with her legal skills. It was probably better that she deal with this Greg guy instead. Less dangerous.

Greg Levine was young. At least he was younger than she expected. The little information she knew about the legal profession told her that even if someone went straight from college to law school, the soonest they'd graduate would be around twenty-five years old. Greg didn't look much older than that, and Serena said as much after they shook hands.

"Good genes. I'm forty, just well preserved."

"I'm sorry."

"No need to apologize. I get that a lot." Greg laughed. "You have every right to ask about the man who's going to represent your brother." His expression turned serious. "And you should."

Serena caught the undercurrent in his tone. "If someone had asked some questions of that pair who claimed to represent Eric at his trial, he might not be on death row. Is that what you mean to say?"

"I may not have been that blunt, and I'm certainly not here to lay blame, but whatever you can tell me about Eric and what happened at his trial might be helpful. The more information I have, the more tools I'll have at my disposal."

Serena sighed and then recounted for Greg the reasons she'd lost touch with her brother, why she wasn't at his trial. Greg was a good listener, but matter-of-fact. Different than Cory. Probably a good thing. The way her emotions were rocketing all over the place, matter-of-fact was what she needed right now. And for facts, she wanted to get an idea of the next steps in her brother's case. "Greg, I may not have a personal account of Eric's trial, but I've read every piece of paper associated with Eric's case. I know what's been done and what hasn't. What I need from you before I head back to Florida is a step-by-step of what comes next."

"Fair enough." Greg started drawing on a piece of paper. "Here's the plan. Stop me if you have questions." He sketched out a flowchart. "Ian has already taken your brother's case as far as it can go through direct appeal channels. He also helped your brother file a writ of habeas corpus, claiming ineffective assistance of counsel, which was denied."

"I don't understand why that claim failed. If it's apparent to a lay person like myself, shouldn't it be easy for a judge to be able to tell those lawyers didn't do everything they should have to defend Eric?"

"Short answer, yes. Complicated answer is that judges are lawyers and lawyers stick together. A lawyer would pretty much have to stand up during trial and scream 'my client's guilty' before an appeals court would decide they were ineffective. I'm exaggerating, but not by much."

"Why do these claims even exist if no one can prove them?"

"Good question. I don't have a good answer. In the meantime, here's where we are—in order to get a stay, we need one of two things: proof that your brother isn't competent and/or evidence that he's innocent that either was withheld from the defense at the time of trial or that is newly available."

Serena had read extensively on the subject of competence and knew how narrow the law defined the term. In order to qualify, Eric would have to be unable to understand the proceedings against him or assist in his defense. He may not have the best judgment, but he knew what was happening to him and he had shared all the information he had with his lawyers and urged them to investigate his defenses. "Eric is a lot of things, but incompetent isn't one of them."

"Agreed. Ian met with Eric on numerous occasions and had the same impression. In fact, it seems like Eric was very interested in assisting his lawyers during trial, but they didn't follow-up on the points he made."

"Again, I don't understand. Why wouldn't they listen to him? His life was on the line."

Greg folded his hands over the chart, and faced her. "I have a probable explanation. You're not going to like it."

"Try me."

"Eric has an extensive criminal history. He was acquainted with the victim. He had no verifiable alibi. A jailhouse snitch testified that Eric expressed remorse over his actions. I hate to say this, but I think his defense team went through the motions, but they believed he killed her."

Serena struggled to contain her outrage. She was angry at the lawyers, angry at the system, but she was also angry with herself. After all, she'd come to believe Eric was capable of pretty much anything. She'd written him off, refused to believe he would ever become a productive member of society. Was it so hard to believe that two strangers, who'd been appointed to represent Eric and received very little money in exchange for a colossal drain on their time, might not bother to dig a little deeper? Who was she to judge?

But she had to know. Before she got on a plane and left Eric's fate in the hands of these new lawyers, she had to know if they too believed he killed Nancy McGowan. She couldn't ask the question the way she wanted, but she did the best she could. "And what do you believe?"

Greg's face reflected compassion and his words, though not what she wanted to hear, were exactly what she needed. "I believe that everyone, regardless of their past and current circumstances, has a right to a fair trial. A trial where all the evidence is developed and presented. I believe that we have a duty to seek the truth. Eric didn't get his fair shake, and I believe it's wrong for the state to want to kill a man under these circumstances."

His words were exactly what she needed to hear. If Eric actually killed this woman, she wouldn't want him to die, but not because she didn't believe in the death penalty, but because he was her brother. She wasn't sure how she felt about the death penalty in the abstract. Of course, now that it was touching her life, the concept would never be abstract again.

"Okay, so after all the bad things about Eric's case you've told me, how in the world do you expect to help him get another shot at justice?"

"We'll have to review every aspect of the case and find the evidence that was missed the first time. In the first trial, the state had to prove he was guilty; he didn't have to prove anything. Now, we're going to have to prove his innocence to even get a second shot."

"How do we do that?"

"We'll start with the investigator you hired. We need to follow-up on any leads the original attorneys let drop, talk to all the witnesses again, make sure we have all the evidence the trial lawyers should have had. Did I hear Paul say you retained Skye Keaton?"

Serena opened her mouth to answer, but another voice beat her to it.

"Did someone call my name?" Skye strode into the room, her black leather jacket a comfortable contrast to the suits in the room. She set an expensive looking midnight blue motorcycle helmet on the table, and slid into a chair. Greg spoke first. "Detective Keaton. When Paul mentioned your name, I wondered…"

"There's only one of me."

Serena looked between them, reading a slight undercurrent to the exchange. "You two know each other?"

Skye answered. "Only as adversaries. We've tangled in the courtroom on many occasions."

Right. Cory had told her Skye was a former homicide detective. At the time, she'd thought Skye's experience on the other side would give her unique perspective. What she hadn't considered was whether her former job might put her at odds with Eric's defense team. Would Cory have recommended her if that were the case? Surely not. She ignored the voice inside her that wondered why she trusted Cory so much and so quickly, and instead floated a question. "Is it easy to shift gears?"

The question was directed at Skye, but Greg jumped in. "Skye's been a private investigator for a while now. I'm confident she's solidly defense oriented."

"Well, I don't know if that's the way I'd characterize my perspective. Let's say this. I've seen both sides. What you want, correct me if I'm wrong, Greg, is objective information." She turned to face Serena. "I can't guarantee you what I find will be good for your brother's case, but I can guarantee that no one is better than me at getting to the truth."

Her assurances sounded sincere, but Serena wanted more. "I can't help but wonder if you won't be inclined to side with the police who did the investigation."

Skye exchanged glances with Greg before responding. "I was a good cop, but I'm a much better private investigator. The reasons why are long and pretty personal. You have no reason to trust me, and I wouldn't blame you if you don't—" A knock on the door interrupted her, and a young woman poked her head in.

"Greg, the clerk's office for the Fifth Circuit is on the phone for you."

He stood. "Sorry, but I have to take this. It may take a while." He extended his hand and Serena reached to shake it. "I have your contact information and I'll keep you posted on our progress. I can't promise you a specific result, but I do promise you that we'll do everything in our power to help Eric." He rushed out, leaving Serena and Skye alone in the room.

Serena looked at her watch. She needed to leave soon or she'd miss her flight. One day hadn't been long enough. She wished she could see Eric again, but the prison didn't allow frequent visits, and not enough time had passed since she'd last seen him. At least she would leave knowing Eric had a decent attorney on his side. And a seasoned investigator. Yet, after yesterday, she'd envisioned Cory hard at work on Eric's case. She'd imagined the calls Cory would make to keep her updated. She'd been looking forward to something that wasn't going to happen no matter how long she stuck around. Time to head back to Florida, to her safe and secure life. She stood. "I need to get going. Thanks for agreeing to work on Eric's case. You can send your invoices directly to me. I don't have a lot of extra cash, but I want to be thorough. Just let me know if your retainer runs low." As she headed to the door, Skye reached out and touched her arm.

"Wait. I want to finish what I was saying before."

Serena didn't need to hear whatever Skye had to say. She trusted her own instincts. If Cory trusted Skye, she did too. "I trust you to do everything you can to help my brother. Enough said. Okay?"

"Okay. Do you need a lift to the airport?"

"No, I rented a car." Serena did her best to act nonchalant. "Did you happen to see Cory when you came in? I wanted to tell her thanks for her help before I leave."

"She was in the office down the hall when I came in. I'll walk you there."

Serena hesitated. She wanted a moment alone with Cory, but wasn't comfortable saying that. "Thanks, I'd appreciate it."

As Skye walked her down the hall, her stomach began to twist. The source was hard to pinpoint. She wanted to see Cory, but she was apprehensive about why she was no longer working on Eric's case. Would Cory want to see her? Had she offended her the evening before? She couldn't get on the plane without answers, but she knew Cory wasn't likely to give her answers with Skye in the room.

"She was in here when I came by earlier." Skye pushed on the door that was already slightly ajar.

Serena's hope fell when she saw the room was empty. "I guess she's gone."

"I'm right here."

Cory's voice was soft, close. Serena imagined she could feel her breath against her neck. She tensed against the onslaught of emotions. How could this woman she barely knew take her to such heights? She turned and met Cory's steady gaze. Sparks flashed between them and she became lost in the moment. Cory reached a hand out and Serena waited, trembling with anticipation. Her adrenaline dropped when Cory pushed the door open and invited both of them inside.

"It's small, but you're welcome in my tiny office." She set a cup of coffee down and motioned to two folding chairs set up on the opposite side of the table.

Serena considered leaving. She didn't need another minute in Cory's presence to know that her self-control was waning. Better to get on a plane and fly back to the familiar than test this uncharted ground. But Skye, standing behind her, eased her into the room, and she found herself seated across from Cory, wondering if she felt any of the raging emotions that Serena was experiencing.

Skye saved her by speaking the first words. "What are you working on?"

Cory pointed at the dozens of files scattered on the table. "Intake. All of these are requests for assistance from the clinic." She waved at a stack of boxes behind her. "Those too."

Serena gasped. She'd had no idea so many waited in line. "There are so many. How in the world did Eric's case get accepted so quickly?"

Cory shifted in her seat, obviously uncomfortable with the question. "The clinic uses a set of factors to prioritize cases. Eric's case scored high on the list."

Of course. Cory may be too delicate to speak the words, but Serena knew what she meant. His execution date could come any day now, at which point the clinic's work would do him no good. She nodded. "I understand."

Cory reached a hand across the table and grasped Serena's hand in her own. Her eyes held pain, sympathy. "I know the clinic will do everything they can for your brother."

"And you?" Serena couldn't help it; the words came tumbling out before she could censor them. "I understand you're not going to be working on Eric's case."

Cory looked uncomfortable again. She drew back her hand and crossed her arms in front of her chest. "I'm not here in that capacity, but I'm confident Greg will do a great job representing your brother."

Serena had taken reading people's expressions to an art form. She both felt and saw the sea change in Cory's demeanor. The subject of what she could and would work on was off limits. Didn't matter. Everything about Cory was off-limits. A crush on a striking woman, whose life was a world away, was a silly consideration. Serena had no time in her life for silliness. Not now, now ever. Time to catch that plane.

She stood. "I just wanted to say thanks for your kindness. For putting me in touch with Skye. I have to leave if I'm going to catch my plane."

Cory stood and walked her to the door, but her arms remained crossed, signaling the new distance between them. "Good luck to you and Eric."

"Thanks, but I think we'll need a little more than luck to get us through." Serena turned and strode back down the hall. She was almost out the front door of the clinic when she realized Skye was at her side. She didn't say a word as Skye accompanied her to her car and took the keys from her shaking hand.

"Are you sure you're okay?"

Serena sighed. "It's all so hard." A vague, but all-encompassing statement.

"Yes. It is. Too bad Cory's not working on Eric's case. I think she'd be great."

"You do?" The question was a throwaway. She didn't want to talk about Cory anymore, but then again, she did. She hung on Skye's next words.

"I do. As a prosecutor, she has a unique perspective. Who better to know what the state should have done, didn't do, and may have hidden from the defense? I know my experience as a—"

Serena cut her off mid-sentence. "What you said about Cory— did you mean she's a former prosecutor?"

Skye looked first puzzled, then uncomfortable with the question. "Well, I may have spoken out of turn. Cory's on leave from the DA's office. Maybe you should talk to her about her specific situation."

Or maybe not. Serena had heard enough. Cory worked for the other side. No wonder she wouldn't be working on Eric's case. Representing the downtrodden wasn't her thing. What was she doing here at the clinic? Serena wanted to know and she didn't. She'd trusted her. Why? Because she'd mistaken her own attraction for something more on Cory's part. She'd been a fool.

Time to leave. Go back home. Try to assume some normalcy in her life. As if that were possible with Eric's death looming and newly awakened feelings stirring in her soul. Being miles away would make the difference. She hoped.

• 78 •

CHAPTER EIGHT

Three weeks in and Cory couldn't wait for the end of her sentence. It wasn't the atmosphere. Everyone at the clinic had been nice to her, but the work was draining, and not in a way she was used to. Every day, all she did was read submissions and scale them. She was the gatekeeper, but she didn't feel a part of the process. While the activity of reading each packet and grading it on a scale of priorities was rote, the substance behind it was what was really wearing her out.

Every letter requested the same thing—help. A last chance. Desperation poured off the pages. It didn't matter that she worked for the other side. The desperate pleas would penetrate even the hardest heart. She'd begun to dream about the cases that consumed her days. Dark dreams with inmates reaching through bars, clawing at her as she walked the corridors of the penitentiary.

Completely unrealistic dreams. She'd have no personal contact with these people. Just like when she was a prosecutor, she would have a shield between her and the person she sought to put away. Except she had had personal contact with one of them. Even though she wouldn't be working on Eric's file, she'd reviewed it in-depth. On some level, she felt she owed it to Serena to know all the facts in case she ever saw her again, in case Serena ever asked. She'd known Serena had only been in town for a day or two, but her departure had still seemed abrupt. Her number was in the file. Cory could call her, feign some case-related reason to talk, but what would be the point? Their brief encounter wasn't real. She knew better. Whatever feelings had passed between them had more to do with circumstance than reality.

Besides, she'd be back at the job soon enough. Julie had promised, and despite the complicated mix of feelings she had toward Julie, she knew she didn't make idle promises. Two months. Almost half of it complete.

The buzzing of the phone on her desk startled her. Besides weekly staff meetings, she barely had any interaction with the rest of the staff. Paul passed it off as the nature of the work she was doing, but she secretly wondered if the lack of contact was more about who she was. She lifted the phone and answered the call.

"A Melinda Stone is holding for you."

Thank God. A friendly voice. "Thanks, please put her through."

Melinda didn't wait for her to say hello before launching in. "You, me, lunch. I'll pick you up and we'll go someplace swanky."

Swanky wasn't in Cory's budget right now. She wasn't being paid either from her old job or her new one. But she knew once Melinda had her mind set, it wasn't worth fighting. "Sure, but you'll have to pick up the tab. I'm still living off my piggy bank."

"Deal. See you in thirty minutes. We have reservations at Capital Grille."

Melinda was a foodie of the highest order. When they arrived at the restaurant, Cory wasn't surprised when the maître d' greeted her effusively and led them to one of the best tables in the place. The waiter practically genuflected, and Cory had no doubt Melinda tipped as well as she ordered.

Once they placed their orders, Melinda started in. "How's life among the less fortunate?"

"Aren't I one of the less fortunate?"

"I suppose. I hope you're not still mad at me. When the attorney for the bar suggested this as a way for you to keep your license, I figured you'd jump at the chance."

"I am grateful, just sulking. I hate it. I'm assigned to intake. I guess I shouldn't be surprised, but on the first day, they had me meet with a new client. I guess I thought I'd actually get to do some substantive work."

"Back up, sister. New client? I thought all their clients were wards of the prison system. Did they really send you out to the pen on your first day?"

Cory laughed at Melinda's attempt to speak the slang of criminal lawyers. "Pen? No. Actually, I met with the new client's sister."

"Dish. What was it like meeting with the family of a murderer? Did I guess right, the guy's a murderer, right?"

Melinda was goofing, and Cory knew it, but her words stung. She didn't like hearing Serena's brother reduced to "murderer" and Serena as the "murderer's sister." She didn't know anything about Eric beyond what Serena had told her, but she knew Serena's layers went deep.

She missed her. Silly, really. How could she miss a person she'd only known for a day?

But it had been a long day, full of disclosures and confidences. She and Serena had talked for hours before they parted, and Cory had hung on to the hope they'd talk again. They had shared more in that single day than she'd shared with Julie during the whole of their relationship. She and Julie barely discussed anything that wasn't related to the cases they'd worked and which hotel would be good for their next meeting. Naked, but never really intimate. She'd felt more intimate with Serena in the few hours they'd spent together than she'd ever felt with Julie.

Cory jerked back to the present when Melinda snapped her fingers under her nose. "Hey, where'd you go? You're missing this wonderful plate of calamari, and I'm not waiting on you."

"Just thinking. You know, the woman I met wasn't what you would've expected."

"I'm sure."

"No, really. Her brother's on death row for murder. Looking at his rap sheet, you'd think he's a piece of shit. Graduated from petty crimes to robbery to rape and murder. I don't know him at all, but I met his sister and she seems perfectly normal."

"So what do you think happened?"

"Well, I do know they were separated when they were young. Druggie mom, both kids went into foster care. Serena turned out great. Eric's sitting on death row."

"Serena, huh?" Melinda put down her fork and stared Cory down. "What's with the tone?"

"Nothing. Just the way you said her name. All gentle and sweet. She's the sister of the murderer, right?"

"There are so many things wrong with what you just said, I don't know where to begin. She's the sister of a guy on death row. The clinic's trying to prove he doesn't belong there. I didn't say her name any particular way, I was just trying to tell you she's nothing like I would have imagined."

"Of course she's not. You're used to dealing with the more obvious victims, not the ones who get burned by your scorch-the-earth prosecutions."

"What the hell's that supposed to mean?"

Melinda speared a circle of calamari and peppers and dragged the forkful through the tasty sauce. "Maybe it's as simple as you've never considered the other side before. Maybe that's why working at the clinic may be the best thing that's ever happened to you."

"I think you've lost your mind. Pushing files and biding my time isn't going to change my life one bit." Cory grabbed a roll from the bread basket and buttered it fiercely. "I was only trying to tell you I thought I'd get to see a little more action. I don't need a lecture from a bleeding heart liberal who makes more money than most CEOs."

"Settle down. You'll ruin my appetite. Let's agree to table the subject. You only have five weeks to go and then you'll be back to locking people up and throwing away the key."

Cory bit back a retort. She didn't need to defend her career. Melinda had given her a hard time about it since the first internship in college, but the teasing had never bothered her before. As Serena's face flashed in her mind, she tried not to think about why it was bothering her now. *You've never hosted a defendant's sister at your house before.* Still, it shouldn't matter. Serena seemed perfectly normal. Better than normal; she intrigued Cory. If they'd met under other circumstances, she'd consider asking Serena out. But they hadn't. Serena's brother was a killer. Accused killer, anyway, and definitely not Cory's problem, which meant Cory and Serena's interaction was over. For the best. At least she was willing to pretend that was the case.

"You like her."

Damn Melinda. Mind reader. "I'll tell you what I like. I like this calamari." Cory stabbed a forkful. "I've been brown-bagging it, and I'm tired of peanut butter sandwiches."

"What, no jelly? You'll never be a gourmet if you forego the little extras." Melinda abruptly switched topics. "You do like her. I recognize the goofy look on your face. Amazing how you ever function in the courtroom since you have no poker face."

"My poker face is fine." Cory knew she wasn't off the hook just because Melinda was up to her usual abrupt changes in topic. "I do like her, but not in the way you think. She's a nice person, that's all."

"Nice, huh? Nice is good. At least it's a step in the right direction. Julie? She's not so nice."

"We're not going to talk about her."

"Which her? I've lost track."

"Don't be a pain the ass. Can't we just eat and talk about mindless things?"

Melinda cocked her head and Cory put on her best pleading expression. "I suppose so, under one condition."

"Name it."

"I get the last bite of this amazing calamari."

"Deal." Cory sank back, relieved that at least she wouldn't have to talk about Serena. She wasn't sure how she was going to stop thinking about her, though.

Two hours later, Cory tapped her foot as Melinda drove them back to the clinic. Melinda reached over and slapped her thigh. "Quit that. You're making me crazy."

"And you're making me late."

"Are you punching a time clock? I thought you didn't even like this place."

"Jeez. You're the one who got me this gig. Don't you care what they think of me? Because I do. I need a clean report to get reinstated. You said so yourself."

"Settle down. I don't think being late from lunch is going to get you any demerits. I bet you haven't taken a real lunch since you started. I bet they'll cut you some slack. Besides, it looks like something more important than your tardiness is on their minds right now." Melinda pointed out the window and Cory swung her head around. "What do you think's going on?"

Whatever it was involved a hook and ladder and a paramedic truck. "Not a clue. Let me out here."

Cory gave Melinda a quick hug and walked toward the bright red trucks. Instinctively, she reached into her pocket, but she quickly remembered she didn't have a badge anymore. No way to flash her authority to those in uniform. She glanced around and spotted Paul standing with one of the paramedics. He looked up at her and waved her over.

He didn't mince words. "Cory, Greg's had a heart attack. I'm going to get his wife. She's a schoolteacher, hard to reach by phone. Will you stick around and hold down the fort?"

Cory nodded. She didn't know what "hold down the fort" meant, but in light of the emergency, she didn't think it mattered. A second later, two paramedics rolled a gurney out the front door of the clinic. Even from several feet away, she could see Greg's face was ashen, and the lines of his tight grimace spoke volumes. She stepped out of the way as they came toward her. As Paul leaned over and spoke to him, she wished there was something she could do. Hold down the fort seemed so trivial.

❖

Serena stared at her desk and sighed. The four weeks since she'd returned home from Dallas had passed quickly. She'd done her best to focus on her work, but thoughts of Eric's case pierced the surface of her consciousness daily. As did thoughts of Cory Lance.

Attraction. Betrayal. Arousal. Anger. In one day, Cory had evoked feelings she'd managed to suppress for years.

She'd dated some, but always cut ties when the other women starting using words like "relationship" and "commitment." Focused on her education and career, she built a wall to keep any distractions at bay, and that wall blocked intense feelings from taking hold. Feelings that could distract, damage, and make her dependent. Her mother had spent her life, lost her life, being dependent on other people for drugs, for sex, for money.

She would never be like her mother. She'd made that vow when she was just a teenager, but she'd kept it all her life. Intense feelings were only distractions. Until she was sure she was independent enough, successful enough that she would never lose herself in someone else, she would stick to her resolution. She'd grown to like her life the way it was. Simple, easy. Loneliness had its benefits. She'd been convinced that was true. Until she met Cory.

The intercom interrupted her thoughts. "Serena, there's a Paul Guthrie on line one for you."

"Thanks, Nancy." Serena took a deep breath and punched the line. "Hello, Mr. Guthrie."

"Hi, Serena. Please, it's just Paul."

"Okay, Paul." She paused. If it was good news, wouldn't he just launch into it?

"I've got a couple of reasons for calling you today. Is this a good time to talk or would you rather call me back this evening when you get home?"

She braced herself. Good news didn't need to wait for a convenient time. Might as well get it over with. "Now's fine. Tell me."

"You're going to get a letter this week. It's a standard form letter, but I wanted to give you a heads-up so you don't worry too much when you read it."

She couldn't take it anymore. "Paul, I do better with bad news when it's delivered fast."

He cleared his throat. "Sorry, Serena. It's from the warden at the Polunsky Unit, and it will tell you Eric's execution date has been scheduled."

She slumped in her chair. Knowing it was coming didn't make the news easier to take. "When?"

"February twenty-seventh."

A little more than three months away.

"But this is just the first notice."

Her laugh was mirthless. "They send multiple notices? Like I'm going to forget the day my brother will be executed? I can't wait for the final notice. As if I could pay a bill and a late fee and stop the whole process."

"Sorry, I'm not being very artful with my explanation. Notice of the stay is pro forma once all the direct appeals have been exhausted, but we'll file an application to stay the execution to give us time to file our final pleadings on Eric's behalf. Skye has turned up some leads, and we're hoping they will provide us with sufficient grounds to get a stay."

"A stay meaning a delay only? No guarantee that the conviction will be overturned?"

"Baby steps. Right now a stay is the most important step. We convince a judge to stay the execution to give us time to develop evidence. Once we have what we need, we file a writ asking that the conviction be set aside or for a new trial."

"Tell me something, Paul, and I want you to be brutally honest. What are the chances that Eric will get a new trial?"

"Serena, I've been honest with you from the beginning. I think we will get a stay, but I can't be as optimistic about anything after that. It's an uphill battle. The law favors finality, and the presumption is that Eric is guilty until we prove otherwise. I know you can appreciate how difficult that is."

"I do. I worry about the toll this roller coaster will take on Eric."

"I've worked a bunch of these cases. Believe me, Eric needs the hope of a new trial to get him through this time on death row. Giving up means he'll be dead before he meets the needle." Paul cleared his throat. "Sorry, that was pretty insensitive."

"You don't have to mince words with me. I've read all about the process. And don't worry. I don't plan to let Eric catch a glimpse of my pessimism. Greg seems like a sharp man. Hopefully, he can persuade some of those hang 'em high Texas judges to give Eric a second chance."

"Well, that's the other thing I called to talk to you about. Greg's no longer working on Eric's case. He had heart surgery last week, and he'll be out recovering for the foreseeable future. His doctors expect him to have a full recovery, but unfortunately, we can't wait for his return to move forward on Eric's case."

"Forgive me, Paul, but who is going to work on Eric's case? I was there long enough to notice the few attorneys you do have on staff seem to be swamped. You have more files than you can handle, even with Greg there."

"Cory Lance is taking over. You met her when you were here. She helped connect you with Skye, which I have to say was a great find."

Serena felt the room spin. She struggled to find her voice. "Did you say Cory Lance is the attorney who'll be working Eric's case?"

"Yes. Is something wrong?"

The list of things that were wrong was long, but only one was appropriate to share with Paul. "Yes, something's wrong. It's my understanding that Cory is a prosecutor."

"Who told you that?"

Serena held back. She didn't want to drag Skye into this. And Skye really hadn't told her much of anything. As she rolled the thought around, she realized she didn't know any details about why Cory, a prosecutor, would be working for the clinic. "It doesn't matter who told me. The only thing that matters is if it's true. Why would you have a prosecutor working at your clinic?"

"Cory is associated with the Dallas County DA's office. She's volunteering her time with us. While she's working here, she's not working at the DA's office, and she won't be working on any cases she may have handled during her time as a prosecutor."

"And she's able to switch off her perspective, just like that?"

"Did you ever take debate in high school?"

"I didn't spend a lot of time doing extracurricular activities."

"Well, debate is classic training for law school. You learn how to argue both sides of an issue. That's the primary skill of lawyers."

"I don't think my brother's life can be distilled down to an 'issue.' Are you telling me that you could make an argument in favor of the death penalty?"

Paul cleared his throat, and Serena was certain he wished he'd never called. Finally, he responded. "I could. I wouldn't, but I could."

"But you wouldn't believe it, would you?"

"No, but—"

"No buts. I want an attorney who believes in Eric's case."

"Cory is one of the finest litigators I know. She'll do everything in her power for Eric. If I didn't believe that, I wouldn't have assigned the case to her."

Serena let several beats of silence pass between them. What were her choices? Have her parents mortgage their retirement for a man they'd never met so she could hire an attorney? The attorneys in the big firms with their fancy framed diplomas and designer suits didn't seem half as committed to death penalty work as the rolled up sleeves attorneys who worked on scuffed desks. It boiled down to whether she trusted Paul or not. She shook her head. No. It boiled down to whether she trusted Cory, and that was a question she wasn't prepared to answer.

Serena looked up when her mother joined her at the table. She'd placed a call to her right after she got off the phone with Paul, but still she hadn't expected her to arrive at the restaurant so quickly. Marion gave her a hug before taking a seat.

"Talk to me. What's wrong?"

Marion's voice conveyed worry, anxiety, concern. Serena instantly wanted to put her at ease. "It's Eric. I'm probably blowing things out of proportion. I need an impartial opinion."

"I'm all ears." Marion settled back in her chair. "I'm not sure how I can ever be impartial when it comes to you, but I'll do my best."

She'd kept her parents up to date on Eric's case, but in vague, general terms. They'd never known Eric, and she imagined their interest in his situation was partly feigned to appease her. Whether they were really concerned hadn't mattered to her before, but she was desperate for affirmation now that she felt Eric's case had been abandoned to an attorney who couldn't care less about freeing a convicted murderer from prison. She took a deep breath and started with the hardest part first. "They've set a date for his execution."

Marion gasped, the look of horror on her face sincere. "It seems so soon."

"It does. Of course, it's been years coming. I guess it just seems so soon to me since I only just found out he's sitting on death row." Serena couldn't keep her voice from cracking.

Marion reached over and grasped her hand. "Not your fault. There's no way you could have known."

"That's the thing. I could have found out. I didn't keep track of him. I wrote him off after the last time." Her last ultimatum to Eric rang in her ears. She'd stayed true to her convictions, but at what cost? She was about to lose the only blood relative she had, and she'd squandered the years apart. For so long, she'd ducked questions about siblings, finding it easier to live a solitary life than answer the banal, yet expected questions that regularly came from friends and co-workers. A closer relationship would naturally lead to deeper revelations, revelations she avoided at all costs. What would, could she say when Eric died from the executioner's needle? *Yes, I had a brother once, but he went to prison and was put to death for rape and murder. By the time he died, I didn't really know him well.* She couldn't imagine sharing these very personal details with anyone she was attracted to. Now that she knew more about Cory, she regretted she already had.

"We have to draw the line somewhere. Even with people we love."

"Is that really true? Would you cut me off if you didn't like the things I did? I find it hard to believe there is anything I could do to displease you."

Marion laughed. "Oh, I'm sure there's something. We would never stop loving you, but yes, there is a line that marks how much we could take. I don't know what it is since you've never even come close to crossing it." She crossed her arms and assumed a serious expression. "Let's talk about Eric. I'm going to ask you a very difficult question, but I think it's important. Do you think he did what he's accused of doing?"

The question struck her like a thunderbolt. Was Eric's guilt or innocence the crux of it? If he's guilty, move on. If he's innocent, fight like hell? If only it were that simple. Problem was, she didn't have an answer for the predicate question. "I wish I knew. But even if I did, I'm not sure it would make this any easier."

"Oh, honey, I didn't mean to imply it would be easier. It's just that I know that you're expending a lot of time and energy, and I hate to know your efforts are futile."

"In other words, if he's guilty, what's the point?"

"Pretty indelicate, but I suppose that sums it up."

"Do you believe in the death penalty?"

"I've always thought I did. That some acts were so heinous no other punishment would suffice."

"I suppose I did too. But now…Now, how can I when I'm faced with so many uncertainties about whether or not he's even guilty? Even if he weren't my brother, I have fears about the weaknesses in the system. What if they kill him and then we find out there is a question about his guilt? The only finality would be the fact he's dead."

"Are there legitimate questions about his guilt?"

"I don't know. What I do know is that there are legitimate questions about whether he got a fair trial, whether all the evidence was examined by his defense attorneys, whether the jury was allowed to consider everything in their deliberations. Ultimately, none of that may matter, but what if it does?"

"Aren't these the things the clinic is looking into? Can they do all that before the…" Marion seemed to be fishing around for a word other than execution. "Before it's too late?"

"I don't know. The attorney who has been working on his case had a heart attack. They've assigned someone else."

"Have you talked to the new attorney?"

"Yes. Well, no. I mean I met with her when I was in Dallas, but I didn't know then she would be working on Eric's case. Well, she helped me find the investigator, but that was all she was doing. Now she's going to be in charge."

"You don't look very happy about the prospect. Did you butt heads when you met?"

Exactly the opposite. "No, not when we met. She was amazing. She was kind and thoughtful. I thought she would be a wonderful advocate for Eric."

"What changed?"

Everything. The moment she found out Cory was a prosecutor, she'd felt violated. Like she'd bared her soul to the enemy. Would her reasons seem petty, spoken out loud? She decided not to take the risk. "I feel like I need to be there. To make sure everything possible is being done." Her proclamation was a surprise. She didn't know where the words had come from, but now that they were spoken aloud, she knew returning to Dallas was what she had to do.

Marion didn't hesitate to jump on board. "Whatever you need. For however long you need. Certainly, your boss will understand. I think these last couple of trips were the first time off you've taken in years. You deserve to take some time for yourself."

Would her boss understand? Was her stability worth risking for the slim chance she could do Eric any good? Her stomach churned as she considered the risk, along with the prospect of seeing Cory again. Seeing Cory would be for Eric, not for herself. Why then did she feel a sense of excitement instead of dread?

CHAPTER NINE

Cory hit the alarm clock, but it took several swipes before she was able to silence its incessant buzzing. When she rolled back toward the middle of the bed, she bumped into a surprise. Julie, propped up on her elbow, flashing a devilish smile.

Cory glanced at the window, noting streaks of sunlight playing across the covers. Julie never spent the night. She cleared her throat, but her voice was still scratchy from lack of sleep. "You do realize the sun is up?"

Julie stretched. "I thought I'd mix things up a bit."

"You're going to be late for work."

"I have a doctor's appointment this morning. Thought I'd enjoy sleeping in for once."

Cory sat up and threw her legs over the side of the bed. "Well, now that you're awake, I'll make you some coffee." She started to move, but Julie grabbed her arm.

"Where are you off to in such a hurry? I thought we could have a few replays of last night."

Of course Julie assumed that if she had time to play, Cory did too. She was wrong this time. "I have to get to the office."

"Office? Can't you do your charity work another day?"

Cory's anger simmered. "Charity work? You know as well as anyone that the work I'm doing is important, at least to my professional future."

"What's that supposed to mean?"

"Right, Julie, like you don't have a clue. Think you can pick up the phone and call the state bar and get them to reinstate me without sanction? Ready to call your boss and fade the heat for my comeback?"

"Why are you so angry? I thought we had an agreement." Julie pouted, sporting a look that Cory had once found endearing, but was not even remotely attractive now. She sighed. They did have an agreement, and she'd promised to keep up her end. The reward would make the struggle worth it. At least she'd hoped that was the case.

"Sorry. I'm just tired and frustrated. Paul put me in charge of one of Greg's cases since it looks like he's going to be out for a while. The work is more exhausting than I expected."

"What case?"

Cory heard the edge in Julie's tone. "Don't worry. I'm not working any Dallas County cases. This is one from a few years back. Out of Rinson County. Kidnapping, murder. Eric Washington."

"Waitress at the bar off I-20? I remember that case from the news. Didn't he work with her? Didn't he rape her too?"

Cory had always been impressed by Julie's ability to remember everything she'd ever heard or read. "He did work with her, but he wasn't working there when she was murdered. He'd gone in to pick up his last paycheck the night she was abducted. Cops focused on him from the start. And they never charged him with the rape, only used it during punishment."

"Probably with good cause. Didn't he have a rap sheet a mile long?"

"Yes, but nothing like rape and murder."

"Robbery?"

"Yes, but never with a weapon."

"Had to start somewhere. I recall she was pretty. College girl. He probably wanted her and she rejected him. He showed her who was boss and now he's going to fry for it."

Not if I can help it. Cory surprised herself with the sentiment. She knew it would send Julie over the edge. Julie gave new meaning to the term black and white. She never bothered with pesky shades of gray since they only got in the way of her view of swift and sure justice. What had happened on the Nelson case had merely reinforced her world view. Julie believed that Ray Nelson had gotten away with murder, and nothing would dissuade her. Cory looked for a way out of this conversation. She wasn't in the mood for a fight.

"Well, maybe he will die, but last time I checked, we don't fry people in Texas."

"Sorry, I meant he'd be enjoying the stainless steel ride."

"Don't do that."

"Do what?" Julie's look of surprise was genuine.

"Joke about it." Julie gave her a blank look and Cory knew she had to name the "it." "Joke about killing someone."

"Lighten up. I'm not joking about killing someone. I'm adding a little levity to a necessary evil. If we want to protect the good citizens of the state of Texas, we have to kill a few of the bad ones." Julie cocked her head. "I mean, it's great for PR that you're doing all this volunteer work for the downtrodden, but you're not going soft on me are you?"

She wasn't, but talking about executions in the abstract was one thing. Talking about strapping Serena's brother to a table and dousing him with a death cocktail was a completely different story. She'd never met Eric, but knowing the pain his death would cause Serena gripped her hard. Whether Eric was a killer or not, Serena was an innocent bystander, and she didn't deserve to suffer. Cory made a silent vow she'd do everything in her power to make sure if the state of Texas was going to kill Eric, his death was justified.

Julie intruded on her thoughts. "Join me for a quick breakfast before my appointment?"

Her sudden desire to act like a couple irritated Cory. "I can't. I told you, I have to get to the clinic. I'm late enough as it is."

"No need to gripe at me. It's rare we have time to be together in the mornings. I just thought—"

"We always have time to be together in the morning; you just choose not to take advantage of it, until now. What changed, Julie? Why the sudden cuddly lover routine?" Cory didn't bother adjusting her tone. Julie's careless remarks about Eric fueled the agitation that always lurked just below the surface. A night of sex had only served to shine a spotlight on their differences. Julie was content with physicality. She thrived on hungry bodies writhing their way toward release. She had no use for attendant feelings like love and compassion. No, she viewed them as a liability. Until recently, Cory felt the same. She couldn't explain why, but suddenly she wanted more.

Julie didn't appear to be fazed. Already out of bed, she pulled on the rest of her clothes and strode over to Cory. "I know you're stressed, and I can't blame you. I promise this will all be over soon and things will be back to the way they were." She brushed her lips against Cory's cheek. "I'll call you later."

In an instant, she was gone. Cory reached a hand to her face. There was a time a kiss from Julie excited her. Now she was only relieved that she was gone.

Eric Washington's case comprised three banker's boxes. One of them consisted of all the post-trial court filings. Hardly seemed right that a man's life could be taken away from him with only a few boxes of paper to show for the fight waged in his defense. After reading through the transcript, Cory was already convinced Eric's lawyers hadn't put up a good fight. It was almost as if they were scared to challenge any of the state's evidence. The ineffective assistance writ Ian had worked on made good, albeit unpopular, arguments that the trial attorneys provided ineffective assistance to their client, but such arguments were always an uphill battle. Lawyers protected their own. Mostly. Considering her own situation, Cory laughed at the irony.

If she'd been on trial for her life, she would have expected her attorneys to take every risk imaginable. After all, what would she have to lose? Eric's attorneys were well respected and they'd had to qualify for death penalty court appointments, but the record was clear. They'd played it safe, dancing around the testimony of the state's experts, trying to poke holes, but never presenting evidence of their own to challenge the damning conclusions. Cory didn't have a clue what it took for indigent defendants to get funding to hire their own experts, but she'd seen defense counsel make it happen before, so she knew it could be done. A death penalty case seemed to make extra financing necessary. The affidavits the trial attorneys had filed in response to the ineffective assistance claim were a study in artful dodgery.

Cory consulted her notes. She'd compiled a list of to-dos, but wasn't quite sure where to start. Probably best to check with Paul for some guidance. A knock interrupted her thoughts. She looked up to see Skye Keaton standing in the doorway.

"I don't remember you being such a bookworm when you worked at the DA's office."

Cory laughed. She'd never been a bookworm. She'd purposefully chosen trial work to be in the thick of things. Appellate attorneys read about cases. She lived them. Until now. "You got me. I'm going a bit stir crazy. Want to grab a coffee?"

"Sure." Skye jangled a set of keys. "On the way."

"On the way?"

"We're going to Huntsville."

"Kind of far for coffee."

"Time to meet the client. I've been doing some digging, and we can talk on the way. Paul's secretary made us an appointment." She glanced at her watch. "We need to hit the road if we're going to get there on time."

Cory fought down a sense of panic. Meeting the client through volumes of paper transcripts was one thing. Meeting him through the bars of a jail cell was an entirely different matter. She'd been to jails before, interviewing witnesses in some of the cases she'd tried. But she'd never had to face a flesh and blood client on the other side of the cell.

As if she could sense Cory's hesitation, Skye grabbed her arm. "Come on. Like you always used to say, there's no substitute for seeing something, or in this case someone, for yourself."

"Should've known those words would come back to bite me."

Twenty minutes later, armed with Starbucks, they sped out of town with Skye at the wheel. Cory checked the e-mail on her phone out of habit, but since she didn't have access to her Dallas County address, the messages were sparse. Melinda wanted to know if they could meet for dinner. It'd have to be a late meal since they were in for about six hours in the car roundtrip. She typed back a quick response, asking Melinda to meet her at the office that night, before tucking her phone into the console between the seats.

Skye waved a hand at Cory's phone. "If you're expecting any important messages, you should check in soon. We'll lose cell signal in just a bit."

"It's been a while since I made this drive. I used to teach at the baby prosecutor school down in Huntsville, but I've been too busy the last couple of years to get away."

"Work busy or personal busy?"

"Is there a difference?"

Skye chuckled. "I used to think that way. Until I got married. Now I know for sure there's a difference."

The laid-back private investigator sitting across from her was substantially different from the hard-nosed police detective she used to know. One particularly prominent detail captured Cory's attention. They were tooling down the highway in a Lexus sedan. "Hey, aren't you a Harley gal?"

Skye couldn't hide a trace of disappointment. "I still have the Harley."

"Way to dodge the question."

"Yes, I'm a Harley gal. I love my bike."

"And the Lexus?"

"Well, first, I don't think I have a helmet that will fit your head. Second, the car was a wedding gift from Aimee."

"I sense there's a third…"

"There is. I decided to cut some of the risk out of my life since I'm about to be a parent. Besides, it cut my life insurance premium by about two-thirds."

"Wow, marriage, kids, life insurance. Who would've ever thought you'd become so domesticated?"

Skye shrugged. "Not me. That's for sure. I'm still the same person, but I have more than myself to live for, so I've decided to be a little more careful in my old age. But don't get me wrong, I still have my bike, and Aimee and I take her for a regular Sunday ride to keep her in tune. "What about you? You have plans for a family someday?"

The direct question took Cory by surprise. She'd worked at the DA's office so long, everyone there had stopped asking about her personal life after she'd made it clear details were off-limits. Funny how she projected an image of keeping professional and personal separate when she did anything but. Certainly some of their co-workers had to know she and Julie were involved, no matter how circumspect they tried to be about their relationship, but they'd never hear any details direct from the source.

A family with Julie was out of the question. They barely even saw each other anymore, and except for the other morning, neither of them seemed to want to hang around once they'd both orgasmed, and even those events were scattered these days. Her attraction for Julie had been all encompassing in the beginning. Aroused by Julie's drive and confidence, she'd welcomed her advances. Their tryst lasted for years, but it never changed. Sex, shoptalk, more sex, and secrets. If news got out about their relationship, both their careers would be damaged—Julie for bedding one of her subordinates, and Cory for climbing the ladder by sleeping with the boss. That last wasn't true, but no one would care enough to sort out the difference between the success she'd achieved on her own and the opportunities she'd been exposed to because of her relationship with Julie. Didn't matter. No one could allege she'd received special treatment after the Nelson case had blown apart. The future promises Julie had made would forever be a secret the both of them would keep.

"I haven't given a family much thought."

Skye gave her a sharp stare and Cory imagined her thoughts were clearly visible. But she didn't challenge Cory's statement. "I think it's one of those things that kind of sneaks up on you."

Not if you're on guard. Despite her guard, Cory's thoughts turned to Serena, and she wondered if Serena would want a family. Maybe not, considering her past. Or maybe her past would give her the resolve to nurture a child of her own, give something she'd never gotten. Why did her thoughts so easily turn to Serena whenever someone broached a personal subject? Time to change the subject. "Probably so. Want to talk about the case?"

Skye seamlessly shifted gears. "Sure. I assume you've read the whole transcript."

"Yes. I probably need to talk to Nivens and Watkins." She referred to the attorneys who'd represented Eric at trial. "I read the affidavits they wrote, and they steadfastly deny they did anything wrong."

"You really think they are going to tell you something different than they wrote in a sworn affidavit? I can tell you right now, it's going to be a waste of time. Those two will say they did everything necessary and they have a plausible sounding excuse for every questionable decision they made."

Cory knew the drill. Defense attorneys weren't going to go on record saying they did a bad job. She moved talking to them down on her list of urgent to-dos. "Okay, so what do you suggest?"

"Client first. Then I made a list of everyone who was working at the bar during that time period along with all the witnesses included in the police report. We need to talk to all of them and the cops that worked the case, but before we do, I want to hear what Eric has to say."

"I can tell you what he's going to say. He's going to say he's innocent."

"Isn't that the point of this whole effort?"

It was and it wasn't. Unless they convinced the court there was a chance Eric was really innocent, he'd die as scheduled. But Cory wasn't interested in buying into the belief herself. When she prosecuted a case, she got worked up about the guilt of the defendant, but she knew defense attorneys often didn't care to know whether their clients were innocent or guilty. Protect their rights, guide them through the process. She'd do that for Eric, but she didn't have to lend a piece of her heart to a man she didn't know, a man with a history of criminal convictions. An image of Serena flashed in her mind. Despite her guarded professionalism, she felt a tinge of compassion. More than compassion, really. She chose not to name the feeling. It would only get in her way.

"Let's just do what we need to do to get Eric a new trial. A jury can decide if he's innocent or not."

"Juries make mistakes."

Cory caught the tone in Skye's voice and knew she was referring to the Nelson case. Time to head her off the subject. "Juries make the best decision they can with the evidence they have."

"Like Nelson? Jury didn't have all the evidence there, did they?"

"Since when did you get so high and mighty? I seem to recall when you worked on the right side of the law and made a few close calls of your own."

"Close calls? Seriously, is that what you call withholding evidence from the other side? Yes, I did my share of making close calls. At the time, I thought I was doing the right thing."

"And now?"

"Now I know better. If someone's guilty of a crime, it will bear out. Nobody wins when you cheat the system."

"And it doesn't bother you when murderers and rapists get off on a technicality?"

"I decided to let the system work the way it's supposed to. Truth rarely leads to injustice."

Cory wasn't convinced, but the firm set of Skye's jaw told her pushing the point was futile. "I know you think I blew the Nelson case."

"I think you did what you thought you had to do."

Skye's assessment was close to right, but a bit off the mark. No way was Cory going to correct the assumption. All she wanted to do was put the whole case behind her. She let the comment go. There was nothing else she could say.

Since their names were on the list, they were bumped to the front of the security line. Despite her experience with jails, Cory had never been to death row. She was familiar with ankle-cuffed inmates sporting jumpsuits, shuffling into the visitor's booth to speak with her. She wasn't prepared for the sight of Eric Washington, in chains, escorted by armed guards bearing electric cattle prods.

She nodded to the guards and spoke loudly to be heard through the Plexiglas. "Thanks. We need to talk to him alone now." She didn't make a move to pick up one of the phone handsets until the guards made their exit. While she waited, she assessed the first client she'd ever had as a defense lawyer.

Pained eyes, gaunt face, haggard expression. He was only thirty-eight, but he looked twenty years older. As she examined him, she realized she was looking for signs of Serena. They shared the same mother, but not much else. Where Serena's bearing was proud and confident, Eric was slumped, and he would barely meet her eyes. What did she expect? They had different fathers and they'd spent a lifetime apart. Nurture had obviously won this round.

"Eric, my name is Cory Lance. I'm working with the clinic and I'm going to be handling your case from here on out." Cory put a hand on Skye's shoulder. "This is Skye Keaton. She's a private investigator that your sister hired to help us gather evidence to help with your appeal."

His eyes signaled distrust. "What happened to Greg?"

Cory shot a look at Skye before answering. "He's had a medical emergency and he's going to be out of commission for a while. Since we have to get moving on your case, I'm stepping in to take over."

"You mean 'cause they scheduled the date they're going to kill me, right?"

Uncharted territory. Cory was used to talking to victims about their rights with compassion, but she was lost when it came to comforting the accused, a deficit made exponentially more difficult when the accused had already been found guilty by a jury of his peers. *What if Serena were sitting across from you? You'd find a way to be gentle, compassionate.* She settled on blunt honesty. Serena would expect nothing less. "Exactly. Now that they've scheduled your execution date, we're working against the clock. I'm sure you know all your direct appeals have been exhausted. What we need to do now is convince a judge that you're actually innocent and get the court to order you a new trial. I'm sure you realize how difficult a task that is."

He cracked a small smile. "Impossible, I'd say."

She'd only seen Serena's smile once, but the impression it left was enough to allow her to recognize it now. Seeing a part of Serena in Eric for the first time made it easy for her to return the gesture. She appreciated his frank appraisal of his situation. "Pretty near, but not quite. I can't promise you I can stop your execution, but I can promise you we'll do everything we can to try and get you a new trial. If the evidence exists to warrant a new trial. Sounds like you already understand how difficult that's going to be."

He nodded. "I do. Folks around here, they dream a lot, talk trash about how they're getting out, but I know the real deal. Once you're here, you usually only leave in a pine box."

His simple assessment of his bleak situation moved her. "Well, let's try and avoid that, okay? Skye and I have a lot of questions for you, but we'd like you to start by telling us everything you remember about that night. Pretend you're on the stand testifying for your life and tell us everything you'd want the jury to know. Leave nothing out, good, bad, whatever. We need to know everything if we're going to be able to help you."

She paused, considering her next statement. She'd discussed it with Skye on the ride down. Chances were good her name had been bandied about the prison, and she could only imagine what some of the inmates had to say about her. Better to be up front with Eric right now if she wanted to gain his trust. "Since I'm asking you to trust enough to tell us everything, I'm going to tell you something about myself first. Up until a couple of weeks ago, I was a prosecutor in the Dallas County District Attorney's Office. I worked on the Ray Nelson case; you may have heard of it?"

Eric nodded, his face tightening into a scowl. Cory took a deep breath and continued, purposefully avoiding Skye's questioning look. She was veering off script, but she knew in her gut she was saying the right things. "There's a long story behind that case. A story I'm not at liberty to tell. But I'm working for the clinic now, part of it is penance for what happened in the Nelson case, but Paul Guthrie, the director, asked me to take over your case and I'm dedicated to nothing but for the duration. I like to win. I've built a career on winning. If you think that changes just because I usually work for the other side, you would be mistaken. I'll work hard to win you a retrial." She met his scowl with a hard stare. "You want to say something?"

"Have you met my sister?"

The question took her by surprise, but she recovered quickly. "I have."

"She didn't boot you out?"

"No."

"Then that's good enough for me."

Cory opened her mouth to explain that when she'd last seen her, Serena hadn't known she was assigned to the case, but she decided against putting anything in the way of the trust her client had just shown. Besides, Paul had assured her he would notify Serena of the upcoming execution date and the change in lawyers. She'd expected to hear from Serena, but figured she was busy, living her life, confident Eric was in good hands. Better get down to business and make sure that was the case. "Great. Let's get started."

Chapter Ten

Serena spent the three-hour flight practicing what she would say to Cory when she saw her. You better do a good job on my brother's case or I'll break your legs topped the list, but she knew her threats needed to be refined. Once she landed, she secured the cheap rental she'd booked online and made her way to the budget motel that was to be her home for the indefinite future. After two recent visits, she found it easier to navigate the busy streets. Everything about this particular trip was easier. Everything except the prospect of seeing Cory again.

After her conversation with Paul, she'd armed herself with information from Google. Cory Lance was a veteran trial attorney who started working for the district attorney's office as an intern while still in law school. She'd risen quickly up the ranks and was a chief prosecutor in one of the felony courts in Dallas County. At least she had been until her recent stumble in the case of the State of Texas versus Ray Nelson. Ray Nelson had been convicted of murder by a Dallas County jury and sent to prison for life. The prosecutors who put him away were Cory Lance and Julie Dalmar.

In a recent election, the former district attorney was unseated by an upstart, Frank Alvarez. Alvarez, in an effort to make a name for himself, instituted a new unit within the office, the Conviction Integrity Unit. He drastically changed the discovery practices of the office and instituted an open file policy. For years, his predecessor had resisted moving toward such a policy, claiming the defense had no right to peruse the work product of the attorneys in his office.

With the new unit and the new policy came a flood of writs on already settled appeals. Nelson's appellate attorneys, now armed with access to the full file available to Cory and her then trial partner, Dalmar, found grounds to challenge the verdict. Apparently, the police had their sights set on several other suspects before they ultimately arrested Nelson. This information had not been shared with the attorneys who represented Nelson at trial. In addition, one of the eyewitnesses wavered about her testimony prior to trial. That information wasn't contained in the DA's files, but once the information about other suspects came out, the whole case started to unravel.

Even though years had passed, now several individuals came forward stating they had information about the case. The new DA cut short the media circus by joining with the defense in a motion for new trial, but as the date got closer for the hearing, he took the surprising move of asking the judge to dismiss the charges. The news was silent on any follow-up. The media crucified Cory, as the lead prosecutor, and the new DA suspended her pending further action by the state bar. Then nothing. Serena couldn't find anything to address what happened with the case once Nelson was released.

What was Cory doing at the clinic? Why did Paul trust her enough to work Eric's case? The clinic had an unparalleled reputation for zealous advocacy. Would they risk their credibility by hiring a lawyer with a reputation for overzealous prosecution? Paul's words still rang in her ear. *Trust me.* She hadn't given him any assurances on the phone. Maybe once she met with him again in person, she'd know what to say. She tried to ignore the fact that seeing him again meant an inevitable confrontation with Cory.

The tiny digital clock by the edge of the bed read six p.m. She reached for the phone and placed a call to Skye. She left her a message, letting her know she was in town, where she was staying, and asking if they could meet the following day to discuss where things stood. Next, she dialed the clinic. As she suspected, Paul was there, still working, and happy to meet with her whenever she wanted to stop by. He didn't express any surprise at her sudden announcement she was back in town. She changed into less wrinkled slacks and a light sweater and was out the door in five minutes. She was starving, but thankful Paul was available now, she put off finding something to eat, figuring she'd have less chance of seeing Cory at the clinic after hours. Some confrontations were better handled on a full stomach and a good night's sleep.

❖

Cory and Skye listened intently, but Eric didn't have a lot to say. He'd met Nancy McGowan when he worked at the Dusty Trail Bar. He'd worked at the bar for about four months. The owner, Gerald Papolos, hired him despite his prior record. After all, how much harm could an ex-con do as a busboy? But on a fateful Saturday night, when the register turned up a hundred dollars short, Eric was the perfect scapegoat. He'd offered to let Papolos search him to prove he hadn't taken the cash, but Papolos brushed him off, saying he could've hidden the money anywhere. The only one who'd expressed any sympathy toward him was Nancy McGowan, a cocktail waitress. She'd spoken up for him, claiming there was no way Eric could've gotten behind the bar and into the register without anyone noticing.

Her protests didn't do any good even though they should have gone a long way toward supporting Eric's defense attorneys' primary argument—why would Eric kill a woman who'd stood up for him? But the prosecutors twisted the situation, arguing that Nancy's support for him caused him to develop an unhealthy attraction for the woman, which ultimately led him to stalk, rape, and kill her.

"After you were fired, when's the next time you saw Nancy?"

"She was there when I picked up my last check, but it was a busy night. I didn't talk to her."

"The police report says you went back to the bar again about three days later. Did you?"

Eric nodded. "My check was wrong. I went back in to get that straightened out."

"Why didn't you take care of that when you were there the first time?"

"Gerald was out of town. The manager told me I'd have to talk to him about the check. Actually, he told me I should be happy I got a final check at all."

"How much was it short?"

"The hundred dollars they claim I stole."

"You didn't take the money?" Cory looked up from her notes as she asked the question, convinced she'd be able to read the truth in his eyes.

"No, I did not." He shook his head. "Look, I know you've seen my record, and I figure you think I'm a thief. Truth is, I used to be. I've had a couple of trips to the pen for stealing other people's shit. I swore the last time would really be the last. Gerald gave me that job, and I was going to work hard. Earn an honest living. I was doing just that. I didn't take that money. I was still on parole. Like I was going to risk my freedom for a lousy hundred bucks. Didn't go down that way."

"Who do you think took the money?"

"Last I heard, I'm not in here over a missing hundred dollars."

Skye interjected. "Eric, every detail is important. I know you've spent a lot more time thinking about all of this than we have, but we do this for a living. We have to look at every detail of your case from scratch."

"Yeah, I get it. I don't know who took that money. All I know is I was told it was gone and they kicked me out that night."

"Who fired you?"

"Lenny. He's the guy Gerald left in charge when he was off."

"Leonard Wilkins?" She'd remembered Leonard was a key witness at the trial, placing Eric back at the bar the night Nancy went missing.

"Dunno. Folks just called him Lenny. He's a white guy. Old, like maybe fifty."

Cory forced herself not to grin at Eric's definition of old. She took over the questions. "Let's get back to Nancy and the night you went back to the bar to talk to Gerald about your check. That's the night she went missing."

"I know, but I'm telling you I didn't even talk to her that night." Eric relayed his every step, from pulling up at the bar to walking back to the office to talk to Gerald Papolos about his check. "Gerald wouldn't agree to give me the whole hundred, but he did slip me a twenty. Told me to get lost before he contacted my parole officer to let him know I'd blown it again. I got the hell out of there before he changed his mind."

"Anyone else there when you talked to Gerald?"

"I don't think so. Well, wait a minute. He wasn't in the office, but Lenny did grab me in the parking lot. Wanted to know what I was doing back at the bar."

"What did you tell him?"

"That it was none of his business. He shoved me around a little. I didn't fight back. I just wanted to get out of there without any trouble. Bad enough I lost my job, I didn't need anyone calling the cops about a fight. I drove off and never looked back."

"Lenny testified against you at the trial, right?"

"That's right."

"Any reason he'd lie to get you in trouble?"

"Just because I can't think of a reason, doesn't mean he didn't do it." His voice rose and he was visibly agitated.

Cory held up a hand, palm out. "Slow down. We're on your side." She waited until he settled down. "You're in the best position to tell us about these people. I know you don't have all the answers, but that's not going to stop me from asking. You might think of something when you least expect it.

"Now, anything else about that night you think might be important?"

"There isn't anything else. I didn't even talk to her that night, let alone rape and murder her."

What happened after that night was all public record. Eric's arrest had been two days later, hours after Nancy's body was found, violated and bloody, in her own apartment. The police interviewed everyone who worked at the bar the last night Nancy had been seen there, along with her family. They quickly concluded, based on Leonard's testimony and an eyewitness account of a black man forcing Nancy into a car in the bar parking lot, that Eric was the prime suspect. From what Cory could tell, the investigation ended with Eric's arrest. He was promptly interviewed, and even though he hadn't confessed to the actual acts for which he was charged, he readily told the police he'd been at the bar that night and had seen Nancy. He "confessed" that she was always nice to him and he liked her. He "confessed" that he thought she was pretty. All facts that were twisted against him at trial.

"This guy who testified he saw you force Nancy into her car. Did you know him?"

"Dale Bolton. No, I never laid eyes on the guy until trial. But his name is burned in my mind for all eternity."

"You never saw him in the bar?"

"No. I've gone over it in my head a million times, but I don't know why he picked me out. I figure it was just another case of some white guy thinking we all look alike."

Cory exchanged looks with Skye. Cross-racial eyewitness identification had become a hot topic in the legal community and defense attorneys with high-paying clients were quick to hire experts to challenge lineups. Of course, Eric hadn't had the money to fund such experts, but his trial attorneys hadn't even petitioned the court for funds to hire experts of any kind. Cory counted back. A few years ago, when Eric's trial had taken place, the topic might have seemed too cutting edge to convince a judge it was worth court dollars. Maybe they could make something of it now. It wasn't enough though. They needed more. Much more.

She and Skye took turns asking Eric questions about his encounter with the police. He admitted he'd gone with them willingly. He'd been on parole and didn't think he had a choice. Besides, he hadn't done anything wrong. As many times as Cory preached to juries that if someone didn't do anything wrong, there's no harm in talking to the cops, she knew she would never follow her own advice. Especially not if she were uneducated and all too familiar with the system, like Eric. People never failed to amaze her.

When they'd exhausted their list of questions, Cory motioned to Skye that they should get going. Skye nodded, but didn't make a move to leave. Instead, she stood and pulled a roll of quarters out of her pocket. "Hey, Eric, there's a whole roll here. What can I get you?"

Cory listened while Eric recited a list of junk food and sodas. Skye grinned at Cory and strode to the vending machines to see the guard standing there. Cory shook her head and smiled at Eric. "Guess you don't have a lot to look forward to in there."

"You got that right." He looked down at his hands, flexing his fingers. "I'm powerless in here. If it weren't for Serena, I'd have already given up."

"Eric, we'll do everything we can for you, but you shouldn't get your hopes up."

"Don't worry. My hope is so low, anything is up. But that's for me, okay? Don't go all negative when you see my sister. Let her think there's a chance. I can handle the truth, but she needs hope to hang on to. You understand?"

"I do."

"Tell her I love her."

"I will." Inspired by his surprising show of strength, Cory started to tell him not to worry, that they would give his defense everything they had, but Skye chose that very moment to reappear, accompanied by a guard whose arms were laden with vending machine junk food. Cory reconsidered. Eric didn't need her words of assurance any more than he needed to eat a healthy diet. She'd save her comfort for Serena.

❖

Serena followed Paul back to his office and declined his polite offer of coffee. "I know you've got a lot to do, but I wanted a chance to discuss my concerns with Eric's case."

He motioned for her to sit and took a seat beside her rather than behind his desk. "We always have a lot to do around here, but I'm happy to talk with you."

She girded herself for the unpleasant confrontation. Faced with his charming smile, getting started was proving harder than she'd imagined. "It's about Cory Lance."

"You've been reading the papers."

With just a few words, he managed to make it easy on her. "Yes, and so far I've read nothing that helps me understand why Cory is even working here, let alone why you would trust her to work on Eric's case."

"I've devoted my life to believing that all people have redeeming traits. No one's all bad and, if given a chance, most folks can turn their lives around."

"So you're letting Cory work here so she can turn her life around? No offense, but that doesn't sound like a ringing endorsement."

"Maybe Cory needs to earn the endorsement from you herself."

"You're not going to take her off the case?"

"I don't think you really want me to. At least you don't know enough about her to make that decision. How long are you staying in town?"

His question caught her off guard. "I don't have any specific plans. I got a room at the Budget Suites down the road. I want to stick around for a while. See if I can be of any help. Keep an eye on things." She stopped talking, certain she was rambling.

Paul's smile confirmed her suspicion. "Perfect. We could use the extra help. It'll give you a chance to get to know Cory, and then you can form a sound opinion about her."

"Did I hear my name?"

The voice preceded her appearance, but Serena would know that husky tone anywhere. She braced herself. Didn't work. When Cory turned the corner, she was every bit as captivating as Serena remembered. She wore her tailored pantsuit like a second skin as she strode into Paul's office with a confident swagger.

"Serena, wow. I didn't expect to see you." Cory's eyes shined with delight and Serena felt a surge of genuine pleasure at their reunion, until she remembered what she'd just said to Paul. Cory glanced between her and Paul. "Am I interrupting something?"

Paul answered. "No, not at all. I was just leaving. Maybe you two can grab dinner. Serena, Cory visited your brother today. I'm sure you both have a lot to talk about."

"Actually, Paul—"

Serena interrupted Cory, before she could get any further. "Don't worry. I have no intention of imposing on you."

Cory's furrowed brow relaxed and her face shifted into a smile. "No worries at all. I only wanted to let you know I already have plans with a friend, but I'd love it if you could join us. Melinda should be here any minute and we were going to grab some dinner."

Paul spoke up. "Melinda? Great. Give her my regards. She'll make a good sounding board about Eric's case. Well, I'm sure you two have a lot to talk about. Have a great dinner." And just like that, he disappeared into his office, leaving Serena alone with Cory.

Melinda. Friend? Conflicting emotions spurred Serena to beg off. "I do want to talk to you, but I don't want to interfere with your dinner plans. Perhaps we can talk tomorrow?"

"No interference at all. I promise."

"I think what I have to say would be better said in private." Serena noted Cory's wolfish grin, and realized her faux pas. "I mean…"

"Cory, are you ready for dinner? I'm starving! Who is this?"

The woman who locked arms with Cory was beautiful, vivacious, and very friendly. Too friendly. Serena had no intention of interrupting their dinner with a confrontation. She offered a hand in greeting. "Serena Washington, and I was on my way out. Have a good dinner."

Cory placed a hand on her arm. Warmth, welcome, want. Normally, such touches or any invasion of her personal space irritated her, but in the span of just a few meetings, she'd come to enjoy Cory's gentle, easy touch. Definitely time to get away. But Cory wasn't giving up so easily.

"Have dinner with us. I'd love it if you would."

Her voice was soft, the invitation almost a whisper, and her eyes conveyed the request was sincere. Serena felt the tug of attraction and dug in to resist. She had imagined their next meeting much differently. A professional atmosphere where she would outline her concerns and make it clear she expected Cory to go above and beyond in her representation of Eric to prove she wasn't biased by her regular job. What difference would it make to have a nice meal first, soften the blow? She could deal with the rest tomorrow. "Okay. If you're sure I'm not imposing."

"I'm sure. Absolutely."

Serena looked into Cory's eyes and read what she was certain was attraction. Was she projecting her own feelings on Cory? Not that it mattered. Their relationship was defined by Eric's case. Cory would represent Eric. Serena would help. The case would end and no matter the outcome, they would each go their separate ways—Serena back to Florida, her job, her life, and Cory back to whatever life held for her. The only thing that Serena could be sure of was that the intersection of their lives was short-lived.

❖

The moment she pulled up at the valet stand, Serena knew the cost of dinner would exceed her budget. She ignored the voice inside that urged her to turn around, and reluctantly handed her keys to the valet. Luckily, she had some cash to tip the eager young man who didn't blink at the fact she was driving an economy car in a sea of Mercedes and Range Rovers. Cory and Melinda were waiting in the foyer of the restaurant, but when she approached, Melinda walked toward the maître d'. Cory was scanning the crowd, and her eyes lit up when they locked with Serena's. She strode over to her. "Did you find the place okay?"

"I did." Serena had insisted on taking her own car. Definitely a good idea. She had yet to see a menu, but she had a feeling she might need to make a quick exit once she saw the prices. "You come here often?"

"Actually, no. It's a great place, but I'm more of a burger and fries kind of gal." She jerked her chin in Melinda's direction. "Mel's a top-notch gourmet foodie. No way would she hang in the dives I like."

"Maybe next time, you'll take me to one of your favorite places." Serena regretted the not so subtle suggestion as soon as the words left her lips, and she rushed to correct the course of the conversation. "I guess what I'm trying to say is that I can already tell this place is a bit rich for my budget."

"Oh, I'm sorry. I should've asked first."

"No, I should have. After all, I'm the one intruding on your dinner, not the other way around."

"You're not intruding. I invited you, and dinner's my treat."

"I don't think that's a good idea."

"Really? Why not?"

"Are you a prosecutor for the Dallas DA's office?"

"Oh, shit."

She wanted to reel the question back in the moment she saw the combination of anxiety and disappointment on Cory's face. Too late. She couldn't take the question back, but she could back out of whatever she thought this meeting would be about. Fast. "Look, I'm sorry. Clearly, this isn't the time or place to have this discussion." She couldn't help notice Melinda's concerned glances in their direction. "Your friend is waiting. Go to her. We'll talk later." Before Cory could respond, she turned and sped out of the restaurant.

CHAPTER ELEVEN

D id she leave something in the car?" Melinda asked.
"Good judgment. Apparently, she thought better of having dinner with a rogue like me."

"Speak English."

"I'm not sure what happened. First she said something about the restaurant being too expensive, and then she asked me if I'm a prosecutor. I'm not certain, but I'm pretty sure it was the prosecutor thing that sent her running."

"Did you tell her yes?"

"I think I said something eloquent, like 'oh shit.'"

"Amazing that you've won so many trials with that silver tongue of yours."

Cory punched her lightly in the shoulder just as the maître d' approached and announced their table was ready. Melinda asked him to wait a moment before she turned back to Cory. "What do you want to do?"

"You heard the man. Your table is ready."

"It's our table unless you've changed your mind. And I think you have."

Melinda's uncanny ability to read her mind annoyed her. "I don't know what you're talking about."

"You invited Serena to dinner. She took off. You have a choice. You can go after her or you can spend the entire dinner with me, being distracted. I'd rather have a rain check than have you ruin my appetite with your regrets. She's absolutely stunning, by the way."

Cory sorted through Melinda's comments, purposefully ignoring the observation. "She's a client."

"She's a client's sister. The lines may be a little gray, but as your attorney, I can confidently say you're on safe ground. Now, go."

"I don't know where she is."

"And here I thought you were one of the best prosecutors around. Seems as if you should have a talent for finding information."

"I don't have a car. You drove."

Melinda turned to the patiently waiting maître d'. "Joseph, I have a bit of an emergency on my hands and I'm going to have to leave. I apologize for the inconvenience."

"None at all, Ms. Stone. We'll look forward to your next visit."

Within minutes, they were speeding back to the clinic. Cory spoke first. "This is ridiculous. She obviously didn't want to have dinner with me. Explain to me why I'm going after her?"

"Tell me again what she said to you, word for word."

Cory did the best she could.

"Think about it. She thinks you're a prosecutor. You're working on her brother's case. For all you know, she's made the connection between your name and recent events that don't exactly put you in the best light as far as defending the rights of the accused."

"And I'm supposed to correct her assumption?"

"Well, it's not an assumption. It's the truth and it bears some explaining."

"I think I'll let Paul handle that. He's the one who put me on this case."

"I think you better handle it yourself."

"Why?"

"Because if you're going to have any sort of relationship with this woman, you should start by being honest with her."

"Relationship?"

"She's the sister of your client, right? That's a relationship. Oh, and the fact that when you look at her, your mouth hangs open and you act like you're love struck."

"I do not."

"You do. Now get out and go find her. I'm going to go scrounge for dinner. You owe me a nice steak."

Cory looked around. They were back at the clinic. No sense responding directly to her crazy theories. She kissed Melinda on the cheek and got out of the car. Once she was seated in her own car, she assessed her options. Go home. Lonely and hungry. Go inside the clinic and catch up on work. Another choice designed to leave her lonely and hungry. Only one other choice. Find Serena. She had no idea what that option would do for her, but she desperately wanted to find out.

She pulled out her phone and dialed a number. "Skye, Serena Washington's back in town. I was hoping you could tell me where she's staying."

Thirty minutes later, as she stood outside of room two thirty-two, one hand clutching a large paper bag and the other raised to knock, Cory resisted the urge to run. When the door opened, she almost gave in. Serena stood in the doorway with an ice bucket in her hand.

"Cory, what are you doing here?"

Cory held up the sack. "I brought dinner." Lame, but she didn't know what else to say. She didn't have a clue why she was here. Serena didn't want to be around her. She'd made that clear when she'd taken off from the restaurant. Coming here had seemed like a spontaneous icebreaker. Now that she was standing here, Cory felt like a stalker. Time to make as graceful an exit as possible. She thrust the bag at Serena. "Here, you must be starving. It's nothing much. Just a burger and fries from one of my favorite places. A total dive. Enough grease in that bag to fuel a small car. Enjoy." She turned to leave, but Serena called her back.

"Wait." Serena hefted the bag. "Feels like more than one burger and fries to me. Why don't you join me? Besides, I want to talk to you."

Shit. Breaking bread, she could handle, but the talk? She wasn't ready for the talk. Would she ever be ready? Not with Serena. She thought about what she would say on the drive over, but every explanation fell short of the full story. Melinda's words echoed in her head: *If you're going to have any sort of relationship with this woman, you should start by being honest with her.*

Honesty. She could do honesty. At least a version of it. She started with a half answer. "I'd love to join you for dinner."

❖

What are you thinking, inviting her into your room? You don't know anything about this woman. Serena tamped down her own silent protests. She invited me into her home; how scary can she be? Despite her strong words, her nerves were frayed. Cory Lance was a mystery, and Serena wasn't in town to solve mysteries. She was here to help Eric.

She motioned to the small kitchen in her suite. "It's nothing like your kitchen, but there's plates and silverware. Can I offer you a Coke?"

"Coke would be great. Forget the silverware and plates. These burgers are best right out of the bag."

Serena avoided Cory's eyes and kept busy fixing their drinks. "Best burgers in Dallas?"

"Best drive-in burgers. Dairy-Ette is an old-style drive-in. You pull up and flash your lights when you're ready to order. One of the waitresses, who's been there since the beginning of time, takes your order, and it's cooked fresh. You can even buy a gallon of root beer from a big ol' keg if you want to take some home."

Serena couldn't help but smile. "You must fit right in."

"Got me. I'm a sucker for grease."

Cory's manner was so engaging, Serena knew she'd have to stay on guard or this meeting would quickly turn too personal. The first bite of burger threatened her resolve. "This is fantastic."

"It is, isn't it? Now, it's just the best drive-in burger. There's still the best gourmet burger, the best eat-in-a-dive burger, the best quarter-pound burger, the best half-pound—"

Serena held up a hand to stop her. "I get the point. If I hang out with you, I'm going to gain twenty pounds."

"You'd still be beautiful."

Cory turned slightly red, and Serena wondered if she was embarrassed. She was a little uncomfortable herself, but she spoke a rough thank you and took a large bite of burger to give her time to think. The comment was inappropriate. Wasn't it? She should be offended that Cory was acting unprofessional. Cory had shown up at her hotel uninvited and plied her way in with food. She complimented her, made her feel special. Completely, totally inappropriate. Yet, Serena felt more confused than offended.

"You must think I'm crazy," Cory said.

You must be a mind reader. "I don't think you're crazy."

"I hear a big 'but.'"

Serena bit back a grin at the double entendre. Focus. "I don't know what to think about you."

Cory leaned back in her chair, her expression serious. "Ask me anything you want to know."

"Why are you working for the clinic?"

"I think you already know that I was a prosecutor for the Dallas County District Attorney's Office." Serena nodded. "And I imagine you also know that I got into some trouble over a recent case."

Some trouble. Serena resisted the urge to point out the understatement. "The Nelson case. I've read about it."

"The disciplinary committee of the state bar placed my license on probationary status, and working at the clinic is how I earn my way back into their good graces."

Serena heard a hint of anger in Cory's admission. Did a deeper resentment lurk beneath the surface? Only one way to find out. "If it were up to you, you wouldn't be volunteering at the clinic?"

"If it were up to me, I'd still be working in my old job. That doesn't mean that I'm not capable of doing the work at the clinic."

"Capable?"

"Probably not the best choice of words. Look, I'm committed to doing the best work I know how while I'm working at the clinic. That includes making sure your brother gets the best representation possible."

"And you think that you, a former prosecutor, can provide him with the best representation?"

"I think the fact that I'm a prosecutor gives me unique insight. So, yes, I do."

The shift in tense wasn't lost on Serena. Cory was still a prosecutor, probably always would be. "What happens when you're done at the clinic?"

"What do you mean?"

"You know what I mean. When your time is up? When your sentence is served? What will you do then?"

Cory fiddled with the wrapper on her burger, avoiding Serena's piercing stare. She wasn't getting off that easy. Serena needed to know exactly how committed Cory was. "You'll go back to what you do best, won't you? Back to the DA's office. Back to sending people to prison. Whatever it takes."

Cory put the rest of her burger down and stood. "I should go." She shrugged into her coat and strode to the door. "I don't know what the future holds. I do know this. I will do my level best for your brother. No matter what happens, he will know that I did everything possible to make sure he got a fair shot at justice. If you want to see for yourself, then meet me in the morning. Eight a.m., at the clinic."

And then she was gone, and Serena was left with more questions than answers.

CHAPTER TWELVE

Cory peered into Paul's office. She couldn't swear, but she was willing to bet he was wearing the same clothes this morning as when she'd seen him the evening before. "Do you ever go home?"

"Occasionally." He motioned to the briefcase she held. "Where are you headed this morning?"

"To file a discovery request in Judge Fowler's court."

"You don't need to do that yourself. One of the interns can run it over."

"If it's all the same to you, I'd rather deliver it myself." She hesitated, unsure about her next question. "If it's okay with you, I plan to take Serena with me."

"Kind of unusual don't you think?"

"I suppose. I think she needs some reassurance that we're doing everything we can to help Eric. Especially since Greg's out of the picture."

"You don't have anything to prove."

Paul's laser perception took her off guard. She scrambled for a strong response. "I don't think I do. Do you?"

His gentle smile broke the ice. "Not in the least. Actually, I think it's a good idea for you to take Serena along. She's a smart, capable woman and she's offered to help out while she's in town."

Cory winced at his use of the word "capable." "She seems like she could be very helpful."

"I'm certain. And, Cory?"

"Yes?"

"She'll come around."

Moments later, Cory found Serena standing in the reception area, reading the framed newspaper clippings of clinic success stories. She was beautiful, and Cory's gut twisted with desire. She should have handled last night differently. Been less abrupt, more understanding. And what would have happened then? Didn't matter. She'd said her piece, hopefully cleared the air. They'd work together, and professionalism would define their relationship. Cory would pretend to like the idea until she got used to it. "Good morning."

"Good morning." Serena pointed at the frames on the wall. "The clinic has a stellar reputation."

"The people here work hard. But not all reputations are built on truth."

"Is that so? What is that supposed to mean?"

"Nothing."

"Not nothing. You have something to say, say it."

"Maybe you shouldn't believe everything you read in the papers." Cory hastily changed the subject. "Are you ready to go?"

Thankfully, Serena followed her lead into the change in subject. "Where are we going?"

"The Rinson County courthouse. If you're going to help out around here, you should see how things work, firsthand."

"Lead the way."

Neither spoke much during the car ride. Cory occasionally referenced points of interest along the way, but otherwise, the forty-five minute trip dragged. Serena stared out the window and Cory flirted with danger as she spent more time looking at Serena's profile than the road ahead. She shouldn't be captivated by the sister of a client, a woman who had no respect for her. She should remain focused on the case, especially if she wanted to earn Serena's respect. Which she did.

Why did she care so much about this stranger's opinion? Maybe because she'd lost the respect of everyone else. Well, that wasn't entirely accurate. Julie respected her. Didn't she? Of course she did. If she didn't, she wouldn't have made the promises she had. But Julie didn't make her feel the way Serena did. And she wanted Serena's respect more than she wanted Julie's. Crazy. Any respect she'd get from Serena would be fleeting. No matter how talented she was,

Eric's case was a loser, and she was destined to have another albatross around her neck the day the state put him to death. Cory Lance, can't keep people in prison or out of it.

"Aren't you going to ask any questions about what's on the agenda?"

"You didn't seem like you were in the mood to talk, so I'm saving them up in my head."

"And here I thought you were the one administering the silent treatment." Cory shook her head as she played the statement back in her head. She sounded like a five-year-old. "I'm sorry, that was unnecessary."

"But probably not far off the mark." Serena turned in her seat. "As I recall, you were the one who walked out last night."

"I probably shouldn't have been there in the first place."

"Don't want to get too close to the real people involved, right?"

If you only knew. Cory pretended to ignore the comment. "Do you want to know the plan for this morning or not?"

"Sure, if you have a plan, I'd love to hear about it." Serena managed to inject a subtle inference into every statement. Trouble was, Cory wasn't entirely sure she knew what she was doing. She'd handled death penalty cases before, at trial. This part of the process was foreign. At least in a big county like Dallas, her work was over once the trial concluded. The post-conviction process was handled by the appellate division, and a lawyer from that unit handled all interaction with the defendant's appellate counsel. The newly elected DA had added another layer to the process. He'd formed a Conviction Integrity Unit. That unit, which consisted of one lawyer and one investigator, was responsible for her suspension. They'd opened the files to Nelson's attorneys and provided full access. All her trial notes and preparatory investigation, normally considered privileged attorney work product, was produced to the other side. Talk about arming your enemies.

As much as she resented the process, the motion in her briefcase essentially asked for the same access in Eric's case. She didn't think she had a chance, but she had to do something to get the ball rolling. "I've prepared a discovery motion, a request for access to the district attorney's files regarding Eric's case."

"Hasn't anyone had access to them before?"

"Partly. Generally, the defense isn't entitled to full review of the prosecutor's files. The files often contain what's called attorney work product. Notes, ideas, strategies—things that aren't considered evidence. Prior to trial, all we're entitled to is the evidence in the case, like the police report, witness statements, copies of photo lineups."

"I recall seeing most of those things in the trial attorney's files and in the trial transcript."

"You're right. We have the stuff that was produced to Eric's attorneys and/or entered into evidence."

"But you're looking for something different."

"Exactly. Reports, statements, evidence of lineups that weren't produced or used at trial because they wouldn't have been favorable to your brother's case."

"Aren't they supposed to share that information anyway? I remember reading about a law that requires them to."

"If it were written on the books as a law, it would be easier to tell. What should be produced in pretrial discovery can be a gray area."

"Lawyers love gray areas."

"What's that supposed to mean?"

"It means that when an attorney doesn't want to do something, it's complicated, but when they've made up their minds, then everything's black and white."

"That's a fairly broad generalization."

"Just my observation."

"Well, you're right about the evidence part. There is a Supreme Court case that says that the prosecution is supposed to turn over exculpatory evidence, evidence that would tend to show that the defendant didn't do what he's accused of doing, to the defense."

"And apparently, most prosecutors don't feel like they need to comply."

"Wow. Talk about black and white. I think most prosecutors do the best they can."

"The best they can? Seriously, how hard can it be?"

"Harder than you think." With every sentence, Cory hoped Serena would lose interest in the subject. No chance.

"I don't believe you."

"Why don't you say what you really mean?" Cory cracked a smile to lighten the atmosphere, but Serena wasn't buying. She took a different tack. "Consider this. You're a prosecutor and the complaining witness in your case is a little girl who claims her dad molested her. Her mother files for divorce, and when the little girl learns that her family is breaking up, she says that she made up the abuse. She talks to a counselor, and finally, realizes she's not responsible for her mother's decision to end the marriage and admits she said she lied about making up the story so her parents would get back together. Do you have an obligation to tell defense counsel about the brief change of story?"

"Yes."

"What makes you so sure? What if the defense attorney makes such a big deal out of it that the child molester goes free? She's a child, for crying out loud. She's susceptible to suggestion."

"Sounds like you're arguing for the other side. Of course a child is suggestible. That doesn't mean they are not capable of telling the truth and sticking to it. The truth is what the truth is. It's that simple."

"You really believe that, don't you?"

"I have to."

Cory thought but didn't speak the logical connection to Eric's case. If Eric really raped and killed Nancy McGowan, then did Serena think he deserved to die? "I don't think things are that simple."

"You sure about that? I bet when you're working at the DA's office you believe the folks you're prosecuting are all bad."

"Most of them are."

Serena shook her head. "Seems simple then. If the bad guys are so bad, they'll get convicted even if you share all the information you have."

"That's a thought, but sometimes you don't have all the facts. Sometimes law enforcement doesn't share the exculpatory information with the ADA working the case."

"Okay, well, that seems like a different situation. Is that what happened to you?"

Cory shifted in her seat, her gaze firmly focused on the road in front of her. They were close to the courthouse, but not close enough for her to dodge the question. "It was a complicated situation." She wanted to shout the answers, clear the air, get Serena to stop looking at her like she was a paragon of evil. Every time she started to share details, she heard Julie's voice in her head, telling her to wait it out, promising redemption. "It's complicated," she repeated.

Serena turned away from her and gazed out the passenger side window. "So what's the plan for today? You march in and ask the prosecutor to just hand over the contents of his file to you?"

"Something like that."

"And you think he will?"

"Not in a million years. But if he doesn't agree, I'm going to ask the judge."

A few minutes later, they arrived at the Rinson County Courthouse. The turn-of-the-century building sat in the center of the town and they parked across the street. As they got out of the car, Serena asked, "Quaint building. Have you been here before?"

"Once, to visit a prosecutor on a case related to one I was prosecuting. It's been a long time."

Serena looked around. "This town seems very…conservative."

Cory followed her gaze. Almost every car on the square sported a bumper sticker supporting Republican candidates, and every face they saw was white. Rinson County was staunch middle-class, and solidly red. "It is. Very."

"Doesn't seem like a good place for a black man from the big city to be on trial for killing a hometown white girl."

And rape. Don't forget the rape. "As much as I hate to admit it, you're probably right. Any idea why Eric was working out this direction?"

"He said that he had trouble getting work in Dallas. I guess small town folks don't run background checks."

"Makes sense." Cory led the way up the steep stairs outside of the courthouse. "When we get inside, I'll do the talking. I'd rather they didn't know you're Eric's sister, so I'm just going to say that you're a paralegal. Okay?"

Serena's expression said it wasn't, but she didn't protest. "Okay."

"You ready to go in?"

"Your assistant is ready."

Cory ignored the sarcasm and led the way into the building. She was accustomed to flashing a badge and bypassing security, but today, she was nobody. She missed the access of her position, but there was a certain comfort in being anonymous. She set her briefcase on the conveyor belt and waited until the deputy sheriff waved her through the metal detector. Even the rural courthouses had instituted some form of security after the Oklahoma bombing and 9/11. To make up for the fact she was being treated like a regular citizen, she chatted up the deputy.

"Where would I find Rick Smith?"

"Docket call should be close to done, but he's probably still in the 578th. Second floor. Take the stairs, the elevator's on the fritz."

"Thanks." Cory waited for Serena to pass inspection and then led her to the broad staircase.

"Want to translate what he said for us lay folk?"

"Most courts hold a morning docket call for cases set that day. That's where you find the prosecutors. He was referring to the 578th District Court."

"Got it. Lead the way."

Cory walked confidently even though she didn't know her way around this particular courthouse. Didn't matter; they were all the same in certain ways. Prosecutors, public defenders, and retained criminal defense attorneys all milled around in the courtrooms. Anyone you encountered could be a probation officer, judge, bailiff, juror, or defendant. The trick was to fake experience until you figured out what you were doing. She remembered it took her months to figure out the ins and outs of the Dallas County courthouse. Years into the job, she knew everyone in the building and could navigate the system blindfolded. Her penance at the clinic wasn't as unpleasant as she had thought it would be, but she was still anxious to return to the familiar. Just over a month to go.

She glanced back to make sure Serena was close by. Her time at the clinic would end before Eric's execution date. And if she or someone else was somehow successful in getting a stay, she'd be long gone before his case was resolved. She shook her head. Eric's case wasn't really hers. It was Greg's and she was just filling in until he was able to return to work. Eric needed a true believer like Greg, someone who would fight without regard to the impossibility of winning.

When she arrived at the doors of the 578th District Court, she glanced through the tiny windows on the outer doors. The judge was on the bench, taking a plea, but a horde of attorneys gathered inside the rails, broken off into small groups, presumably discussing pending cases. Cory motioned for Serena to take a seat in the gallery, and then she stepped into the well of the courtroom and approached one of the bailiffs.

"Can you point Rick Smith out to me?" Before the bailiff had a chance to answer, Cory found herself wrapped in a bear hug. She stiffened, but quickly relaxed when she turned to face her attacker. "Kyle Hansen, you dog! I thought people in small towns shoot folks that creep up on them like that."

"Right, Lance. We all carry six-shooters in holsters. Oh, and don't forget the ten-gallon hats."

Cory leaned back and appraised her old friend. She and Kyle had been hired at the Dallas DA's office at the same time. They'd gone to baby prosecutor school together and had a friendly competition between them as to who would be promoted to felony court first. She'd won. Kyle had left the office a few years ago, and she'd heard a rumor he was moving back to his family's ranch. "Are you working here?"

"If by here, you mean the DA's office, the answer's no. I'm in private practice now."

"Ah, defense attorney."

"Among other things. Actually, I don't do much criminal work anymore. I'm general counsel for the family business and I do some other transactional stuff on the side. I've got a civil trial in here next week, and I just came by to file some last-minute motions. I can't believe I ran into you. What the hell are you doing here?"

Cory shot a glance at Serena who was staring daggers her way. "It's complicated. We'll have a beer sometime and I'll catch you up."

They wouldn't have a beer and she wouldn't catch him up. The explanation was more than complicated; it was personal. Too personal to share with someone she hadn't seen in years. No doubt he'd read the news stories, and she wasn't up for the inevitable questions. Time to cut this chance meeting short and accomplish what she came to do. "Do you know Rick Smith?"

"Sure, he's in the jury room. I'll take you back." Before she could protest that she could find her own way, Kyle grasped her arm and led her through the door at the back of the courtroom and into the jury room. Cory looked back at Serena and mouthed that she would be right back. Serena's response was a disgusted shake of her head, and Cory wondered if she could ever do anything right in her eyes.

❖

Serena took about fifteen minutes to decide she was tired of doing what Cory told her to. She didn't take an indefinite leave from work, fly all the way out here, and rent a hotel room to sit around and wait for someone else to make things happen. She certainly wasn't going to watch Cory yuck it up with other attorneys, attorneys who probably thought whatever wrong she'd done was for the greater good. Put those criminals away; fry them if you have to. Doesn't matter if they're innocent; at least we can sleep at night knowing we erred on the side of caution.

She made her way to the edge of the crowded row and was about to leave the courtroom, when one of the bailiff's approached her, a clipboard in his hand. "Ma'am. Have you checked in?"

She was confused at first. Were she and Cory supposed to check in? Had Cory done so? She'd seen her approach one of the bailiffs. Had she taken care of it?

She'd waited too long to answer and he tapped the clipboard with his hand. "Are you sure you're on today's docket or that you're in the right courtroom?"

Realization dawned and it wasn't pretty. This man with his uniform, badge, and gun, thought she was a defendant. That she'd committed a crime. That she was here to have justice meted out to her. She surveyed the rest of the people in the gallery. Lots of Hispanics, a few poor looking whites, and about a dozen African-Americans. Of course she fit right in. Didn't matter that she was wearing her best suit, the color of her skin lumped her in with the rest of the ne'er-do-wells of Rinson County. She kept her reply short. "I'm definitely not in the right place."

Once out in the hallway, she wasn't sure what to do. The halls were teeming with people, and it didn't take long to separate the accused from their counsel. The conversations were all laced with a thread of desperation: is that the best deal you can get? What am

I looking at? I'll lose my job. I'll never get a job if this stays on my record. She walked as far away from the crowd as she could and took a seat on a wooden bench.

Thirty long minutes later, Cory burst into the hall. Serena saw her looking around, but wasn't in the mood to help her out. She waited until Cory finally found her and let her have the first word.

"Obviously, that didn't go as well as it could have, but I've laid some groundwork."

Serena stood. "Can we go now?"

Cory looked confused. "Sure. I know a great place for a late breakfast if you're up for it."

"I'm not hungry." She didn't wait for Cory's reaction. Instead, she walked as quickly as she could, her entire focus on getting out of the building. Cory followed, but wisely didn't try to engage her in conversation. Once they were in the car, she turned to Serena. "You want to tell me why you're so angry?"

"I'm not angry."

"The hell you're not. I know an angry woman when I see one. Come on; tell me what has you in such a huff."

"You honestly don't know, do you?"

"Wouldn't ask if I did."

"Why did you bring me out here?"

"You wanted to see how things were done. I thought this would be a good opportunity."

"Oh, I saw how things were done. I saw you be all buddy buddy with the other attorneys while the rest of us sit in the audience and mind our manners."

Cory's shock was genuine. "Were you in the same courtroom I was? Rick fought me on every point. The judge is taking my discovery motion under consideration, but I don't think we're going to win access unless we raise solid issues in our writ."

"Didn't look like a fight to me. At least most people I fight with don't hug me first."

"Hug?" Cory looked puzzled for a moment. "Oh, you mean Kyle? Uh, no. He used to be a prosecutor, but he's in private practice. He took me back to the jury room to find Rick. I've known Kyle for years. Wait a minute. Were you even in the courtroom when we approached the bench?"

Serena felt stupid. She was angry at the bailiff for making assumptions about her, and she was doing the same about Cory. Time to fess up. "You mean that guy you hugged wasn't the prosecutor?" Cory shook her head, and Serena felt sheepish. "I left right after that."

"Why? I thought the whole reason you were coming along was to check up on me. Hard to do that when you're not even in the room." Cory's anger was palpable, and Serena wished she were anywhere else.

"I'm sorry. I don't know what to say. I had to leave." She didn't feel like sharing the humiliation of having been mistaken for a defendant, so she fished around for a change in subject. "I may be hungry after all. How about that breakfast?" She silently prayed Cory would let the change in subject pass without question. "You can tell me what I missed."

Cory's stare bored into her. Serena sensed she was trying to read her mind, and she also sensed she'd lost more than a few notches of respect in Cory's estimation. She'd have to steel herself if she wanted to be involved in Eric's case. Besides, if she weren't careful, she wouldn't get to spend time with Cory, and as much as she didn't understand it, as much as she resisted it, her desire to be with Cory was strong.

❖

Cory ushered Serena into the diner. She hoped for all her bragging it was as good as she remembered. She hadn't been able to impress Serena with her courtroom skill; maybe she could at least provide a good meal. Impressing Serena wasn't going to be an easy task.

Why had she left the courtroom before they were done? What had at first made Cory angry, now had her puzzled. Maybe facing the reality of her brother's case and the uphill battle ahead proved to be more than she could handle. She could hardly blame her since every desperate move wore at her confidence as well. How did attorneys do this for a living, knowing that wins were scarce and losses cost lives?

After Kyle had directed her back to the jury room, she'd confidently strode into the room, asking which one of the attorneys standing behind buckets of files was Rick Smith. When a middle-aged balding man with a slight paunch had stood to shake her hand, she felt a vague sense of recognition.

"Cory Lance, nice to see you again." He must have noticed her puzzled expression, because he followed up with, "You taught that class on homicide investigations last year, down in Huntsville."

She remembered. She and Julie had laughed about him later that evening when Julie had snuck into her room. He'd spent the class falling all over himself in his attempts to impress her and the rest of the class with his extensive knowledge of the law. Talking over her and the other panelists, shouting out answers, preaching his own courtroom methods as the only way. She'd been anything but impressed. That he was the prosecutor who'd sent Eric Washington to death row was a stinging blow. As much as it pained her, she knew his type would be more susceptible to flattery than intimidation. She did her best imitation of a southern belle.

"Of course I remember you, Rick. You were the star student."

He beamed and she did her best not to choke on her next words. "I'm sure you're just the person to help me. I'm doing some work for the Justice Clinic, you know that little group that operates out of Richards University? Well, anyway, they're working on a writ for a case you handled, and we'd like to see if we can get an agreed discovery order to review your file. The name Eric Washington ring any bells?" She waited and watched while he digested her request. She could tell he was trying to wrap his head around the fact she had just said she was working for the Justice Clinic, but he'd be too kiss-ass to admit he wasn't already aware of her current predicament.

"Eric Washington, eh? I remember that case. Brutal. Jury didn't take long to decide his fate. Not long at all." He motioned her over to a corner of the busy room. When they were out of earshot of most of the occupants, he let his guard down. "What's a nice woman like you working on a case like this for? I mean, I heard about your recent troubles, but the Justice Clinic? What's the point of all the years you wielded the sword of justice if you're going to use your talents to put murderers and rapists back on the street?"

Cory drew on reserves deep within to keep from slapping the pious expression off Rick's face. Wielding the sword of justice? Had she ever thought of her job in such grandiose terms?

She had. She may not have the insufferable personality traits of this bozo, but their differences weren't as vast as she would like to think. Prosecuting crimes, putting away bad guys—she'd lived for the thrill of those victories her entire legal career. She'd always believed the guy on trial deserved the worst the jury could mete out. She had to, or else what was the point?

"Rick, we all do what we have to do. Right now, I'm working this case and I'm going to give it everything I've got. Now, how about you show me your file? Come on, one prosecutor to another. If Eric Washington was good for the crimes, then what's the harm?"

His expression quickly turned from affable to sour. "I can't believe you, of all people, would be asking that question."

"Care to explain what you mean by that?" Cory abandoned charm and settled in for a fight.

He glanced around. Their conversation had begun to draw attention from the other lawyers in the room. To her relief, he lowered instead of raised his voice. "I know you need to make a show of this for PR and all. Let's go into the courtroom and you can argue your little discovery motion to your heart's content. But you and I both know you don't have a chance of saving Eric Washington's life. And I don't think you really want to anyway."

Cory didn't bother replying. Instead, she directed her anger into a well-crafted argument before Judge Fowler. Fowler had unseated the former judge, the one who'd presided over Eric's trial. She'd hoped his lack of investment in the original case would make him more receptive to her motion. He'd listened to her arguments and asked thoughtful questions, but at the end of the day, he did what she expected and ruled against her.

"I can't authorize what amounts to a fishing expedition. If you file a writ that raises genuine questions of fact regarding Mr. Washington's innocence, then I'll authorize discovery." Her only comfort was that he instructed Rick, on the record, that everything in the file should be preserved, at least until time ran out for Eric.

She couldn't believe how naive she'd been, thinking she could bounce into court and use her law-and-order cred to get a fellow prosecutor to hand over his file. Cory was thankful Serena hadn't witnessed the behind-the-scenes confrontation, but she wished she'd been there to see Cory argue in the courtroom. Impressing Serena seemed to be high on her list of priorities these days.

"What's good here?"

Serena's question brought her back to the present. "Everything. Precisely the reason I'm glad this place isn't on my way to work every day."

They settled on pancakes and split an order of bacon. When their food arrived, quick and hot, Serena groaned after the first bite. "These are amazing. I can never get pancakes to turn out right. They're either too tough or runny in the middle."

"I know, right? I don't even bother trying to make them myself. Nothing can compare to my mom's except this place." Cory immediately regretted the reference to her mother. Did Serena feel a sense of loss whenever anyone else talked about their parents?

"We had pancakes every Saturday morning when I was a kid. My adoptive parents, the Clarks, were big on tradition."

Since Serena had opened the subject, Cory forged ahead. "Do you call them Mom and Dad? Are you close? How does that work?"

"You sure ask a lot of questions." She looked more amused than annoyed.

"Occupational hazard."

"It varies. I love them, but when I first went to live with them, I'd been ripped away from everything familiar. I was angry because Eric couldn't come with us. I didn't understand why my mother was no longer in the picture, not that she ever really was. I couldn't process all the changes at once. It took me a while to warm up to the idea of having replacement parents, let alone acknowledging their roles by calling them Mom and Dad."

"And now?"

"Now, they're Mom and Dad to their faces, but I still have a habit of referring to them as Don and Marion Clark when I'm talking to other people."

"You didn't take their name?"

"They let me choose. I had this strange idea that if my mother ever came looking for me, she wouldn't be able to find me if I changed my name." Serena grunted. "Like she'd ever find her way out of whatever crack house she happened to be in to give it a go. She lived the life of a junkie and died with a needle in her arm."

Cory stretched her hand across the table and placed it over Serena's. "I'm sorry."

Serena didn't pull away, but when she looked into Cory's eyes, her stare was blank. "Not your problem."

Cory knew from experience that sometimes the most extreme pain burrows so deep it looks like nonchalance. Time to veer away from this subject. "What do you do in Florida?"

"I'm the head teller at a bank. Nothing glamorous."

"I know all about non-glamorous occupations."

"Really? I know plenty of people who think attorneys are at the top of the food chain."

"Not those who work for the county. Prosecutors probably make the least money of anyone in the law biz." Shit. She'd stepped in rough conversational waters again. Bad enough she regularly worked on the other side, she didn't need to call attention to it.

Serena didn't let her off the hook. "How long did you work as a prosecutor?"

"I started right out of law school. Actually, I interned at the office before I graduated, so besides a stint serving ice cream at Braum's, it's the only job I've ever had."

"Guess you liked it?"

Cory didn't read any sarcasm behind the question, only a genuine interest. "I did. It felt good representing victims, some who couldn't speak for themselves."

"You became successful."

"I've won more cases than I've lost." Cory didn't feel like bragging about her ninety percent victory rate. She knew some defense attorneys would say she came by that number by cherry picking her cases, but it wasn't true. She worked harder than anyone she knew. That's why Julie had noticed her. Taken her under her wing. Promoted her through the ranks. At least that's what she had to believe.

"I think you're being modest. I Googled you."

"Well then, you've probably read just as many bad things as good things." Cory didn't try to hide a smile, flattered that Serena had taken the time to get to know more about her. "I'm sure the recent news has you a bit on edge."

"Understatement. Prosecutor hides evidence and man lingers behind bars. Not a confidence builder, for sure."

Cory fiddled with her pancakes, her appetite gone. The master litigator was at a loss for words, but Serena wasn't going to let her off so easy.

"Care to tell me what happened?"

Cory flashed to an image of Julie, placing a finger over her lips, telling her, "Let's get past this, and everything will work out just fine. You do your part and I'll do mine." For once, she didn't care what Julie thought. She wanted to tell Serena the whole story. But she wouldn't. Too much at stake. She did want what Julie promised—just to get past this, no matter what respect she could buy from Serena with the truth. She settled on a half-truth. "Maybe someday."

"Right." Serena didn't have to say it. Cory knew she didn't believe her. Didn't believe she would ever share what happened, ever tell the truth, ever come clean. Didn't matter. They would work Eric's case together and it would all be over soon. Serena would go back to her noncontroversial job at a bank in Florida, and Cory would try to survive the swirl of bad PR and return to her life as it had been. Their lives could not be more different. So why did she desperately want to find similarities?

Serena's cell phone rang and Cory feigned disinterest as she answered it. Would it be her parents, calling to check on her? A significant other? The thought made her seethe with jealousy. She was surprised when Serena passed the phone to her.

"It's Skye. She's been trying to reach you, but her calls are going straight to voice mail."

"I turned my phone off when I was in court. I must've forgotten to turn it back on." She spoke into the phone. "Skye, where's the fire? You're kidding? What time?" She glanced at her watch. "We're about forty minutes out. We'll meet you there." She ended the call and handed the phone back to Serena. "Want to tag along on a witness interview? Skye just located Leonard Wilkens and he's interested in repenting before he dies."

CHAPTER THIRTEEN

Leonard aka Lenny Wilkins's house was not much more than a beat-up shack with paint peeling from the siding and only a few uncracked windows. Lenny was in worse shape than his house.

After a brief discussion on the front porch with Skye, Cory decided no harm would come from letting Serena sit in on the interview as long as she understood the ground rules. Skye and Cory would ask all the questions. When the time came for Skye to get a written statement from Leonard, Cory and Serena would both leave to keep him from claiming that he felt undue pressure from having Eric's entire legal team standing over his shoulder.

"You sure you're up for this?" Serena's presence was Skye's idea. She'd hypothesized that having Eric's sister on hand would motivate the old man to tell the truth, especially if it meant the telling might spare Eric's life. Cory's reservations were more about protecting Serena's feelings than for any other reason. She'd read the statement Leonard gave to the police. It was laced with racial epithets. They'd cleaned up his language for trial, and Eric's attorneys were ineffective at pointing out the difference in his polished courtroom presence and the bigoted self he'd shown the cops. But here, in his own home, he wouldn't bother hiding his coarse manner, and Cory wanted to protect Serena from any further harm.

"I've read the file. I know guys like this. They don't change. If anything, the older they get, the worse they are. I can handle it." Serena's face was steel. Cory knew she had to hurt inside, but the last thing she needed was to be patronized. She offered an encouraging nod and held open the door. Skye introduced them to Wilkins. She didn't bother explaining Serena's role, probably assuming he would get the connection by the fact she and Eric had the same last name.

Wilkins sat in an aging vinyl recliner, his lower body wrapped in a dingy afghan. Tubes ran from his nose to the oxygen tank on the floor beside him. He motioned at the couch and gasped a welcome. "Come in. Sit down."

Cory wished she had a tarp or something to put between her suit and the filthy piece of furniture. The entire room, with stacks of newspapers and magazines, used fast food containers, and half full abandoned mugs of coffee was a showpiece for one of those reality shows that featured hoarders or people who didn't know the definition of sanitary. The faster they heard what he had to say, the faster they could leave. She took a seat on the couch and tried to ignore the slight crunch when she made contact with the upholstery. Serena sat close beside her. The only bright light in an otherwise dismal room.

Skye opened the interview. "Mr. Wilkins, I'd like you to tell Ms. Lance what you told me. Can I get you something to drink?"

"No. Don't want anything. It'll just make me have to piss. You have no idea what that involves."

And we don't want to know. Cory tried to summon some reserve of sympathy for Wilkins. He'd been diagnosed with testicular cancer the year before and the disease had advanced rapidly. Skye had found all of this out from the woman who came by once a day to help him with his bodily functions. Lucky lady. She'd also pumped the woman for helpful information, like what time of day he was likely to be in the best mood. They were still in the window of supposedly pleasant behavior. Around lunchtime, he got surly. They had a short time frame to get the information they needed.

"Where do you want me to start?"

"Start with what you told me about firing Eric."

"I fired him all right. Pretty sure it was him that stole that money out of the drawer."

"The cash that was short, that was from a drawer behind the bar, right?"

"Best I remember, yes."

"Did Eric work back there?" Skye did a stellar job of keeping her tone easy and even. Cory was pleased to see her interrogation skills had only gotten better over the years.

"He did all kinds of stuff. Odds and ends. He did take a shine to that McGowan girl. I do remember that."

"How did she react to his attention?"

"That girl? She was smooth as silk. I'm sure she was used to getting all sorts of attention. She didn't act like it bothered her."

"The police, they seemed to think she might have been annoyed by his attention. That he may have made unwanted advances. What's your opinion?"

"That detective, can't remember his name now, but he was hot on the idea. Had a theory that boy got a little too familiar and was rebuked."

"He ask you to feed into that? Play it up at trial?"

Cory tapped her foot, just enough to try to get Skye's attention. Exaggeration wasn't fabrication. If they filed a writ stating only that Wilkins had embellished his testimony, they'd be bounced out of court. She prayed this wasn't the extent of his coming clean. Skye caught her stare and patted the air with her palm. Cory bit her tongue and tried to be patient.

"I may have made a bigger deal of it than it really was." He shrugged. "Detective said they had a rock solid case."

You lying bastard. Cory could imagine how the questioning went down. The detective had probably worked with him for hours, asking leading questions so many times that when he took the stand, the lies were easier than the truth to tell. She couldn't resist getting to the heart of the matter. "Tell us about the night that Eric came by to ask questions about his final paycheck. The night Nancy McGowan disappeared."

The police had assumed Nancy disappeared that night because no one had seen her the next day. Fact was, she hadn't been scheduled to work, and it wasn't that abnormal for her not to have been seen. The medical examiner placed the time of death in the range of twenty-four to forty-eight hours from when she was found, so she could have died much later.

"That boy didn't know his place. I fired him and he comes back in here, trying to cozy up to Gerry." He stopped and placed the oxygen mask over his face and drew several wheezing breaths.

When he finished, Cory asked, "Was Gerald there?" She knew the answer, but she asked anyway to prompt him along. An objective observer might conclude her behavior toward the old man was callous. She didn't care. The only person's feelings she cared about right now were Serena's. The sooner they could get out of this hateful man's wretched house, the better off she would feel.

"He was there and he fell for that boy's sob story. I figured he'd already taken whatever he might be owed, but Gerry apparently saw things differently. I saw him in the parking lot after he squirrelled some money out of Gerry, and I told him to get the hell out."

Cory couldn't help but glance in Serena's direction. She admired her stoicism in the face of Wilkins's callous remarks. She pressed on. "Did he do what you asked?"

"You bet he did. I don't make idle threats."

"He drove off? You watched him."

"Yep, that's right."

"How late did you work that night?"

"Same as always, 'til they closed. Around three."

"Did Eric come back?"

"Didn't come back in the bar. I know that for a fact."

"How late did Nancy work that night?" Skye posed the question and Cory scooted forward, sure that they were finally getting to the reason they were here.

Wilkins glanced around as if he were afraid of an invisible disapproving audience. "Same as me. We all walked out together."

Cory heard Serena expel a heavy breath. If Nancy hadn't walked out of the bar until three a.m., no way did the other witness see her arguing in the parking lot with Eric hours earlier. Still, it wasn't enough. She nodded to Skye to keep going. They had to pin him down.

"Are you aware an eyewitness testified at trial that he saw Eric Washington arguing with Nancy, and that he forced her into his car and drove away?"

"I heard that. Didn't happen."

"And you're sure?"

"Damn straight. She worked in that bar all night. Didn't leave until we all walked out. She got in her car and left."

"Any idea why," Cory glanced at her notes for the name of the eyewitness, "Dale Bolton, would have lied about what happened?"

"I don't pretend to know what goes on in the mind of anyone but me. All I can tell you is it didn't happen."

His insistence rang true, but Cory pressed on. "If you knew he was lying, why didn't you say something at the time?"

"Weren't my business and nobody asked. I'm not the law. I'm just a hard-working man who didn't want any trouble. That boy, he wasn't ever up to any good."

Cory knew he was talking about Eric. She despised this miserable human being. Talk about no good. She didn't even try to hide her disdain. "What gave you a sudden attack of conscience?"

He took a deep breath from the mask before fixing her with a stare. He picked up a Bible from the table next to him. "Death. I'm going to meet my maker soon. Time to unburden my soul lest it's too heavy to enter the gates of heaven."

The Bible in his hands didn't show any signs of wear. Cory bet it was brand new, just like his born-again conscience. Death makes people do strange things; maybe he was telling the truth. She wanted to believe him. After all, he had nothing to gain by coming forward now. It still wasn't quite enough, but she needed every piece of evidence she could get to make the puzzle of Eric's fate come out differently.

"How sick are you?" She knew the question seemed blunt, but if he was going to keel over soon, they needed to work fast to preserve his statement. The potential irony of him dying before Eric and thereby sealing Eric's fate, was too much to handle.

"Doc says it could happen any time."

Cory stood. "Thanks for coming forward," she said with gratitude she didn't feel. All she really felt was anger. Anger that he'd lied in the first place. Anger that he still held on to his bigotry even in the face of death. But displaying her anger now wouldn't do Eric any good. Besides, Serena was the one who had the right to be angry. She forced herself to focus on what they still needed. "Ms. Keaton's going to need to get your written statement, and you'll need to swear to it. You'll do that?" She barely waited for his nod before addressing Serena. "We should go. Skye, can I speak to you outside for a minute?"

Serena stood, but before she left the room, she stuck her hand in Wilkins's direction. "Thank you." Wilkins actually teared up at the exchange. Cory scrutinized Serena's face, but she read nothing but sincere gratitude. Serena had a bigger heart than she did.

Once out on the porch, Cory turned to Skye. "You know what to do, right? His statement has to be ironclad. It might be enough to get that discovery order we need. I don't want us to lose because he dropped dead before the judge gets all his questions answered."

"I know what to do." Skye bounced on the balls of her feet, obviously anxious to get back in there and do what she did best.

"I know you do. Call me when you have it. I'm going to head back and start drafting the motion now. As soon as you're done, we're going to need to find this Dale Bolton. He's the key." She turned to Serena. "Ready to get out of here?"

Serena shot one last look at Wilkins's door, but Cory couldn't read her expression. "Absolutely."

The ride back to the clinic seemed long. Cory didn't speak and Serena didn't try to engage her in conversation since it was obvious her brain was whirring at top speed. Her brow was furrowed and her lips moved in silent conversation as if she were ticking off items on an internal checklist. Beautiful, kissable lips. Cory, focused and fierce, aroused her. Serena turned her gaze out the passenger side window and forced herself to remember how little she'd trusted Cory just a short while ago. She didn't need the distraction of anything personal. Neither of them did.

She didn't want to talk anyway. Her mind churned with possibilities. If Wilkins had lied, maybe other witnesses had lied as well. Would Skye and Cory be able to use this new information to get Eric a new trial? Would a new trial have a different result, or would Eric be back in the same position all over again? Had Eric's trial attorneys spoken with Wilkins and this Dale Bolton before the first trial? Had they even tried to figure out the truth, or had they only played defense?

If Eric got another chance, Serena vowed to do everything within her power to make sure he was well represented. She'd ask Cory for the name of the best defense attorney she'd ever tried a case against and she'd figure out a way to get the money to hire that person. If the dying old man they'd just left was an example of the type of witness the state had used to send Eric to death row, then he had to get another chance. Didn't he?

When they turned into the clinic parking lot, Cory finally spoke. "I want to get a draft of this motion done today so we can file it as soon as possible. Sorry we won't get to spend the rest of the day together, but this is the boring part of the job. Me, sitting at my computer, typing." Cory offered a grin and Serena smiled back.

"I understand." She opened the door. Cory wanted to get to work. She wanted Cory to get to work. But she wanted something more. She hesitated. "About today, this morning, I'm sorry for assuming…you know…" She didn't remember the last time she'd been this much at a loss for words.

Cory shook her head. "Don't worry about it. You love your brother. You want the best for him. I get it."

Serena nodded. Cory got it. She should trust her. She wanted to. "Thanks. I'll see you tomorrow?"

"Yes. Maybe Skye will have some info for us on Bolton."

"Great." Serena turned to leave, but Cory called her name. "Yes?"

"Are you tired of eating in your motel room?"

The non sequitur threw Serena for a moment. "What?"

"Why don't you come over tonight? For dinner?" Cory looked as flustered as Serena felt, but she kept talking. "At my place? I mean, I could pick up some groceries and we could play around in my big kitchen." She actually blushed. "I mean cook. Nothing fancy, but a home-cooked meal. I can write down directions for you to get there." Cory ended her ramble abruptly. Adorable. There was nothing Serena would rather do than join her for dinner. Lost in Cory's blush, she realized there *was* something she would like to do more, and the realization made her own face flush.

"I'll get the groceries. And I remember how to get there. Call me when you're ready." Serena walked away before either one of them could change their minds.

Chapter Fourteen

Cory uncorked the best bottle in her collection. Serena would be there any minute. With groceries. For dinner. With her. Why had she asked her over? Silly question. She knew the answer. She wanted to see her, outside of the office, not about the case. She wanted their proximity to be about the slow boil of attraction instead of their circumstances. Did Serena feel it too? Surely she wouldn't have agreed to come over if she didn't. Or maybe she thought this dinner was a business meeting, an opportunity to discuss the work Cory had done after they parted ways earlier in the day.

She hoped not. Especially since she didn't have anything noteworthy to report. She'd rushed into the clinic offices, excited about the prospect of penning a winning argument. Her excitement fizzled quickly when she greeted the somber faces of the other staff attorneys in the conference room.

She'd completely forgotten about the execution scheduled for the next day. Michael Young. A clinic client who'd killed his entire family with an axe in a bloody evening killing spree. He'd been caught literally red-handed and there was no doubt he'd committed the crime, but Michael was mentally retarded and the state wasn't allowed to kill those folks whose IQ was so low they may not understand the process. The problem was no one had raised the issue previously even though the evidence was readily available. If they couldn't figure out a creative argument, they might be barred from raising the issue now and Michael would meet the needle the following evening. All hands were on deck to work on a brief to the appellate court.

She had cornered Paul at the coffee maker and given him a snapshot of what she'd learned from Wilkins.

His reply was rushed. "Sounds like you got something to work with, but we need your help on this case today. A couple of the interns are researching the jurisdictional part of the brief. They need a guiding hand. We need to get it filed by six to allow the Criminal Court of Appeals time to reject us and still be able to refile with the Supreme Court tomorrow. Eric's case has to wait."

Cory had worked her ass off the rest of the day, cobbling together an argument to convince the higher court to overlook technicalities in favor of justice. Appellate work was new for her. She spent her days in the courtroom, making things happen, not hunkered down in the law library figuring out how to reverse events that had already taken place. She wasn't afraid of a good fight, but she couldn't imagine spending her days fighting uphill battles the way the clinic attorneys did. Every day, every fight was an all-out war. And because of the nature of the cases, they came out bloody and their clients remained incarcerated, or worse, were killed by the state. Depressing.

The doorbell rang and Cory shook herself out of her blue mood. In seconds, Serena would be in her house, drinking her wine, cooking dinner with her. She couldn't think of a better cure for depression.

❖

Serena shifted the grocery bags and struggled to reach the doorbell. She'd blown her food budget to live up to Cory's amazing kitchen. The front desk clerk at the hotel had recommended Central Market when she'd asked for the best grocery store around, and she'd spent over an hour wandering the aisles selecting the perfect fresh foods for their dinner. The abundance of choices stood in stark contrast to her memories of her childhood when she and Eric spent only seconds figuring out which can to open or which box to defrost in order to feed themselves every evening.

After checking out everything in the store, she settled on a simple meal of steaks, salad, and new potatoes. She'd add her own special touches, but she knew she didn't want her entire focus to be on preparation of the food. When she arrived at Cory's house, she murmured a quiet thank you for her own good judgment. Cory wore faded blue jeans like a second skin. A slightly rumpled, untucked, white oxford shirt was open just enough to tease her gaze. No, food would not be the focus of their evening.

"Hi, there."

"Hi. I hope you're hungry."

"Starving."

"Good."

Serena shifted the bags again and Cory jumped forward, arms outstretched. "I'm sorry. You must think I'm the rudest person on earth."

Serena pushed one of the bags into Cory's arms. "Not the rudest."

"Thank goodness. I have something to work toward." Cory stepped closer, but she didn't reach for the other bag, instead merely lingering in Serena's personal space. Serena struggled not to step closer. "Come on. Show me back to your kitchen. I'm going to put you to work." She didn't wait for an answer, but walked confidently in the direction she thought she remembered the kitchen was located. Cory trailed behind her, and she could smell the musky hint of her cologne. Even out of her sight, she was captivating.

Cory set the bags on the counter and offered her a glass of wine.

"A small glass. I have to drive later." She didn't intend to drink even that, but she didn't want to break the spell between them with her personal fears.

"Hopefully, you'll stick around long enough to wear off a full glass of wine." Cory stood close, the bottle in one hand, a glass in the other. She poured the glass, a three-quarter full compromise, and placed it in Serena's hand. Seconds ticked away as they both held the glass. Serena stopped breathing as if she could suspend time long enough to bask in the light touch of Cory's fingers barely meeting hers. Cory pulled closer. "At least I hope you will."

Torn between surrender and keeping her guard, she resorted to her favorite method of personal protection, avoidance. She stepped back and pointed at the grocery bags. "I recall you said you were starving."

"I am."

Uh oh. Cory's knowing smile conveyed her hunger had nothing to do with food. More distance necessary. Now. She reached into the nearest bag and began pulling out several bags of produce. "Then start chopping. When you're done, you can put these in a bowl and bring them back to me. Make sure and wash them first." She tried to think of more steps to keep Cory busy, but those would do for now. "Now, tell me where you keep your bowls."

Cory used a knife to point out a couple of cabinets. "Care to tell me what we're making?"

"You're working on the salad."

"I see peaches in here."

"You are very observant. That come in handy in your line of work?"

Cory tossed a slice of peach across the kitchen. Serena pointed to the floor where it landed. "Not much of an athlete, are you?"

"I can hold my own. Would you like me to show you my particular skills?"

Damn, the banter only kept getting more suggestive. Serena bent over the skillet she had heating on the stove. She knew if she made eye contact with Cory or even bantered back, she'd be finished. Finished preparing this meal, finished avoiding the attraction, finished denying what she desired. Ignoring Cory's suggestive query, she asked the most innocuous question she could think of. "How do you like your steak cooked?"

"In my kitchen, by a beautiful woman."

Enough. Serena whirled around. Ignoring Cory's innuendo wasn't working. "What do you mean by that?" She was surprised at the angry tremor in her voice.

"Um, excuse me?" Cory's voice reflected a tremor of its own, but one of genuine surprise, not anger.

"What am I doing here?"

Cory's eyes darted around the room as if seeking escape, but when she answered, her voice took on a slight edge. "I've obviously done something to make you mad. If you don't want to be here, you don't have to be." She paused and when she spoke again, she softened her tone. "I'd like you to stay. I can't remember the last time any appliance in this kitchen besides the Keurig and microwave got any action. Not to mention—" Cory stopped midsentence and her face flushed.

Serena didn't need to ask her to finish. Her instincts told her Cory had been about to make another suggestive remark. And why shouldn't she? Clearly, they were attracted to each other. Serena had recognized the looks that passed between them, the rising heat beneath her skin when they drew close. She loved the way Cory aroused her, but she resented her inability to control her own reactions. Was Cory torn as well? Did she struggle against her feelings? If her actions this evening were any indication, the answer was no. At least not tonight. Tonight she seemed hell-bent on exploring the minefield between them, risks be damned. Could she meet Cory halfway? Would she?

"I don't know what I'm doing here." The words tumbled out before she could censor her thought. She was no longer talking about her physical location. She had no idea how to navigate this situation since it was one she'd avoided her whole life. But here she was again, and this time she wanted to take the next step more than she wanted to protect herself from the pain of the unknown.

Cory walked across the kitchen. She was close, but not too close. Her eyes bored into Serena's, questioning, compassionate, kind. "I'd like you to stay."

"I think I want to."

"That's a start."

"I think I want to do a lot of things."

Cory moved mere inches closer, but already Serena could feel the sparks igniting between them. The heat fueled her forward, pressing her into Cory's space. Cory leaned forward to close the gap, and she gave in to soft lips and fiery passion. Her first surrender made her wonder why she'd ever fought. Every nerve in her body surged, and she both feared and hoped she would explode.

Eons later, she pulled slightly back. She felt drunk, or at least what she thought drunk felt like. Heady, hazy, she gasped for air.

"Are you okay?" Cory murmured the question. She looked like Serena felt, eyes half shut, her lips puffed in a dreamy smile.

"I've never done this before."

Cory grinned. "Never kissed an attorney? Never been kissed in a kitchen?"

Serena started to answer, but stopped to examine Cory's expression. She was kidding around, but her eyes were kind. She wanted to trust her. She resolved to trust her. "I'm feeling things for you I've never felt before. Never allowed myself to feel. I'm afraid…Well, I'm just afraid of what happens next."

"Oh." The one-word response landed between them with a thud. Serena started to turn away, but Cory pulled her back.

"Hey, don't go."

Paralyzed, Serena didn't know what to do. Whether she left Cory's house or not was of no consequence. After that kiss, she could never go back. The question now was, could she go forward? "I shouldn't have told you."

"You surprised me; that's all. Tell me something."

"What?" Serena both dreaded and welcomed the conversation. Talking meant they weren't kissing. Kissing led to confusion. Or did it? When her lips met Cory's, she'd never felt anything so right.

"Did you enjoy it?"

Enjoy it? Was Cory kidding? Kissing her was rapture. All she could think about was doing it again. "I adored it."

"May I kiss you again?"

Cory's question was tentative, sweet. Serena wanted to shout yes, but years of not giving in to want took their toll. "If I say I need to think about it, will you want me to leave?" She saw a flicker of disappointment in Cory's eyes, but her response was perfect.

"Don't be silly. You haven't cooked me dinner yet."

Serena opened her mouth to say more, but decided instead to lean into the levity Cory had thrown between them. Later. Process your feelings first, and you can talk to her about them later. You can't think straight, while she's standing beside you looking completely kissable. She answered by gently pushing Cory back toward the cutting board. "You do your part, and I'll do mine." As she watched Cory walk across the kitchen, she knew with every fiber of her being that she already knew what she wanted and no amount of thought was going to change her mind.

❖

Cory couldn't remember the last time she'd eaten a home-cooked meal, let alone one that tasted like it had been prepared in a five-star restaurant. She swallowed the last bite of her perfectly prepared filet and tossed her napkin on the table in surrender. "Dinner was amazing. Do you always cook like that?"

Serena laughed. "If I did, I'd be big as a house. I love to cook, but it's not as much fun when it's just for me."

"I survive on takeout. This spread spoiled me rotten."

"Thanks. I'm addicted to the Food Network. It's nice to take some of what I've learned for a test drive." Serena started to stack their plates.

"Hold it right there." Cory pushed her chair back and stood. "I'll do these dishes later. Come relax on the couch while I put some coffee on." She started to ask if she wanted another glass of wine, but she noticed Serena had cleaned her plate, but her wine glass remained full. "You don't like wine, do you?"

Serena glanced at the glass and frowned. "I'm sorry I wasted it."

"I'm not worried about that. It's just I should've offered you something else. Sorry to be such a lame hostess."

"Not your fault. I could've said something. To tell the truth, I don't know if I like wine, which is a little embarrassing."

"Don't be silly. So you've never tried wine before. Not a problem. I can make sure you meet all the right grapes."

"Well, that's the embarrassing part. I've never tried any alcohol. When all your blood relations are junkies, you learn to be on guard against the possibility it might be in your DNA."

"That's nothing to be ashamed of. Actually, it's pretty damn smart." She reached for Serena's hand and led her to the couch, careful to keep a conversational distance away. She sensed the significance of Serena's revelation and didn't want to crowd her comfort zone. "You could've told me."

"I guess I should've been honest. As I recall, you were a bit distracted while serving the wine." She offered a subtle smile and let a few beats pass before she added, "And I'm still trying to navigate the distance between you and me."

"Are our worlds that far apart?"

"Not as far apart as I first thought."

Cory heard a slight inflection. "I hear a but."

"Do you feel badly about the man who spent all that time in prison? That one who was just released?"

Damn. The Nelson case was the last thing Cory had expected Serena to bring up, and it was definitely the last thing she wanted to talk about tonight.

Actually, she did want to talk about it, but after weeks of resisting the constant pressure of the press, her peers, and even Melinda, to tell her side of the story, she'd become resigned to letting everyone assume the public facts spoke for themselves. As much as it pained her, she'd made a promise and, contrary to what everyone now thought, she valued her integrity more than she valued other people's opinions.

Except Serena's. Her opinion mattered and it mattered a lot. Cory considered her options, but she knew there was no way to tell even part of the story without compromising promised loyalties. "I wish I could talk to you about it, but—"

"But your lawyer probably told you to stay quiet," Serena interrupted.

"Yes." Not the entire truth, but it was the easier explanation.

"I just find it hard to believe, based on what I've seen, that you would be the kind of person that could sit by while someone went to prison for something they didn't do."

If only it were that simple. But guilt and innocence rarely was. As sure as she might ever be that she was prosecuting the right person, she never really knew. She'd made peace with the conundrum long ago. She'd had to or she would've gone crazy. Nelson was a bad man. Despite the mistake that put him away, she didn't lose any sleep over the time he'd spent in prison. How could she expect Serena, whose brother spent his days counting down to death, to understand?

"Then don't believe it. Instead, believe I'm a good person who does her best to do the right thing." The minute the words tumbled out, Cory felt lame asking for Serena's trust with nothing to offer in return.

Serena let out a deep breath. "I want to. I really do. I can see you're working hard for Eric and you don't have any reason to. Do you think the judge will grant a hearing on the motion you wrote today?"

Cory held back a flinch as guilt pinched her conscience. Now would be the time to explain to Serena she hadn't been able to work on Eric's case when she got back to the office, but she held back. She supposed she could have worked on the motion this evening, after they'd filed the brief on the Young case. But then she would've missed this evening. Would Serena think she'd made the right decision?

"I think we have a good chance at a hearing. I promise you I'll fight hard for him. And you're wrong. I do have good reasons to work hard for him. I need you to trust me." She hoped Serena wouldn't ask her to list the reasons since they started and ended with the magnetic pull she felt between them.

"I'm starting to."

Cory heard her own hope reflected in Serena's simple words. She took a chance. "Have you had enough time to think?"

"About?"

Cory leaned in close. If she expected Serena to take a risk, she had to be willing to take one first. As she drew closer, she heard Serena take a deep breath, but she wasn't to be deterred. Serena's eyes dilated and she exhaled. Cory brushed her lips past Serena's cheek and whispered soft and heavy in her ear. "Another kiss?"

Serena answered by placing a hand on her cheek and she drew Cory closer. Their lips met and Cory had her answer. The kiss in the kitchen had been perfection, everything a first kiss should be. But this embrace was packed with portent. Deeper, stronger, their entire bodies were engaged. Cory took her lead from Serena and reached out to pull her closer. Passion drove her. She wanted more, more closeness, more heat, more than she'd ever wanted before. Serena's thirsty lips signaled she wanted the same. For the first time she could ever recall, no thoughts, only feelings crowded her conscious and she surrendered to the siren call.

So deep was her surrender, she didn't hear the doorbell at first, but Serena pulled back from the embrace, the spell broken.

"Do you think you should get that?"

Still in Serena's arms, thinking didn't factor into Cory's world view. "What?"

"The doorbell," Serena whispered in her ear. "Someone's at the door, and I don't think they're giving up easily." She smiled. "How about you answer the door? I'll wait right here."

Cory pulled back from Serena's embrace, reluctant to break the connection they'd finally forged. "Promise?"

"I promise." Serena nudged her off the couch. "Hurry back."

Cory blew a kiss through the air and trudged to the door. The clock in the hall showed it was close to nine o'clock. When she was a prosecutor she was used to late night calls. Detectives sometimes wanted her input before waking up a judge to sign a search warrant or requested her presence at an impromptu interrogation, but even those events were rare. Her neighbors only knocked when their kids accidentally threw their ball over the fence, and it was too late for backyard games on a school night.

She peered through the peephole. *Damn.* Julie stood on the porch, tapping her foot, finger poised to ring the bell again. Judging by her wrinkled suit, she'd come straight from the office. Julie liked to have sex after a long day at work. She claimed it was the only way for her to settle her nerves. Of all the possibilities Cory had considered when she heard the doorbell, Julie dropping in for a booty call hadn't merited a fraction of her attention. She jerked the door open before Julie could press the bell again.

"Hey, baby, what took you so long?" She held a hand against the doorway, but she couldn't hide the sway of the rest of her body. Waves of pungent whisky breath hit Cory in the face. As if the situation couldn't get any worse.

"What are you doing here? Do you know what time it is? Did you drive like this?" What started as a whisper quickly became a growl. She glanced over her shoulder, hoping Serena couldn't hear their exchange.

"I came to see you. It's late. And, yes, I drove, but I probably shouldn't have." Julie giggled as she delivered the last line, a sure sign she was drunk. "Aren't you going to invite me in?"

Cory glanced over her shoulder. Her plan to quickly and quietly get rid of Julie was fizzling as fast as she'd made it. She couldn't send her packing. What if she got in an accident on the way home or got pulled over? Her DA badge could only work so many miracles, and it didn't have the power to save lives. She'd have to call her a cab. "You're drunk and it's late. I'll call you a cab." She paused to consider what to do next. She didn't trust Julie to wait outside without trying to take off, but she didn't trust a drunk Julie to not embarrass her in front of Serena. Before she could decide what lesser evil to choose, Julie pushed past her.

"You have some wine open? I'd love a glass. The stuff they pour at The Shack is rank. I had to drink bourbon instead." She draped an arm over Cory's shoulder and nestled her face against Cory's neck. "I'm glad you're home. I've missed you."

"I'm calling you a cab."

"I don't need a cab. I need some of this." Julie made it clear exactly what "this" was by snaking her hand under her shirt. Cory backed away, but Julie wasn't so easily deterred. "What's wrong? We had a great day today and I want to celebrate. With you."

A replay of numerous other encounters flashed in Cory's mind. All the times she shared celebratory sex with Julie after she'd had a great day at the office. It always started with Julie gushing about her victory and ended with Cory bringing her to orgasm. In this moment, Cory realized there was only ever one winner and it wasn't her.

She thought about the amazing woman waiting in her living room. She'd given more of herself to Cory in one evening than Julie had offered in their entire relationship, if one could even call what they had a relationship. Suddenly, she didn't care about embarrassing Julie. All she cared about was getting rid of her as quickly as possible. "I have company, but I'll call you a cab. You'll have to celebrate on your own tonight."

Julie frowned, then cocked her head. "Company?" She started walking toward the living room, but Cory grabbed her arm. As Julie whirled back toward her, Cory spotted Serena walking toward them. She pushed Julie away and held a hand out, but before she could say a word, Julie beat her to it. "I don't want to celebrate on my own, baby. Tell your company to go away, and I'll show you what a good day I had."

Cory stepped toward Serena, an apology on her lips, but Serena shook her head. "I'm leaving."

"Don't go." She reached for Serena's hand. "Please. I can explain."

"No need. You stay with your *friend*. She looks like she has a little bit more celebration left in her."

Cory followed her to the door, but Serena rushed out. She wanted to go after her, but she couldn't say the things she wanted with Julie weaving her way through her house. She'd get rid of Julie and then go to Serena's hotel and explain. As she reached for her phone to call a cab, its loud ring startled her. She jammed her fingers against the buttons to answer it, daring to hope Serena would be on the other line. She listened to the voice on the other end and murmured appropriate responses. She'd still have to get rid of Julie, but the rest of her plan would have to be put on hold.

Chapter Fifteen

Serena could barely see to drive through the tears. She couldn't believe she'd been so foolish. Everything about the evening had been perfect. Dinner, conversation, kissing Cory. And what she'd hoped would happen next made her feel foolish. She never should have come so close to risking her dignity, her heart.

You didn't give her time to explain. She pushed the thought away. She didn't care to hear what Cory had to say. The explanation was clear. Whoever the woman was who had appeared at Cory's door late that night had obviously been there before. The way she held on to Cory, leered at her, grabbed at her. Serena didn't need it spelled out. The woman wanted Cory with a passion Serena felt but dared not show. Serena was thankful she'd held back. She could at least face Cory again without the humiliation of being second in line.

Or could she? Could she stroll into the clinic offices tomorrow, reporting for duty, knowing that Cory had spent the night with another woman? And not just another woman, but a gorgeous, expensively dressed, confident woman. If the woman who'd appeared at the door was Cory's type, Serena had no business picturing herself in Cory's arms, in Cory's bed. Damn her. She lay in bed, but sleep wouldn't come. It was barely ten o'clock, but back home she would've been well on her way to sound sleep by this time. Early to bed, early to work, late coming home. She'd spent years constructing her defenses, and she wasn't going to allow them to come crashing down in one night. But right now she felt lost and longed for the familiar. She reached for her phone. A quick call to Marion, just to check in, catch up on old news and hear a friendly voice. To her surprise, she saw that she had numerous missed calls and several messages waiting. She'd turned her phone off when she'd arrived at Cory's, not wanting any distraction from the outside world.

She thumbed her way through the call list. Cory had called six times, all within close succession. She'd left two messages. Serena couldn't resist the urge to hear her voice and she tapped the phone to start the first message:

Serena, I'm so sorry. Julie is my boss. Well, she was my boss. At the DA's office. I didn't know she was planning to stop by. I had no idea. She was inappropriate and I'm sorry you had to see that, but I'm even more sorry you left. I was going to come see you as soon as I put her in a cab, but I got a call to come into the office. Please call me. I want to talk to you. Please.

If she weren't so angry, Serena might have laughed at Cory's rambling message, but there was nothing to laugh about. *Boss.* Right. Did Cory take her for a fool? She must or she wouldn't have dared spout such nonsense. And she got called to the office this late at night? The truth might hurt, but she couldn't stomach lies. She deleted Cory's second message unheard. Drained, she quickly scrolled to the next message, from a familiar number. She listened to Marion's long message, telling her about her day, the current events in the quiet suburb where she lived, and the pretty birds she and Don had seen on their morning walk. The one-sided conversation was tame to the point of dull. Serena played it back seven times, craving the sameness of her life before she'd received Eric's letter, before she'd flown back to Texas, before she'd met Cory Lance.

As she listened to the message one last time, she made a decision. She was going home. She'd go by the clinic tomorrow and explain to Paul that she couldn't take any more time off work, but she'd come back for any court proceedings where her presence might make a difference. She wasn't doing Eric any good here. If she'd thought her presence put any pressure on Cory to do a better job, she'd been mistaken. She'd talk to Skye before she left. Skye was solid and she trusted her to keep Cory focused. Her own presence was likely doing just the opposite. Time to return to being the person she'd worked her whole life to be.

❖

Cory guzzled her fourth cup of coffee even though she was certain it no longer had the power to keep her awake. Maybe the action alone would suffice. It was eight a.m. and she'd been at the clinic for almost nine hours. She would have worked longer, but the cab service had been slow, and it was after eleven before she'd been able to push Julie out her front door. Paul's call had interrupted her plan to go see Serena, and Julie hadn't believed that was where she was really going anyway, but right now, she was tired of caring what Julie thought. Caring about what Julie thought was exactly the reason she was working at the clinic in the first place. Of course, if the only upshot of her current situation was the opportunity to meet Serena, she should be thanking Julie. But any chance at something more with Serena was probably as tanked as her career. Julie had finally agreed to get in the cab, but not after spewing a string of threats about how Cory had put her job in jeopardy and she could expect dire consequences from her decision to reject her advances.

When she had her energy back, she would care. The all-nighter she'd spent working on the amended brief the clinic team had just filed had drained her. Paul's call the night before was to let her know that the lower court hadn't waited until morning to respond to their appeal, but they hadn't rejected it or granted it. Instead, they'd had their clerk call to ask if there was anything else they planned to file. An odd question, obviously designed to make them question whether their original brief included all the arguments they should've advanced. Unfortunately, no clues accompanied the question. The team had spent the night poring over their arguments, second-guessing their own best work, and losing valuable hours in the process. The problem was they couldn't proceed to the next rung until they were rejected by this court, and this court apparently wanted more. So while half of the team struggled to rewrite the original brief, the other half prepared the brief they would file if they lost their arguments and had to appeal to the next level. Everyone in the room had worked at a crazy pace throughout the night, and Cory was amazed that any of them were able to string together any coherent thoughts after the marathon they'd endured.

Paul clapped his hands to get their attention. "Great work, everyone. I think we can count on at least an hour until we get a ruling. I want everyone to take a breather." The group working on the contingency brief groaned, but he insisted. "Seriously, you can't polish your arguments any more until we get the ruling. Take a nap, grab some breakfast, run laps. I don't care what you do, but for the next hour you're off the clock. We'll meet back here and regroup at nine thirty sharp."

Cory grunted. As a volunteer, she wasn't on any clock, which was a subtle, but persistent source of stress, especially after Julie's slurred, but very real threats from last night. She couldn't afford to lose her job at the DA's office, her pay, benefits, the retirement plan. Not to mention, it was the only career she'd ever known and she'd come to define herself by her success in the courtroom. She'd given her heart and soul to the job, yet here she was offering up the same level of devotion to working the other side. No wonder Julie was pissed. No doubt she viewed Cory's rejection as not only a slight against her personally, but against everything they'd both worked for. Cory hated to think what her reaction might have been if Julie had known Serena was the sister of a man awaiting execution.

The realization was like cold water in her face. She had no business mucking up her personal life until she had her professional affairs back in order. Besides, when Eric's case was over, no matter how it ended, Serena would get on a plane and fly back to her life. Everything about their situation was transient, from their geographic proximity to the fact their only connection was a case with a looming end. She needed stability, and she wasn't going to find it in a volunteer temp job, sleeping with a client's sister who had no other ties to keep her around. She needed to get through the grueling pressure of the day and then contact Julie, make nice, and lay a foundation for her return to the life she knew.

She'd start by taking full advantage of the break in activity. She needed to get away from the computer, the research, the stacks of drafts piled on her desk. She needed air, but the moment she stepped outside she ran smack into a reminder that later today when the Young case was over, she'd have to turn her attention back to Eric Washington. And his sister.

"Hi, Skye. What brings you here first thing in the morning?"

"Might be first thing to you, but I've been up for hours. I have a lead on Mr. Bolton. Care to take a ride with me?"

Cory cast a wistful look at the clinic building. She'd much rather be out in the field than cooped up with pages of legal briefs. "Wish I could, but I've got to stick around here today. Michael Young's execution is scheduled for tonight. We'll be working up until the last minute."

Skye nodded. Texas executions might seem plentiful, but each one still commanded the attention of the entire criminal bar whether they were directly involved with the case or not. "You think he's got a shot?"

"I've given up predicting these things. Technically, the state can't execute him. He's clearly mentally retarded."

"I thought that term wasn't PC."

"It's not, but it's what the case law says. Besides, I don't feel like being PC. I'm actually pretty beat right now. I've spent the entire night trying to save the life of a guy who killed five people and got caught standing in their blood with the murder weapon in his hand. I'm all out of warm and fuzzy feelings right now."

Skye changed the subject. "Did you get what you wanted done on Eric's case yesterday?"

Cory shook her head. "No chance. When I got back to the office everyone was working on Young."

"I'll let you know what I find out about Mr. Bolton. Maybe it'll be something juicy that'll make the wait worthwhile."

"Sounds good. Call me as soon as you talk to him." She started to walk back to the office, but stopped when she saw Serena pull into the parking lot and get out of her car. Paralyzed, she watched Serena hesitate, and then head her way.

Skye raised her eyebrows, then followed the direction of Cory's transfixed gaze. "You look a little pale. You okay?"

"Fine," Cory muttered. She willed her legs to move, but they betrayed her desire to make a hasty exit. What was the point anyway? Serena had already seen her, and she was heading straight for them. If Serena could handle a direct confrontation, then she could too. She couldn't deny she welcomed the sight of her as much as she dreaded the fallout from last night. While she was bleary-eyed and rumpled, Serena looked rested and, as usual, her outfit was perfectly put together.

Skye waved as Serena approached. "Hey, Serena. We were just talking about Eric's case."

Serena flashed Skye a bright, friendly smile that fizzled when she turned to look at Cory. "Good to see you, Skye. I was hoping to talk to you today." She didn't acknowledge Cory's presence other than with a slight nod. Her next words seemed directed into the space between them. "When do you think the judge will rule on your motion in Eric's case?"

Skye shifted in place, looking decidedly uncomfortable. Cory knew the question was meant for her, and now she wished she'd told Serena she hadn't even written the motion and why. But when she'd been with Serena last night, work was the last thing she'd wanted to discuss. Even now, her resolution to keep her distance was fading fast against the pull of attraction she felt. Who was she kidding? Distance was necessary. Besides, she wasn't used to having a client to deal with, someone standing over her shoulder, watching her every move. If she wanted that, she would've gone into private practice. She didn't feel like sugarcoating every bit of this process because Serena was the sister of the man she represented, and without any consideration, she threw her former desire to protect her out the window.

"I didn't get to it."

"What?"

"I didn't finish it and I didn't file it."

"Care to explain why? And would you also care to explain why you didn't tell me?"

"Actually, no." Cory caught a glimpse of Skye shaking her head, warning her from this path, but she plowed on. "I don't report to you."

"Is that so?"

"Absolutely. Now, if you'll excuse me, I'm going back in to do the work I've been assigned to do. Skye, call me after your meeting." As she turned to leave, the mix of hurt and anger on Serena's face brought back memories of her passion, a completely different kind, from the night before, but she shook away the reflection. She had a plan, and passion wasn't part of it.

❖

Serena bored holes into Cory's back with her eyes, to no effect. She stood, fixed in place, as Cory marched into the clinic offices without a backward glance. After several silent seconds, she realized Skye still stood next to her and she felt silly for arguing with Cory in front of her. "I'm sorry."

"You don't have anything to be sorry for."

Skye's voice was gentle and kind, but she was dead wrong. She had a lot to be sorry about. Letting her guard down, succumbing to her feelings for Cory. The list was long, but it no longer mattered. She'd be on her way home today if she had to sit at the airport all day waiting for a seat on standby. "I appreciate the work you're doing, and I'd like you to keep me posted on your progress directly. Is that okay?"

Skye looked puzzled. "Sure. I'll report everything I learn to both you and Cory. Is there a problem?"

"No problem, but I'm leaving and I just want to make sure that even though I won't be here, I'll be in the loop." She'd sent Paul an e-mail late in the night, a cursory explanation about her planned departure. He'd asked her to stop by before she left, and she decided she owed him a face-to-face, even if she dreaded having to explain in person. She'd prepared a list of reasons to give Paul about why she was leaving, all purposely vague: family, work, pressing needs at home. She'd planned to make the meeting short and quick and any follow-up discussion could take place on a long distance call. Bottom line, she'd made up her mind. She had a list of possible afternoon flights in her purse, and once she packed, she'd plant herself at the airport until a seat opened up. She did feel guilty about abandoning her promise, but she couldn't face the idea of working in such close proximity with Cory after they'd crossed the line.

"Why are you leaving?"

Serena hadn't expected the blunt question from Skye, and she sensed Skye would see through her "pressing needs" excuse. She stared at her feet, but she couldn't admit the real reason she had to go. What would she say? That the heat of Cory's closeness threatened to burn through the layers of protection she'd worked her whole life to build? That Cory was obviously a player, and she couldn't protect her heart? Both things might be true, but she didn't feel comfortable sharing either of these reasons with Skye, no matter how much she trusted her. She settled on something innocuous. "I don't think my presence is adding anything. I'm on my way in to talk to Paul and let him know my plans."

"Let me buy you breakfast." Skye shot a look at the clinic building. "You're due for a change of atmosphere, and I happen to know Paul's super busy right now. If you still want to talk to him in an hour, then it'd probably be a better time."

Serena hesitated for a second, but then gave in. She could use the time to find out what steps Skye had planned, since Cory had obviously back-burnered Eric's case.

Ten minutes later, they were seated in a crowded diner. Serena marveled at the crowd still present even though it was almost nine o'clock. "Popular place."

"Dallas has a ton of diners, but in my opinion, this is the best one for breakfast. You can't go wrong with anything on the menu."

"I wish I were more hungry, but frankly, I'm feeling a little drained."

"I bet. But don't lose hope. Eric has a good attorney. She'll fight hard for him."

Serena started to say that wasn't the reason she felt drained, but she quickly realized how that would sound. Of course she was worried about Eric. The thought of his death pierced her, but right now she was still focused on her own shaken vulnerabilities. Seeing Cory so soon after last night had only heightened the loss she felt. She was now committed, but with no one to commit to. She couldn't help but feel foolish for thinking Cory could be that person, a lover, a trusted confidant.

"I guess so."

"I can tell you're concerned. Talk to me. Maybe I can help put your mind at ease."

"How well do you know Cory?"

"Personally, not well. At least not anymore. When she worked—"

Skye stopped abruptly, but Serena urged her on. "I know she works for the other side. That secret is out of the bag."

Skye cleared her throat and resumed. "When she worked for the DA's office, we spent quite a bit of time together. We worked some pretty gruesome homicides. When you spend that much time together, you necessarily get to know a little about their personal life."

Okay, so Skye was a great source for all things Cory, but now Serena wasn't even sure where to start. She considered for a moment, then blurted out, "Is she honest?"

"Wow, you don't beat around the bush, do you?"

"When you've had the life I've had, you figure out what really matters."

"And by honest you mean?"

"Seriously, is honesty really that difficult to define?"

"I'd say no, for the most part. But if you're asking about what I think you're asking about, what you really want to know is does she do the right thing. Because if she did what she got suspended for, I'd bet my Harley, which I love dearly, that she did it because she thought it was the right thing to do."

Serena noted the "if she did" part of Skye's declaration, and filed it away for future reference. "So it's okay to do the wrong thing for the right reason? What if the reason turns out not to be so right after all? I mean, who gets to judge?"

"All good points. I don't pretend to have all the answers, and I may not be the best one to ask about this particular subject." Skye suddenly couldn't seem to look her in the eye, and her change in demeanor piqued Serena's curiosity.

"Well, you can't just make a remark like that and then let it drop. Spill."

"I hid evidence once because I was sure I had the right guy and I didn't want the defense to be able to muck up the case. In my case, I was dead wrong. I arrested the wrong guy."

"Oh my God. What happened?"

"The truth came out. I eventually realized maybe I don't know everything and my detective skills aren't perfect. I told the defendant's attorney what I'd done and they were able to get the case dismissed."

"Bet that made you pretty popular around the police department."

"They waited a respectable amount of time and then allowed me to either resign or be dismissed. I quit, but it was one of the hardest things I'd ever done."

"And now?"

"Now, I work for the other side and I do my best to keep my head clear about the difference between the process and the result. I have to tell you, it's not always easy. When you see what you're sure is an injustice, you don't always want to take the careful route to right it." She stopped to take a big swallow of her coffee. "I'm willing to bet Cory got herself in trouble for that very reason."

"So if her motives were pure, she shouldn't suffer any consequences for putting an innocent man in prison?"

"I didn't say that. Truth is, neither one of us know the whole story."

"I wish I did." Serena whispered the words, a personal reflection. She wanted to know the whole story. Good or bad, the truth might allow her to either detach from or embrace the strong attraction and powerful arousal Cory elicited. If she knew more, would she have compassion, be able to forgive what she perceived as global slights? Didn't matter. The only person who could tell her the truth wasn't interested in having anything to do with her. Cory had made that clear during their curt exchange this morning.

Wait a minute. Surely someone besides Cory could give her details, at least enough to give her more of the picture instead of the partial glimpse the press had provided. Serena stared at Skye, chowing through a plate of pancakes, and realized she might have already found what she was looking for. "You ever do any work that doesn't directly involve a criminal case?"

"Huh?"

"I want to hire you."

"You already did."

"No, I mean I want to hire you, not on behalf of someone else, I want to hire you to find out the rest of the story." She grew frustrated at Skye's puzzled look, but mostly it was directed at herself. "You know, with Cory."

Skye pushed her plate aside. "You're kidding, right?"

"No." Serena spoke the single word with more confidence than she felt. She shouldn't care. She certainly shouldn't spend the money. What she should do is get on the next plane and return to her life in Florida. Her stale, boring, sequestered life. No passion, no problems, no Cory Lance.

But what if she left hope behind? She braced herself for a battle and faced Skye. "Will you do it? Don't you want to know more? Surely, you still have the connections to get some answers?"

"I still have some connections, but I don't think many of them would be willing to talk to me about Cory. Law-and-order types tend to close ranks when it comes to one of their own."

"I'm not asking you to implicate her in anything. I only want to have some peace of mind. Maybe you're right. Maybe the situation wasn't as simple as the media made it out to be."

"What if I find out that isn't the case, that Cory broke the law to put Nelson away?"

"Then we're back to the status quo."

Skye shook her head, and several beats of silence passed between them. "I can't believe I'm saying yes, but yes, I'll see what I can find out. You don't have to pay me."

"That's sweet, but I'm paying you. Whatever you find out belongs to me. Fair?"

"Okay, fair, but on one condition."

"What?"

"You stay in Dallas, like you planned."

"I don't see why that's necessary."

"Maybe you don't, but I do. Stay here and I'll find out what you want. Leave and I'm off the job."

"Blackmail."

"Yep." Skye didn't try to hide her evil grin. Serena shook her head. "Fine. I'll stay, but you have to keep me updated on both cases you're working. Directly, not through Cory."

"What's going on between you two?"

"Nothing." Serena faced Skye's probing look with what she hoped was a mask of indifference. She could tell Skye didn't believe her and she didn't blame her. There was a lot going on between her and Cory, and a whole lot of nothing she could do about it.

Chapter Sixteen

Cory, along with the rest of the staff and volunteers, stared at the clock on the clinic wall. Five minutes past six p.m. By law, the warden had from six p.m. until midnight on the scheduled execution date to carry out the sentence. Liz Martin, the staff attorney who had worked Michael Young's case from the moment the clinic had taken it on, was down in Huntsville, waiting to be ushered into the room where she would watch her client be put to death. While she waited, she talked to Paul and the rest of the clinic staff through the speakerphone, second-guessing every decision she'd made as lead on the case. There was still time for the governor or the court to intervene, and the warden had been informed that a writ seeking a stay of execution was pending before the Supreme Court at that very moment.

Everyone in the room was silent, and the only sounds were Paul's gentle voice on the speakerphone, reassuring Liz that she'd done everything she could, and the play-by-play offered by the *Execution Watch* radio show. The host of the show echoed what they already knew. The warden wasn't legally bound to wait to carry out the death warrant, but it was customary to give deference to the slow moving legal system. To a point. Liz told them the warden had been particularly receptive in Michael's case. Michael had been a model inmate, content to sit in his cell and draw and read and reread the same two picture books without complaint. The guards had treated him with respect on his final day on earth, but respect didn't mean they held back on carrying out their execution day duties. Hours ago, he'd been taken from his cell at the Polunsky unit to shower, change, and ride in the back of a secure van to the Huntsville unit where he sat in a room waiting with a prison chaplain and his attorney until the guards collected him for his final walk to the death chamber. He was likely strapped to a gurney right now, waiting for the execution team to place the IV lines that would be used to put him down.

Only five of the nine Supreme Court justices had to vote for a stay for it to become effective. Of course, a stay only meant a delay to allow the courts to consider the evidence they'd either ignored or hadn't had the opportunity to consider up to now. A win tonight could mean that Michael might have to go through this entire ordeal in a month or a year. Cory couldn't imagine the toll that kind of uncertainty would have on Michael. On anyone.

She thought of Eric. So young, so vibrant. How had he managed to stay hopeful while counting the days until he met the same fate as Michael Young? Because he believes in you, in the work the clinic does. He believes the truth will set him free. If only the truth was a concept Cory could believe in. She'd given up thinking she could nail down that concept long ago. All she could do was trust her instincts and believe they would lead her in the right direction. She'd never questioned her convictions. Not until Nelson. Now she had no idea if Eric was innocent or guilty, but she wanted him to have the benefit of her doubt. She'd file the motion on his case first thing in the morning, no matter what Skye found out from Bolton. She would fight as hard as she'd ever fought to give him a chance at a fair trial. If he was really guilty, the truth would bear out.

As for truth, she owed Serena the truth too, not the brush-off she'd delivered this morning. The truth wouldn't win her any points, but Serena, who'd trusted her enough to share her most private thoughts and feelings, didn't deserve the cold morning after Cory had served up. She hadn't had any business kissing a client's family member in the first place, no matter how attractive she was, no matter how she made Cory shiver with pleasure whenever she was near. She was the professional, and it was time for her to act like it. As soon as she filed the motion tomorrow, she'd go see Serena, tell her she was sorry, and throw herself into the work she'd promised to do.

Resolution made, she turned her thoughts back to Michael Young. Six thirty p.m. Time was ticking away. The hosts of *Execution*

Watch droned on with their experienced speculations about whether the governor or court would intervene. Cory had only met Liz a couple of times during her stint at the clinic, but she was a spitfire. She was probably marching around the prison, making all her best arguments in an attempt to get the warden to wait. Liz would take it hard if Michal Young died that night. Cory glanced around the room. The entire team would take it hard, herself included. Every one of them had worked furiously throughout the night, researching, writing, rewriting, in pursuit of zealous advocacy for their client. Cory knew in her gut the team had risen to the challenge with the same vigor for every one of their clients. When Eric's time came, they'd do the same. Except she wouldn't be here.

Her time at the clinic would end before Eric's execution was scheduled to be carried out. If she couldn't stop the process in advance, some other attorney would be on the ground in Huntsville, overseeing Eric's deathwatch. Would Serena choose to attend the execution? Would she sit with one of the other attorneys from the clinic while she watched her brother utter his last words and then breathe his last breath? Cory shuddered as she imagined how Serena would feel, wracked with guilt and loneliness as she watched her only blood relative meet such a terrible fate.

If she couldn't be there with Serena at the end, she could do everything in her power to change the ending. She walked across the room to where Paul was standing, no longer on the phone. Liz had gone into the viewing room, along with the other witnesses to the macabre death show. Their only direct connection to the execution was the radio show, which was winding down. She tapped Paul's shoulder and he turned to face her.

"I know this isn't the best time, but I'd like to get the writ on Eric Washington's case filed first thing in the morning. Would it be okay with you if I snagged a couple of the interns to help me with the research?"

His smile was tired. "I appreciate your dedication, but everyone has worked all night. Take a day and then come back to it with a fresh perspective. Besides, I think the interns all skipped class the last few days. At least let them catch up on their assignments before you load them up."

"Okay for them, but I think I'll get it done by myself. Since Eric's sister is in town, I feel an extra sense of urgency to get the process rolling."

"You're free to work on the writ whenever you want. I'll even help you. But if you're trying to get it filed tomorrow because you think Serena will be here breathing down your neck, you needn't worry. She sent me an e-mail this morning saying she's headed back to Florida."

Serena was leaving? Headed back to Florida? "When?"

"Today, I think."

Cory struggled to digest the news. Today? Serena was leaving today? Today was almost over. So the last time she'd seen Serena, she'd been cold and unfeeling. Serena had left, and doubtless her only memories of Cory were sour ones. Had she told Paul why she was leaving? Did it have anything to do with Cory crossing the line? She wanted to ask, but this wasn't the time. Paul was distracted, defeated. She had no business advancing her personal interests when the rest of the group was focused on what was going on in a room far away. She had no business being here in the first place. She felt like a traitor in their midst. When she'd sent someone to death row before, she'd kept a similar vigil, but she'd wished for a different outcome than the one wished for here. She should slip out, go home, let the rest of the group mourn their loss without having to wonder if her own grief was truly genuine.

No one was paying any attention to her. The perfect time to slip away. She walked toward the door, but as she started to push it open, she froze in place when she heard the loud ring of the office phone.

❖

Serena sat outside Cory's house in her rental car. She'd been here for an hour, but the house remained dark. She wondered how much longer she could sit there until one of Cory's neighbors called the cops.

She'd spent the balance of her day organizing her life. After she'd made her promise to Skye to stay in town, she realized she should use the day to catch up on all the personal errands she'd let fall by the way while she volunteered at the clinic. She'd checked in at work, talked to her parents, balanced her checking account, and did a few loads of laundry. Now it was time to clear the air with Eric's attorney. She had to think of Cory in that role because that's all she was and all she could ever be to her. No matter what tides of passion swept through her whenever Cory came close, her own pleasure had created a rift in the professionalism between them. She couldn't risk the harm that rift might do to Eric, and she certainly couldn't resist the damage it would do to her heart.

Tonight she would let Cory know, in clear and certain terms, the parameters of their relationship. She'd help with Eric's case in any way she could, even if that meant sharpening pencils while Cory drafted the arguments to set her brother free. She didn't have any preconceived notions about their chances, but she needed to know that even if the end came on schedule, they'd done everything they could to fight for his life. And she would not let her own feelings interfere with her brother's future.

Just when she was about to give up and head back to the motel, she saw a light flick on inside Cory's house. She must have parked in the rear drive. Serena steeled her will and walked toward the front door, determined to maintain professional boundaries despite the late hour and the fact she was at Cory's home. When Cory answered, her resolve melted.

She wore the same clothes she'd had on the night before. This morning, they'd been wrinkled, now they looked as if she'd slept in them. But Cory's tired, red eyes told her she probably hadn't slept at all in the past twenty-four hours. Now was not the time for conversation about boundaries. At least not right away. Serena walked through the door without waiting for an invitation.

"You look terrible. When's the last time you slept or ate?" She placed her hands on either side of Cory's face and stared deep.

Cory managed a half smile. "Slept? Not sure. Ate? I'm pretty sure the last real meal I had was the one you made me last night."

Serena wanted to pull her into her arms and tell her that whatever caused the hollow look in her eyes, the lines of worry on her forehead, would go away. Instead, she resorted to less intimate caretaker skills. "Follow me." She made her way to the kitchen without waiting for

Cory to follow. She started pulling ingredients from the refrigerator and reached into the cabinets for a small pan.

"What are you doing?"

"I'm thinking an omelet. Surprisingly, you have some eggs that aren't out of date. I'll use the leftovers from dinner last night for the filling. Sound good?"

"If you manage to salvage anything from last night, I'd consider that good." Cory's expression was contrite. "I'm sorry. Last night was perfect until…well, until it wasn't."

"I think we should start over."

"I'd like a chance to explain."

"You look like you're about to fall over, and you don't owe me an explanation." Truth was, Serena wasn't sure she wanted to know the truth. The woman who'd appeared on Cory's doorstep the night before had acted possessive and territorial. She wouldn't call Cory a liar to her face, but no boss she'd ever seen acted like that, at least not outside the workplace. No, there was more to the story and, since she'd decided to maintain professional boundaries with Cory, the details shouldn't matter. She wasn't sure she even wanted to know.

"You may not need an explanation, but I need to tell you." Cory reached out for her hand and led her to the big kitchen table. Serena settled in, bracing herself against the truth. "Julie is my boss, and that's the truth. But she's also been my lover for the past six years."

Cory paused and the silence was deafening. Serena felt compelled to break its hold. "That's a long time."

"A long time, but not much in the way of substance. We've worked together since we met, and our time in the courtroom is the only time we spend together outside of…" Cory let the sentence fade off, but Serena knew where it was headed. An image of Cory, naked, filled her mind, but it quickly became unpleasant when the reality of another woman enjoying the real version struck her.

She spoke before Cory could continue. "That's none of my business."

"Last night I wanted it to be your business. I thought you might be interested in something more personal as well, or did I completely misread the situation?"

"You didn't. When you kissed me, I felt…" Serena struggled to capture the essence of what she'd felt. Chills, heat, the realization she'd finally found the passion she'd purposefully avoided, but deeply craved. She wasn't ready to speak those words or anything like them. Instead, she attempted to minimize her feelings. "I've never felt better, but—"

"But I'm not what you're looking for, and the way I acted last night was extremely unprofessional." Cory hung her head. "Totally my fault. I apologize."

Serena took a deep breath. She'd come here to clear the air, restore their professional relationship, but she hadn't counted on it being so difficult to contain her feelings once she saw Cory again, fatigued and adorable. Her resolve had begun to fade, but apparently, Cory felt last night was a mistake as well. Time to concede that their circumstances had flamed passion when it shouldn't have. At least they'd stopped before things got more heated or serious between them. Still, she wasn't ready to hear more about Julie, so she abruptly changed the subject.

"Talk to me while I cook. Tell me about your day." She selected a knife from the cutting block and focused on the task of making dinner. She didn't dare face Cory while she worked for fear she wouldn't be able to hide the sadness, the pain of the distance their mutual decision had placed between them.

"It was a hard day."

"I can tell that just by looking at you."

"I want you to know, up front, that I didn't finish writing the brief on Eric's case, let alone get it filed."

Serena mentally counted to five before she responded. "I'm sure you had a good reason."

"I suppose. I wanted to work on it, but Paul put the entire team to work on another case. In fact, he called me in last night."

That explained the tired eyes, the rumpled appearance. "You worked all night?"

"Yes."

"Care to tell me about it or is it confidential?"

"Let's talk about something else."

Serena set the knife down and walked back over to the table. This conversation felt like pulling teeth. Cory was hunched over and on edge. She looked miserable. Serena rested her hands on her shoulders and began to gently knead them. "I think you need to talk about your day or it's going to eat you up. If you are allowed to talk about it, I'm a good listener."

Cory leaned back into the comfort of Serena's touch, and the words came tumbling out. "Michael Young killed five people. With an axe. He chopped them into little bits, each one, while the others watched, too paralyzed from fear to do anything but scream. He didn't give a damn what happened to those people. Probably still doesn't to this day, years later." She paused and let Serena's soothing touch sink in. She wanted a drink, but to get one she'd have to break the connection. Instead, she spat out the reason behind her angst. "The people he killed will never enjoy a spring day, have children, grow old, but today his life was spared."

Cory leaned back as Serena stopped the massage and wrapped her in strong arms. Neither of them spoke. Cory was out of words. She'd used the power of language all day in her quest to save Michael Young's life. No words were left to adequately express the pain, the conflict that came from having to use her powers of persuasion to defend a murderer. The comfort of Serena's embrace was a surprise. She hadn't meant to share any of the details of her day, her struggle to align her principles and her gut feelings, especially not with Serena since it might be too easy to draw a parallel between Eric and Michael.

"Was it this hard to work the other side? As a prosecutor?"

Cory took a deep breath and settled on honesty. "I didn't let it be. I think my perspective from the prosecution side makes working these cases more difficult."

"I think that might be horseshit." Serena resumed her gentle massage, but the action didn't soften the blow of her remark.

Cory twisted around in her chair. "What's that supposed to mean?"

"It means you, miss high and mighty prosecutor, are not the only one who is conflicted about saving the lives of criminals. This man whose life you all saved today, was he the one who had mental issues?"

"Understatement, but yes, that's the guy."

"You think I don't have mixed feelings about whether life in prison is adequate retribution for murder? Well, I do, and I imagine that if someone I loved was one of his victims, the decision would be a whole lot harder. So quit acting like you're the only one who has all this conflict to deal with."

Cory grinned. "Why don't you tell me how you really feel? Seriously, do you really have mixed feelings? Even about Eric?"

"Let's be clear. We don't know yet if Eric did what he's accused of doing. But if he did? Well, I wouldn't want him to die, because he's my brother, but I do think he should be punished. If I were Nancy McGowan's mother, I might want him to die a slow and painful death. Point is, it's not an easy issue."

"Okay, but back to what you just said. If Eric did what he's accused of doing. What if you don't know and could never find out? Michael Young got caught at the scene, bloody axe in his hand, covered in victim DNA. Cases don't usually pan out that way. Usually, only two people know who committed a crime and, when the crime's murder, the murderer is often the only one alive to tell the story."

Serena sat next to Cory. "Why, in cases where you never hear from the victim, do you automatically think the person you've put on trial is the one who did the crime?"

"Victims speak through evidence, and as a prosecutor, it's up to me to give them a voice by presenting that evidence. Today, I spent all my energy saving the murderer. That's why I didn't get Eric's motion filed."

Serena shushed her. "I understand. I was totally out of place to get angry with you this morning. I think I had a little residual anger left over from the night before. Had nothing to do with Eric's case."

"I'm sorry. Julie really is my boss. She worked with me on the Nelson case." Cory wasn't sure why she divulged that detail, but she regretted the remark as soon as Serena posed her next of many questions.

"What happened in the Nelson case?"

Why did everything circle around to that? Her relationship with Julie, her career. Everything started and ended with that damn case. If not for Nelson, she'd never have met Serena, the only good outcome from a huge cluster fuck.

"I wish I knew. Judge Yost let Nelson free. Does anything else matter?"

"Yes. I find it hard to believe you'd fight so hard against something unless you had good reason to believe it."

"Doesn't matter what I think. Only matters what I can prove."

"Life is full of things you can't prove."

"I know and I hate it." Cory laughed, but she wondered if Serena recognized how much she really meant it.

"I know you do and that's one of the truly adorable things about you. A true idealist. Infuriating, but sweet at the same time." Serena turned her chair and pulled Cory into her arms. "Tell me about the Nelson case. I need to know and you need to tell it."

Cory sighed and gave in. She'd shared bits and pieces with her circle of friends, but she'd never tried to tell the whole story in a single sitting. She and Julie, as close as they'd worked on the case, never hashed the details other than to work out their arrangement at the end, when everything fell apart. She suspected Serena needed the telling as a barometer of sorts, to allay her concerns that Cory may not fight hard for Eric because she was predisposed to believe a convicted felon deserved whatever he had coming. She could understand that. Maybe sharing the details would be cathartic. Surely her promise that she'd give only "no comments" didn't extend to her personal life.

"Ray Nelson and his wife had a rocky relationship. In the two years they'd been married, the police had been called to their house seven times after receiving complaints of abuse. A couple of those times, he'd been the one to make the call, but the rest were neighbors calling to report that Ray was beating up on Helen again. The first few times, she'd refused to talk to the police, said she wanted to drop the charges. Then the DA's office started making her go through extra hoops to make things go away, and at least two of the cases were dropped because she didn't show on the day of trial.

Finally, we got smart and sent one of our investigators to get her before the next trial date, keep an eye out to make sure she showed up. When he finally racked up three convictions, we had him on a felony.

Yost wasn't on the bench at the time, and the "they all can be saved" judge gave him probation after he gave some sob story about how drugs and alcohol had led to his problems and if he only had a chance to get clean, he could manage his anger and his fists.

Three years into his seven-year probation, several rehab programs behind him, police were called out to their house. Helen had been stabbed to death. The neighbors heard the noise, but they'd long since given up on trying to intervene. Nelson was nowhere to be found.

Two days later, they found him, drunk off his ass, trying to buy crack from an undercover cop. They arrested him right away for a probation violation and took him into custody. Judge Yost was on the bench then and set the bond high enough to keep him under wraps until we could figure out the situation with his wife."

Cory stood and walked to the fridge. "I'm going to have something to drink. Can I get you anything?"

"Some cold water would be great."

Cory fixed Serena's water, and pulled a cold beer from the fridge for herself, not bothering with a glass. While she fiddled with the drinks, Serena asked, "What kind of evidence did you have against Nelson?"

"You mean besides his long history of violence, which should definitely not be minimized? Statistics show that most family violence deaths were signaled by numerous prior events in the household. The recidivism rate for family violence offenders is not only high, the offenders tend to escalate in the number and severity of assaults." Cory didn't try to hide her anger about the situation.

"I didn't mean anything by my question. I was just asking."

"I'm sorry. I'm not mad at you. I just can't help but get a little touchy about the whole subject. Most of these crimes can be prevented." She took a long pull from her beer. "Neighbors testified about fights they'd had, including a rather loud argument the night of the murder. Based on the time of death the medical examiner gave, Nelson had no alibi. There were a few other things, a particularly violent movie he'd rented the night of the murder. Aspects of his wife's death could be tied to the events in the movie. The cold, callous way he acted when the police questioned him after her body was found. Everything we had was circumstantial, but like I said before, sometimes that's all there is."

"So what went wrong?"

"I'm not sure. We got our conviction, but years later, Nelson's mother-in-law tells some reporter who wants to write a book about the case that she told one of the detectives that Nelson's son, who was left alone with his dead mother, said that his dad wasn't home when the murder occurred, that some 'monster' broke in and did the deed. The kid was three years old at the time.

"The reporter tells Nelson's lawyers, and they get the Innocence Project involved. They file a writ and our new DA, who's made a national name for himself as the conviction integrity guru, opens the entire DA file to the defense attorneys. They found not only a taped conversation with the grandmother that says exactly what she told the reporter, but also supplements to the police report that were never produced at trial, in violation of a court order."

"What did the police reports say?"

"Someone tried to use Nelson's wife's MasterCard ten days after she was killed. And her paycheck had been cashed at a bank in a neighboring town, the signature forged."

"You didn't know about these reports?"

"Damn right. I'd swear on my life those supplements weren't part of our file when we tried this case. All I can figure is that when the current DA agreed to open the file, he had our appellate division check with the law enforcement agency that investigated the case and requested copies of their files to be included as well. Apparently, no one logged the files. It all got lumped together, so there's no way to tell what we had at the time versus what turned up later."

"And because everyone assumes you had this info and didn't turn it over, you got blamed?"

"Pretty much. This case went high profile fast. They needed a scapegoat. Someone high enough up to matter, but not so much that all their aspirations would be ruined. I won." Cory sighed as she recited the party line she'd memorized. She could hear Julie's whispered urgings as if she were there in the room. *When I'm the DA, we'll be able to put this unfortunate episode completely behind us. Take the heat now, and I'll make sure you're taken care of.* Julie had never given her a reason to distrust her, but the fallout had been more than she bargained for. Still, she cared about Julie who, unlike her, had fiery political aspirations. She was the only other attorney who'd worked on the case. If she took the fall, she'd have been ruined. Cory felt ruined, but she would survive. She'd been pressured by promises. Julie assured her that no matter what happened, she wouldn't lose her license and she would always have a job. She'd have to claw her way back to the reputation she'd worked her entire career to build, but if she and Julie both went down, she'd be left without any options. At least this way she'd have some assurances.

She felt a twinge of guilt that she hadn't shared any of the backroom arrangements with Melinda, her lawyer, but she felt more than a twinge that she wasn't sharing any of it with Serena right now. But she couldn't. She'd given her word to Julie, and no matter what anyone else thought of her, her word meant something.

Serena sensed there was more that Cory hadn't shared. Her feelings, for one. She wanted to pull her back into her arms and hold her tight, murmur comforts to smooth away the edges of her sadness. She could tell Cory wasn't entirely convinced Nelson hadn't killed his wife, but none of that really mattered in the face of what she'd lost as a result of the high-profile fiasco. While comforting Cory was all she wanted to do, she remembered her vow, the reason she'd come to Cory's house in the first place. Restore the boundaries, show she could work with Cory on Eric's case and not get emotionally involved, either in the right and wrong of the case or the tangle of feelings she had for Cory that was twisting her into knots. She pushed back her chair and walked to the fridge. "Would you like another beer?"

"You don't have to wait on me."

"I only asked if you wanted another beer. I didn't say I was going to get you one."

Cory laughed. "Good point. I think I'll pass. It's getting late."

It was. Serena returned to the table. "I should go."

"I know, but I don't want you to."

I don't want to. Serena didn't dare speak the words. To do so would send a river of want tumbling out of control. "I'd like to keep working with you on Eric's case. You could use the help, and I promise I won't get in the way."

"What if I want you to get in the way?" Cory moved closer, her hands dangerously close to taking Serena's into their grasp.

"I don't think we can let what we want matter," Serena lied. The passion she felt when Cory touched her, bared her soul to her, mattered more than anything else had ever mattered to her before. She'd stay close long enough to see Eric's case to conclusion, but she'd have to keep her distance the entire time.

Chapter Seventeen

Cory tumbled out of bed the next morning wishing for a few more hours sleep. Her dreams had been punctuated with images of Serena. Images she shouldn't be having, images she couldn't shake. Didn't matter. She'd blown off all pretense of professionalism the night before and Serena had rejected her advances. Even her rejection was as tender as the caresses she'd delivered when Cory had needed comfort. Maybe when this case was over Serena might welcome more.

Cory quickly dismissed the idea. When this case was over, Serena would go home to Florida. And if this case wasn't over soon, Cory might not be around to see it through. She only had a few more weeks of her penance to serve. She needed to talk to Paul about a transition plan. She'd file the writ today and make sure all her notes were in order in case another attorney had to conduct the actual hearing. Would Serena be relieved to have a different lawyer make the arguments in support of her brother's case? Would she feel more confident? Cory tried not to care, but she didn't have a choice. Without even trying, Serena had dug her way into Cory's heart. Whether destiny would give them a chance or not, Cory resolved to make the brief supporting Eric's case the best legal work she'd ever done. She needed to show Serena who she really was, that she was capable of seeing more than just one side of an issue. How else could she ever hope to earn her respect? Cory knew she wanted more than Serena's respect, but she didn't dare name her desire for fear she would doom her chances.

After she showered and dressed, she checked her phone for messages. She hadn't bothered to reconnect with the rest of the world after Serena had left the night before. Melinda was right; she was notorious about blocking out the rest of the world when she was involved in her work or her relationships. She didn't even try to convince herself that failing to check last night had been about work. She hadn't wanted to invite anyone or anything else into what could have been, preferring instead to fall asleep with hope and promise for what might be.

She had several messages. Julie had called three times, sounding increasingly apologetic each time she failed to reach a live voice. She ended the last message with an emphatic, urgent plea for Cory to call her back as soon as possible. Cory deleted each of Julie's messages. As much as she needed her job, she needed to focus more. At least for today. Tomorrow, after she'd smoothed the way for whoever would take over Eric's case, she'd call Julie and make nice.

The last message was from Skye. Her lead on Dale Bolton had panned out and she had an appointment to interview him this morning. She gave Cory the when and where and suggested she come along. Cory looked at the clock. She barely had time to make it. She should get started on the writ and let Skye handle the interview alone. But if Bolton had something really useful to say, Cory wanted to hear it, directly from him. She told herself it was because she would have an easier time incorporating the evidence into the brief if she'd heard it firsthand, but she couldn't help feeling a bit like there was more to it than that. One more day. Could one more day make a difference? She could only hope.

Serena shot up in bed. The dream she'd awoken from had the combined effect of thrilling her and scaring her to death at the same time. She leaned back on propped up pillows and dissected its meaning. Just before waking, she'd been in Cory's arms. The two of them were naked, panting from sex. The vivid detail of her dream surprised her. She recalled the hum of anticipation as Cory had gently removed her clothes and urged her into bed. The hum quickly grew to a steady roar as Cory undressed and stood before her, strong, beautiful, vulnerable. Every inch of her craved contact with Cory and she gave in to long suppressed urges, pulling her down on top of her, rising to meet her. Struggling to be closer, she ground her pelvis against Cory's, reveling in the slick wetness of their arousal. She licked and sucked Cory's breasts and delighted in the moans she elicited with each new touch, her own pleasure mounting as Cory stroked her in response.

She'd woken before the dream could progress. A loud noise from the neighboring room had been to blame for the interruption. She considered closing her eyes and trying to recapture the pleasure she'd been robbed of, but she knew the chance that she'd drift back to the same dream was slight. Better to take a cold shower and forget the dream since that was all it was. But it was hard to forget. She'd always gone further in her fantasies than in real life, and up until now she'd been okay with that. Convinced that women who wanted to get in her bed, would want to be a part of every aspect of her life, she was content to keep things light. She'd kiss them, touch them, but naked and steamy wasn't part of the deal. Her education, her job, her entire approach to life was sensible and cautious. After witnessing firsthand what a life of abandon had brought to her mother, she wouldn't give everything she had to offer until she was ready. Was she ready now?

Rather than face the question, she considered going back to sleep. No, better to leave her dreams and face reality. She'd promised Cory she'd help her while she worked on Eric's brief. As much as it pained her to think about being in close proximity to Cory all day, knowing Cory wanted her and knowing she wanted her as well, she had work to do and it was more important than satisfying her cravings.

After she showered and changed, Serena grabbed her purse and phone and started to head out the door when she heard her phone beep, signaling she had a voice message. She listened to Cory's message that she had gone to see a witness with Skye and wouldn't be at the office until later, and sighed with relief. Cory's message said that Paul had given the rest of the staff the day off after working solid the past forty-eight hours. She ended with a promise to call later to check in.

Serena wasn't sure what to do. She'd finished all her personal errands the day before. She could explore Dallas, but for once, she wasn't in the mood to be alone. She wished she had some family or even a friend here, some tangible connection to the city where the most formative events in her life had occurred.

She realized she did have family, and even though he wasn't in Dallas, he was close enough. She glanced at the calendar on her phone and confirmed that today was a visitor's day. Who knew how many more times she might get to see Eric alive? She needed to make the most of whatever time they had. The thought resonated on more than one level. What she felt for Cory wasn't the bond of family. Why did it have an even stronger pull?

❖

Cory pulled up to the open parking lot outside of the Lew Sterrett Justice Center. Fancy name for the Dallas County jail. She'd been uncomfortable about this visit from the moment she'd gotten Skye's message telling her where to meet. The building in front of the jail was the Frank Crowley Criminal Court Building, and she hadn't been back there since the hearing that set Ray Nelson free.

She still had a parking card to the garage that connected to the court building, but she didn't want to risk running into any of her fellow prosecutors who also parked there. Better to slip into the jail without being noticed.

Skye was waiting for her in the courtyard between the court building and the jail. She shook her hand. "He's in the south tower, thank goodness." She led the way without waiting for a response. The south tower, also known as the Kays unit, was the newest addition to one of the largest county jail facilities in the country. The unit was the easiest to access, and it hadn't been open long enough to acquire the sour scent and layers of grime of the other two towers.

Cory jogged to catch up. "How do you know he'll talk to us?

Skye stopped. "Oh, I guess I forgot to mention we're not going to see Bolton. I have a little surprise for you."

She started to walk off, but Cory tapped her on the shoulder. She hated surprises. "Hold it. I need a little more intel. I thought you were tracking down Bolton."

"Oh, I found him. He's here."

"What's he in for?" Cory asked.

"Aggravated sexual assault. It's not his first."

"Tell me Bolton didn't have a felony conviction when he testified at Eric's trial." If he had and Eric's trial team hadn't been told, that was an egregious offense. The DA's office had an obligation to provide the defense with any criminal history information on Bolton, a witness they sponsored. The record showed that Bolton only had a couple of misdemeanor convictions that the defense hadn't been allowed to use to impeach him. Only certain misdemeanors could be used to challenge the credibility of a witness and Bolton's DWI and marijuana possession convictions had been deemed not relevant by the trial judge. A felony conviction would have been a different story.

"He didn't. At least not technically. He was on deferred adjudication probation for his first sexual assault. State didn't disclose, but I'm not sure they had to. That case was from Michigan."

Deferred adjudication was a special kind of probation, a huge carrot with an even bigger stick. If the defendant completed his probation successfully, he would not have a conviction on his record. If he fucked up, then the judge could haul him back into court and sentence him to the maximum prison term. "Gray area. Eric's lawyers wouldn't have been able to mention the sexual assault since he wasn't actually convicted, but if I were them, I sure would have wanted to know about it. Do we know any of the details?"

Skye handed her a folded up piece of paper.

"What's this?"

"Ann Arbor police report. You're going to love this. He picked his victim up at a bar. Got into her car, rode back to her place, raped her, and took off."

"You're right. I do love it." The similarities to Eric's case were several—using the victim's car, her house, the rape. "But he didn't kill her."

"Didn't have to. She couldn't remember anything beyond being at the bar and meeting him there. Cops suspected he used a date rape drug, but since those flush out of your system in about twelve hours, they couldn't prove it. He claimed any contact was consensual."

"How did he wind up on deferred?"

"With his claim she asked for it and her inability to remember anything, could've gone either way at a trial, so the state offered him probation."

Cory nodded. A plea in a case like this saved everyone, especially the victim, the pain and anguish of a public trial. Getting rape victims to the stand was an arduous process, and while they wanted justice, closure was often more of a priority. "You think he may have been involved in McGowan's case, don't you?"

"After hearing more about Bolton's past, don't you?"

"Yep. He'd be a fool to talk to us."

"And that's why we're going to talk to his cellmate instead. I reached out to a guard I know. He said Bolton's got a big mouth. Guard put a bug in his cellmate's ear and cellmate said he'd be happy to talk to us. Guy's name is Derek Lanard."

"Does he have a lawyer?"

"Yep. Johnson Lithgow with the PD's office. I already spoke with him. He gave the go-ahead for us to talk to Lanard. Told me to steer clear of any questions about his new case, which is fine."

"Guess Johnson trusts you." Many public defenders viewed both current and former police officers as enemies.

"I have a lot of friends in the defense bar now. More so than prosecutors. Funny how things change."

Real funny. Skye's remark sparked an idea, but Cory stowed the thought away and focused on the reason for their visit. She had enough to deal with today. After they showed their credentials to the guard and received their visitor badges, they took the elevator up to Derek Lanard's floor and settled in to wait for the guards to bring Lanard to the attorney visitation room.

"What makes you think he'll talk to us?"

"It's a gamble. What have we got to lose?"

Skye was right. In this uphill battle, every shot fired was a chance at victory. Of course, victory was subject to interpretation. At a minimum, a writ in Eric's case would net a stay of his current execution date to allow for a hearing. If they were lucky enough to get a hearing, the end result might be a recommendation from the court that the case be retried. New lawyers would be appointed, new jurors selected, and the entire affair would begin again, maybe a year from now depending on the court's docket. Serena would go home to Florida, and perhaps return to watch some other lawyer fight for her brother's freedom.

In the meantime, Cory would return to the DA's office, her relationship with Julie, both personal and professional, and the steadfast conviction that she could do the most good on the right side of law and order. A month ago, the prospect would have been exciting. Now all she could think about was how Serena didn't fit into her future. The realization dulled her enthusiasm.

The loud click of the bolt on the other side of the room jolted her out of her pity party. A tall white man shuffled into the room and settled on the steel stool. He picked up the phone handset on his side of the Plexiglas and Cory did the same. She took a moment before she spoke to size him up. His skin hung in folds where she imagined muscle used to be. Bulked up, he would be a formidable opponent. He stared at her with cold, dark brown eyes. She waited him out, knowing that whoever spoke first would lose leverage in their exchange.

He blinked first. "Visitor slip says you're an attorney. You're not a PD. You're dressed too nice."

"My name's Cory Lance. This is my investigator, Skye Keaton. We were hoping you would talk to us about an old case."

He leaned back on the stool and flexed his legs. "Why not? I got all the time in the world. Johnson says we're going to have to go to trial. Prosecutor's not being very friendly toward me."

Likely an understatement. "Who is the prosecutor?"

"Can't remember. It's changed a few times. Whoever it is has been giving Johnson the runaround. Maybe a free world lawyer like you could do a better job than him." Cory had worked in the system long enough to know defendants preferred lawyers in private practice. No small wonder, when she considered Eric's case. The problem occurred when defendants assumed a public defender wasn't going to do a good job before they ever had a chance to prove otherwise. This guy was in good hands. Johnson Lithgow was one of the more experienced public defenders, and contrary to general misconception, she didn't know many who worked harder. When she'd had to do battle with him, she came prepared.

"I'm not in the market for a client. Just want to talk to you about an old case."

"What's the story?"

"Nancy McGowan, you ever heard anything about that case?"

He scrunched his forehead in a show of brain activity. "Need a few more details."

Skye cut in. "Nancy McGowan was raped and murdered over in Rinson County, about six years ago. Eric Washington is waiting on the needle. Ring any bells?"

"Oh, yeah, that case." He tapped the glass with his finger. "I heard about it. What do you want to know?"

Cory took back the reins. "Anything you can tell us." She was extra careful not to lead him. The testimony of a jailhouse snitch wasn't the strongest foundation on which to build a case. Whatever he had to say had to be corroborated in order to be admissible in the courtroom.

"I might know a thing or two. My cellie's Dale Bolton. Word is he was a star witness in that case."

"I heard the same thing," Cory responded. "I wasn't there. I'm more interested in whether he's saying anything about the case now."

"He's got plenty to say. You tell me what you want to hear and I'll let you know if he had anything to say on the subject."

Cory shot a what the hell look at Skye. Skye prodded him. "I heard you had stuff to say. Guess I was wrong. Cory, let's get going." She stood and waited, but Lanard wasn't finished.

He jabbed a finger in Cory's direction. "What's your name again?"

The question caught Cory off guard for a moment. She chose to respond honestly. "Cory Lance."

"I heard of you. Aren't you that prosecutor that's been in the news?"

Of course her name was probably a regular topic of conversation at the jail. Cory turned to Skye. She should've sent Skye alone instead of risking their chance at information by showing her face back in the Dallas County system before memories faded. She decided to shade the truth a bit in her reply. "I used to be a prosecutor. Now, I'm helping out on the other side. I represent Eric Washington."

"You like representing killers?"

"I like finding out the truth. You want to help me with that or should I leave?" The back-and-forth was tiring. She'd already decided they weren't going to get anything from this guy. If his only motive to talk to her was what he could get out of it, she had nothing to offer. She stood to emphasize her point. She motioned to Skye that she was leaving. She only made it two steps before Lanard called out.

"I wanna help you."

She stopped, but didn't sit back down. "Okay." She'd caught the inflection in his statement and she waited for what he hadn't yet said.

"I'll help you, if you'll help me."

Decision time. She could bluff him into talking. His earlier reference, that he knew who she was, hung in the air. She could barter her prosecutor credentials, her reputation that she'd do anything for a win. Why not do what everyone thought she'd already done in Nelson's case for the benefit of Eric? She could do it for Serena.

Like a slap back to reality, she could hear Serena's protests. What about honesty? Integrity? Doing the right thing? Values Cory had clung to, both personally and professionally even though everyone else thought she'd compromised. Her only compromise had been that she'd allowed everyone to believe she was someone she wasn't—a scheming, end-justifies-the-means shark. For once, Cory found only cold comfort in the fact she'd considered using those tactics now in a selfless act, a way to protect someone she cared about, respected.

Serena's face flashed in her mind. Serena would never ask her to do the things she'd done for Julie. She had too much honor. Cory desperately wanted to deserve Serena's respect, so she said, "I can't help you. Not the way you want. I'm not a prosecutor any—" She stopped before she said anymore, and changed course. "I'm defending Eric Washington, and I need information that can help him, but I don't have anything to barter."

She held her breath, hoping she hadn't tanked her chance with this guy. He stared her down, but she couldn't get a read on whether she'd passed his appraisal until he spoke. "I'll talk. But you gotta at least tell Johnson what a stand-up guy I am. Maybe he'll treat me better if it comes from you."

Small price to pay. "Yeah, I can do that."

"Okay. This Bolton guy's a scary dude. Doesn't really care what he says out loud. Guy like that, been in the joint before, should know better about watching his mouth."

"Some people don't ever learn. What's he saying?"

"He dances around it, but he talks about his case then says he got away with more than they'll ever know about."

"What makes you think he's talking about anything we'd be interested in?" Cory didn't hold out much hope for anything solid. As a prosecutor, she'd dealt with jailhouse snitches on a regular basis, especially among the defendants in the county jail where they weren't likely to be around long enough to reap much in the way of nasty consequences from ratting out their cellmate. At least half the time, the snitch didn't have anything useful to report.

"Female bartender, black guy went down for it? That all sound familiar?"

"Sure. Also sounds like details anyone could read in the paper, some of which we mentioned when we showed up here today. Maybe Bolton likes to read." She spoke her next words carefully, deliberately. "Maybe you do too." If this guy was jacking them around, Cory wanted him to know she wasn't in the mood.

He took the hint. "Okay, I got you. You need proof he knew something no one else would know. Am I right?" He didn't wait for her to respond. "How about this? He says she had a stack of *Playboy* magazines in the trunk of her car. Said he took one when he was done, to remember her by."

Cory forced her features to remain casual, but inside she was shouting. Finally, they had what they needed. The court record she'd reviewed meticulously over the past month contained a sealed motion, and the sealed transcript of a hearing in the judge's chambers on the subject of those magazines. The defense had argued they should be able to bring up evidence that Nancy was no stranger to sex and, since one of the issues had a particularly racy story about rape fantasy, the magazines were relevant to whether she'd consented to the play that had turned deadly. Cory remembered thinking the theory was crazy— to assert the defense, they'd have to admit Eric had been at the scene of the crime, but hadn't meant to force sex or kill his sex partner. The point had quickly become moot. Because rape shield laws protect the personal lives of rape victims, the judge had ruled neither side could bring up the magazines, and he'd ordered the record on the issue sealed. Cory had scoured the clinic's file, and she was confident the issue had never hit the press. Yet, Bolton knew. Bolton, a known rapist who was currently awaiting trial on another violent crime. She had what she needed to file the writ. She let Skye ask all the follow-up questions while she mentally ticked off the points she'd make in her brief. Or at least she tried. Her ability to concentrate was divided between the work she had to do and the person she wanted to tell about it.

❖

The guard held up five fingers to signify time was running out, and Serena groaned. This visit had been way too short. Would she ever see Eric again? As much as she hoped Cory would be able to pull off a miracle, she didn't place much trust in a system that was better at doing than undoing.

Seeing him now was painful. He was gaunt, hollow, restless, likely counting down the days, maybe even hours until his death. She'd produced enough quarters to buy out one of the vending machines, and then done her best to project a cheerful demeanor, but she feared he could see through her despair. This visit hadn't been about the legal and factual issues in his case. She'd made the long drive to demonstrate solidarity, support, love. Those things didn't translate into much in the way of conversation, and soon the conversation drifted back to the case.

"Ms. Lance, she's a good attorney."

Serena, surprised by Eric's words, couldn't tell if he'd asked a question or made a statement. She'd deliberately avoided the topic of Cory because she couldn't stop thinking about her and she worried her attraction would shine through any discussion on the subject. Their closeness from the night before, combined with the torrid sex of her dream, had whipped her into a frenzy that she'd driven hours to keep at bay. She didn't need to stir up that trouble again. Still, Eric deserved some response. "She's working very hard on your case."

"I know. She keeps me up to speed. I hope this writ gets me a hearing at least."

"When did you talk to her?"

"This morning. She gave me a call. Said she was on the way to talk to one of the witnesses in the case and then she was going to finish the writ and get it filed later today or tomorrow."

"Does she call you often?"

"If you listen to what the guards say, she calls me more than any other attorney with a client on the row."

Serena smothered a huge grin and filed away the intel. She'd give Cory a big hug when she saw her.

No, she wouldn't. They'd been too close to crossing boundaries last night. Still, she couldn't help but be happy to hear Cory had taken such a personal interest in Eric's case, and she wondered if personal rather than professional interest played a part.

The guard signaled it was time to go. The visit had been both too long and too short. Serena leaned as close as she could get to the divider, and whispered into the handset, "I love you."

She fought back tears as Eric echoed her sentiment. He added, "Don't cry, sis. I'll be okay. No matter what happens, I'll be okay." He cleared his throat. "I need you to promise me some things."

"Anything."

"Don't come watch. If I'm going to die, I want this to be the way you see me last, not strapped—" She put a hand up to stop him before the gruesome image could stick in her mind. He shook his head. "I'm not done."

Serena braced herself.

"Don't let them bury me in a pauper's grave."

Serena couldn't stop the tears this time. Both she and Eric wept. Neither of them had any idea where their mother was buried. She'd died alone and penniless, a victim of her addiction, at a time when neither of her children had the means or were even old enough to deal with the details. She'd been cremated and her ashes buried in a county plot. Eric's fear of meeting the same anonymous fate as her mother was palpable, and Serena rushed to reassure him. "I swear. I'll take care of the details. I promise."

"Thank you. One last thing."

She took a deep breath, bracing herself for his last wish.

"Don't let the past hold you back. I let everything that happened to us growing up shadow my life. I didn't even try to break free. I just lived my life like the criminal everyone expected a junkie's son to be."

As Serena drove away from the prison, she realized she felt a deeper connection to her brother days before his death than she'd felt their entire lives. She turned his last request over and over in her mind. Ostensibly, she'd already outshone her roots. She'd graduated college. Hell, she'd graduated high school. She had a steady job, a modest savings account. She didn't have to rely on the random charity of others for food and clothes. Yet she was empty. None of the trappings she'd accumulated filled her mind, fueled her heart, fed her soul.

She was more like her mother and brother than she cared to admit. They'd had choices to make, and although they'd chosen differently than she, they'd all wound up without the things that really mattered. What a waste. She was done wasting time and emotion. She sped her way back to Dallas. To Cory.

CHAPTER EIGHTEEN

Cory's car was the only one in the clinic lot when Serena pulled in at seven o'clock. Serena had driven straight there after she'd retrieved the message Cory had left on her voice mail letting her know she'd be working late on Eric's case. Her only stop had been to pick up dinner.

The front door was unlocked. Serena pushed through the door and tiptoed to the back where Cory had taken over Greg's office. She stood in the hall, peering in at Cory who was so intent at her keyboard, she didn't notice she had a visitor. It didn't matter how rumpled and fatigued Cory was; she was still beautiful. Serena wished she could freeze time, put Eric's case on hold, and take advantage of the intimacy Cory had offered her. But she couldn't. Eric's clock was ticking and any day now, Cory might return to her former job. What would she do? Go back to her solitary life in Florida, content to the be the celibate daughter of an aging couple in a job she only mildly enjoyed?

As stressful as the last few weeks had been, she felt truly alive for the first time. Even with the looming execution date, she'd felt renewed hope in her relationship with her brother, but mostly in her ability to have a relationship of her own. Would she have the courage to face her fears once she was back in Florida? The question rocked her, and she realized it wasn't the fear of being in a relationship that scared her. She feared leaving the world she had created here. She may only be pushing paper, but unlike the same activity at the bank, here she had a chance to affect lives. And she wanted to take that chance.

She stared across the room and realized that was the crux of it. She wanted Cory. More than want, she craved her. Despite all the reasons why she shouldn't. The list of negatives was long: Cory was her brother's lawyer, Cory would return to her job putting people behind bars, Cory was still entangled with that other woman. Why then, did none of these reasons outweigh the pull of attraction?

"Hey, you, what are you doing here?"

Serena returned Cory's greeting by hefting the bag of dinner. "I got your messages. Thought I'd bring you dinner." Short and choppy sentences were all she could manage, but what she really wanted to say was "I missed you today and came straight here. I wish you didn't have to work because then we could…" She couldn't finish the sentence even though she knew what she wanted. Asking for intimacy, speaking her desires out loud, would shatter the shield she'd built around her heart. She should give Cory the food and leave.

"Hope you brought enough for two. I could use your help. I want to get this brief filed first thing in the morning."

A harmless invitation. A working dinner. But Serena knew if she decided to stay she would cross a line, and her life would never be the same again. She set the bag down on Cory's desk. "I came prepared."

Hours later, Cory hit the print button on her computer. "Pretty sure this is the final draft, but I want to read it one more time. In the morning, with fresh eyes."

Serena yawned and pointed at the clock on the wall. "Um, I hate to be the one to break this to you, but it is morning."

Cory laughed. It was two a.m. "I lose track of time when I'm deep into a project. In fact, I usually forget to eat too. Thanks again for bringing dinner."

"Couldn't let you starve. Besides, I wanted to see you."

A sense of urgency lay within the tentative declaration. Cory turned away from her monitor and faced Serena. "I'm sorry. I put you right to work and didn't even bother asking if you needed something. Is everything okay? Did visiting Eric upset you?"

"Yes. I mean, no." Serena cleared her throat. "Visiting him didn't upset me, but it did put some things in perspective."

"You want to talk about it?"

"I don't think I want to talk at all. I think talking…actually, I think thinking is what keeps me from doing the things I want."

The air between them was heavy with anticipation. Cory sensed they teetered on the edge of change. Would Serena pull back? Or would she? "Tell me what you want."

Serena crossed the few steps between them. Cory stopped breathing when Serena placed her hands on either side of Cory's face. She was the one with the power to pull back now. All the reasons she should clamored loudly in her head. Serena's lack of experience. Serena's relationship to her client. Serena, Serena, Serena. The reasons fell away until all she cared about was the beautiful, compassionate woman standing in front of her, offering herself, completely. She couldn't pull back, but Serena had to be the one to jump first. "Show me what you want."

"I will." Serena's whisper turned up the heat. "But not here."

"My place?" Cory hoped the comfort of her home would outweigh the memory of Julie's late night drop in.

Serena took her hand. "I'll drive."

Cory gladly let her take the lead. She'd worry about her car later. All she cared about now was taking this path, seeing where it led. While Serena drove way too carefully through the streets, Cory sat on her hands and focused on everything but Serena to get her through the ride. When they finally arrived at her house, she felt like she was going to explode. When they crossed the threshold, she forced herself into hostess mode, determined not to force anything else on Serena before she was ready.

"Can I get you a Coke, maybe some water?"

"Why don't you make me breakfast?"

"What?" Really? She wanted food? Of course, it had been hours since dinner. Serena had cooked for her before; she should return the favor. "I think I have a few things in the fridge. I can probably come up with something. If you don't mind if it's inedible. Did I mention

I'm not much of a cook?" She wasn't done babbling, but Serena's finger over her lips stopped the ramble.

"Hush. I was kidding." Serena removed her finger and replaced it with her lips. Soft and hard, strong and gentle. Cory melted into the embrace, savored the light caress followed with sure strokes.

When she could no longer breathe, she ducked her head and said, "You're an amazing kisser."

"So are you."

"What other amazing talents do you have?"

"Not much else, I'm afraid." Serena stepped back. Cory could feel her hesitation, and she gave her the space to voice it. "Truly. I don't know what I'm doing."

Such unbridled trust deserved acknowledgment, solidarity. Cory closed the distance between them. Serena had jumped off the cliff; it was time for her to follow her off the edge. "Do you want to?"

"Desperately." She breathed the word and Cory felt her need, her want, full-force. She held out her hand and led her to the bedroom.

Serena took in her surroundings. Cory's room was cozier than she expected. Scattered pillows, framed photos featuring Cory with what appeared to be groups of friends and family, a stuffed Scooby Doo in a chair by the bed. She'd exhausted all her confidence with the kiss, with the not so subtle hints she was ready for more. Now she found herself stalling for time to decide if this was what she really wanted. "Scooby Doo? I bet there's a story to tell."

Cory's whisper grazed her neck. "Scooby's great. Gag gift from my brother. Kiss me."

Serena barely digested Cory's breathless words before they were kissing again, but this time the kiss was different. Instead of being all-consuming, it felt like a prelude, and Serena ached to see where the passion led. She pulled back. "I want more. Show me." A simple request. She could only hope Cory respected the strength it took to ask the question.

"May I undress you?"

"How about you go first? I want to see what I'm getting into." She was only partly kidding. She didn't know if she could handle standing naked in front of Cory, worried whether she would pass inspection.

On the other hand, she already knew Cory would be stunning. Maybe seeing Cory vulnerable would make it easier to expose herself.

"Fair enough." Cory slowly unbuttoned her shirt. Too slowly, yet Serena forced herself to wait, to let the gathering tide of arousal sweep her up in its embrace. She licked her lips as Cory shrugged out of her shirt and tossed it on the floor.

"Messy little thing, aren't you?" She needed the levity to maintain her composure.

Cory grinned in response. "Just anxious, I guess."

"You took so long taking it off, I was beginning to wonder."

"Seems every time we've gotten close, we've been interrupted. I suppose I just wanted to prolong the moment."

"You're killing me."

Cory stepped close and placed a hand on the hem of Serena's blouse, tracing a finger just underneath. "Any chance I could help you with this?"

"Please." Serena could barely get the word out, though she was desperate for Cory to touch her. She groaned as Cory took her time, accompanying the release of each button with increasingly intense kisses against her neck, her shoulder, her chest. When Cory's tongue dipped into her cleavage, she could wait no longer. She pulled Cory's head up and kissed her deeply, then gasped, "Too slow. I'm going crazy."

"Me too. Bed?"

Serena could only nod and then follow as Cory led her across the room and gently pushed her back against the pillows. She reached for Cory's fly as Cory tugged off her pants and then watched as Cory tore out of her own trousers. Despite the frantic lead-in, once she was undressed, Cory stood frozen in place, staring down at Serena's naked body. Serena started to panic. "Change your mind?" She didn't even try to hide the undercurrent of nerves racing through her.

Cory shook her head. "Are you kidding? You're gorgeous. I can't believe you're here with me." She trailed her hand down Serena's thigh. "Like this." Cory climbed into bed and pulled Serena into her arms. "You're sure?"

Serena was as sure as she'd ever been about anything in her life. Whatever they were to each other outside of this moment, right now, all she felt was the rush of arousal, the ache of wanting, the surge of need. Being with Cory, naked and vulnerable, was coming home. "Kiss me."

As their kiss deepened, Serena's confidence grew and she let her hands explore Cory's body, her breasts, her tight abdomen. She reached lower and grazed the inside of Cory's thigh and sighed as Cory shuddered against her.

"Ah, that feels wonderful." Cory opened her eyes and asked again, "Are you okay? Do you feel good?"

Serena answered with another deep kiss. When they were both breathless, she pulled back. "Being with you, like this...nothing has ever felt more right. I want to please you."

Cory reached for her hand and moved it to her breast and gently guided her to squeeze her nipple. She groaned. "Touch me like this. Your touch is wonderful." As she teased Cory's breast, Cory leaned over and swirled her tongue around both her nipples, murmuring, "Does that feel good? Do what feels good." Serena arched her chest toward Cory's hungry mouth until she felt she would explode, then she inched down and savored Cory's nipples with her lips and tongue.

Cory's hand moved down her body until she reached her sex and she began caressing, coaxing her to levels of fervor she hadn't known she could attain. Her first orgasm was a quick, shattering blast of wonder. She rose from the bed, taking Cory with her as the powerful waves of arousal coursed through her. Cory held her close, whispering unintelligible comforts in her ear until finally she lay spent in Cory's arms.

Her dreams had not prepared her for the onslaught of feeling. She'd spent a lifetime confining what she wanted, what she craved, to what was safe, or what she thought was safe, denying the risk of her desires. But right now, even in the throes of ecstasy, she'd never felt more safe, more loved. She'd vowed she would never suppress her desires again. And she desired Cory most of all.

Chapter Nineteen

Cory sat in front of Paul's desk, tapping her foot as he read the writ she'd prepared the night before. She wanted him to give his stamp of approval, but beyond that, she wanted to get the brief filed so she could take a few hours off. Take Serena to lunch. With or without food.

Serena had dropped her at the clinic pre-dawn, her desire to be circumspect about their relationship only slightly stronger than the urge to stay in bed. Naked, sated, and warm.

"Get in your car and drive back home. We can go back to bed."

Serena's face flushed as she delivered the invitation, and Cory almost gave in. It was still early, but she knew if they went back to bed, she wouldn't return to the clinic that day. She hadn't wanted to leave that morning, and a repeat performance would only weaken her resolve to work at all today. She remembered the other night, when she'd left work undone to be with Serena. She'd hate herself if she didn't put responsibilities before play. And as much as Serena seemed to want her now, she'd feel the same way.

"I'd love to, I really would. But I need to put the finishing touches on the brief, show it to Paul, and get it filed today." She softened her pull back with a deep kiss that left them both panting. She shook her head to gain perspective. "See what happens when I'm with you? I lose my head."

"I'll come in with you. Help you work."

"Oh, no you don't. I won't get a thing done. You go. Get some sleep. I'll call you when I'm done and we'll go to lunch."

"I don't think the Budget Suites does room service." Serena's wicked smile signaled food was the last thing she wanted for lunch.

Cory leaned in and kissed her again, savoring the touch since it would need to last for the next few hours. "We'll figure something out. I'll hurry."

Cory spent the next few hours working, her mind divided between remembering the pleasure of Serena and worry about the plight of her brother. She was lost in thought when Paul cleared his throat.

"Your arguments are well-articulated, your writing is top-notch. You're sure you haven't done any appellate work before?"

"What? Uh, no, not a lick. I'm good on my feet, but brief writing is not my favorite way to get my point across."

"Maybe it should be. You have a gift for it."

Cory wasn't sure how to respond. "So you think it's ready to file?"

"I do." He handed her the sheaf of papers. "Just change the signature line and it's ready to go."

Cory was confused. "I'm sorry?"

"I figured you'd want me to sign as lead counsel. The judge will expect whoever files the writ to argue at the hearing. The judge will probably want to review the record before setting a hearing. Even if we're lucky and get a quick hearing, I doubt Greg will be back in time. I'll handle the arguments. You can bring me up to speed on anything you think I need to know."

Of course. It would be awkward if her name were on an appellate brief for a death row defendant after she was back at the Dallas DA's office, working as a prosecutor. Still, the prospect of handing over her work, walking away from Eric's fate, left her numb.

"Cory, are you okay?"

She looked at Paul, hearing his words, but not really processing his question. "What?"

"I asked if you're okay?"

She needed to pull herself together. "I'm fine. Just tired I guess."

His stare told her he thought there was something more to her distraction. "Why don't you take the rest of the day? Rest, relax. I've got some candidates coming in later this week, possibly to fill in for Greg on an interim basis. You can help me bring them up to speed."

"How is Greg?"

"He's itching to come back, but his doctor was clear about his need to take time off. And I have to agree. Even in the short time you've been here, you've come to realize what a stressful job this is."

Was working on death penalty appeals more stressful than prosecution? She hadn't given the comparative stress level much thought. It was different, that was for sure. As a prosecutor, she'd been convinced she was defending the rights of the downtrodden, society's victims, but she'd worked on the side of a different kind of downtrodden over the past two months, and she had to admit, many of the clinic's clients were also victims. Just not the popular kind. Did that make the work more stressful? Maybe, but righting wrongs was fulfilling, no matter what the circumstance.

On some level, she would miss the work at the clinic, but she could do one last meaningful act. "Hey, Paul, you mind if I file the writ? After you've signed it?"

"You don't need to drive all the way out there. We can have one of the interns run it to the court."

"I'd like to do it myself." Symbolic though it was, filing the brief she'd poured her heart into would be the one last thing she could do for Eric, for Serena. "I'd like to be able to tell Serena I personally delivered a copy of the writ to the judge."

He didn't ask her motivation, but he did study her for a long moment. She didn't know what she would say if he asked why it was so important for her to do this for Serena. A variety of thoughts flashed through her mind—because I care about her, because I'd do anything for her, but one idea shone more brightly than any of the others. Because I'm falling in love with her.

"Sure, you can file the writ."

Paul's words barely scratched the surface of her trance. She took the packet from him and drove to the Rinson County courthouse, as if on autopilot, desperately trying to process her feelings. The realization she might be falling in love with Serena consumed her. She couldn't be falling in love. As Paul had just reminded her, she would be back at the DA's office soon, and Serena had her own life, back in Florida. Eric's case was the only thing connecting them, and except for the clerical act of filing the stack of paper, her involvement was over. Ostensibly, nothing could hold them together, but she couldn't deny the powerful pull of something more than physical attraction, affection. Could it really be love?

Whatever it was, she felt emboldened. She filed the writ with the clerk and hand-delivered a copy to Rick Smith. Then she asked him to approach the judge with her to discuss a possible hearing date, and she surprised both him and herself by taking the opportunity to take another stab at her motion for discovery.

Judge Fowler took a moment to glance through the brief before putting Rick on the spot. "Looks like we have grounds for a hearing, Mr. Smith. I'm sure you don't have any objections to opening your file at this point."

"Well, actually, Your Honor, I'll need to talk to my supervisor about our current policies."

"We'll be happy to adjourn for a moment if you'd like to take care of that now. Let him know that if you can't come to an agreed discovery order, I plan to enter an order of my own today." A hint of a smile played on the judge's face, and Cory enjoyed watching Rick squirm. It was his file, his call. She knew it, and apparently, the judge did too.

"Thank you, Judge. I think we can agree. I'll need some time to gather the files and do any necessary redactions." He cleared his throat as the judge fixed him with a stare, and then added, "We can probably have most of it ready later today."

Cory chimed in. "That's fine with us." She paused for a moment, but then decided she should make her role clear. "Judge, Paul Guthrie, will be handling the case from here on out. I'll let him know about our agreement and he'll contact Mr. Smith directly to make arrangements to review the file."

"I haven't seen Paul in a while. I'll look forward to seeing him in my court. Thanks, Ms. Lance. It's been a pleasure meeting you."

Cory left the courthouse with mixed feelings. A sense of accomplishment with the developments in the case mixed with confusion about what to do next. She needed to see Serena, but she didn't have a clue what she would say, what she would do when she did. She picked up the phone to call, but it rang before she could punch the numbers. She recognized the incoming number. Not Serena, but still someone she needed to deal with if she had any hope of figuring out her life. And she wanted—she needed—to figure out her life. She answered the call.

❖

"Paul, have you seen Cory?"

Serena had waited in her motel room as long as she could, but it was almost noon and she'd driven to the clinic to surprise Cory. After making love the night before, the few hours away had seemed like forever. She poked her head in Cory's makeshift office, but she wasn't there. As much as she didn't want to be obvious about seeking her out, she finally gave in and knocked on Paul's door.

"Hi, Serena. She was here, but she left about..." He paused to glance at his watch. "About nine this morning. She finished up the writ on Eric's case and took it to Rinson County to file it. In fact, I have a copy for you, somewhere around here."

As Paul searched through his desk, Serena did a rough mental calculation. The trip to Rinson, took about forty-five minutes. Seemed like Cory should've been back way before now. She considered calling her, but if Cory was in court, she didn't want to risk interrupting. Maybe she'd see if she could do some filing while she waited for Cory to return. Paul's voice cut into her thoughts.

"Here you go." He handed her the stack of papers designed to save Eric's life. She couldn't resist flipping through, feeling the weight of the arguments in the heft of the document. When she reached the last page, she saw Paul's scrawling signature in the space where Eric's counsel was to sign, and she was surprised. She'd expected to see Cory's name, since she'd put in all the work. Maybe it was customary to have the head of the clinic sign all the documents they filed. "I know Cory worked really hard on this. Is there a reason she didn't sign it?"

"My call. She may be back working at the DA's office by the time the case is set for a hearing. The judge will expect whoever signed the writ to make the arguments. I thought it would be easier on everyone this way. Cory has brought me up to speed on all the arguments, and I promise I'll do his case justice."

Serena had no doubt Paul would do a great job on Eric's behalf, but she couldn't help being distracted by his reference to Cory's return to the DA's office. She shouldn't be surprised. Working as a prosecutor was Cory's career, her entire livelihood. Did she think that would change because of one night of sex? She had to admit, she'd dared hope it might. A tinge of worry settled in. Had she risked too much? She'd finally experienced true intimacy, but without knowing what came next, the satisfaction was hollow.

You're being too dramatic. You should talk to Cory, see what her plans are for the future before you write yourself out of them. "Do you have any idea when Cory will be back? I'd like to thank her for her work."

"I'll be happy to pass along the message. I told her to take the rest of the day off, and I heard someone say her supervisor at the DA's office called here looking for her earlier. I don't expect to see her until tomorrow, if then."

If then. Serena struggled to process the implication, but she could barely breathe. Cory's words from this morning echoed. "I'll call you when I'm done…I'll hurry." But those promises flew out the window when the call came from her past. She hadn't even called to say there'd be a change of plans.

Julie Dalmar's face loomed in her memory. Possessive, controlling, gorgeous. Seemed like Cory found another call more worthy. Serena thanked Paul for his work and rushed out. When she reached her car, she let out a bitter laugh. She had nowhere to be, no one to meet, nothing she had to do. Before Cory, she wouldn't have cared, would have even enjoyed the lack of connection to anyone or anything that could evoke feelings of affection, want, love. But now, she'd glimpsed what was possible when she let herself feel. The thought of losing what she'd barely found was the loneliest feeling of all.

❖

Cory stood as Melinda approached. She'd been waiting in the lobby of the Dallas DA's office for thirty minutes and Julie had stuck her head out several times, impatiently asking if Cory was ready for their meeting. She'd held her off each time. She could handle a meeting with just Julie, but she'd been called back to meet with the elected DA, Frank Alvarez, and since Julie had made it clear her future with the office was on the line, she wanted her attorney present.

"Hey, girlie, where's the fire?"

Melinda made her usual ruckus entrance, and Cory was grateful. She needed someone she could trust to be completely in her corner. Julie's phone call had left Cory wondering if she even wanted to take this meeting.

"I talked to Alvarez, told him I wanted to go ahead and bring you back on board. He wants to meet with you. This morning."

"Okay." Cory kept her tone cautious.

"Wow, thought you'd sound a little happier than that."

As usual, Julie hadn't even considered that Cory might have mixed feelings. She'd been ousted from her job and forced to work against everything she believed in just to have the chance of getting back to her chosen profession. Julie had made promises at the onset, but she'd done nothing in the interim to bolster the blind trust Cory had placed in her, in their relationship. They'd handled the Nelson case as a team. The only reason Cory had taken the fall on her own was because Julie had more at risk. She'd been at the office longer; she was on the fast track for a leadership position in the new administration. An accusation of prosecutorial misconduct would have meant sure termination. On the other hand, Cory had no aspirations to be part of "management." Her goal was to be the best litigator she could be, and Julie had assured her when things blew over, she could return to the work she loved. Yet, now Julie expected her to jump when she called and pant with joy at the prospect of possibly getting her job back.

"I am happy," Cory said, even though she wasn't entirely sure she was. Things had changed. Not just between her and Julie. Being with Serena had given her new perspective about not only relationships, but her career path. She wasn't sure she could return to the job with the same sense of righteousness she'd had when she left. Maybe she'd be a better prosecutor for the experience. But was that what she wanted?

"Good, because this was harder than I thought it would be. I had to do a lot of talking to get Alvarez to come around. I convinced him that all this do-gooder work you've been doing makes you more well-rounded, and since he's really into the whole integrity of the process crap, he agreed to meet with you and at least talk about it."

"Well, aren't you generous?" Cory didn't try to hide the sarcasm, but Julie was unfazed.

"Do you want the meeting or not? I told him your schedule was flexible since you're just a volunteer at that place and he's got an opening in an hour. I suggest you be here by then."

She'd disconnected the call and studied her internal angst. She had always trusted Julie, but her confidence that Julie would do the right thing had shifted recently. Julie took and took, only giving when she could benefit from the bargain. She'd admired Julie's tenacity, her willingness to sacrifice everything for success, but witnessing Serena's situation gave her a different perspective. Serena had given up her home and risked her career for a brother she barely knew anymore. Her willingness to sacrifice meant giving up what she wanted, not what others needed. The difference was stark.

No longer sure Julie would protect her interests, Cory had called Melinda and asked if she would join her for this meeting. She wasn't sure what she wanted Melinda to do, other than level the playing field. Cory had filled Melinda in but left out the part about how she'd agreed to take the fall for Julie when the Nelson case fell apart. She'd keep that secret as long as Julie kept her end of the bargain.

"I feel a little silly for dragging you down here. Guess I just want a witness for this meeting. I think Alvarez is going to reinstate me, but I don't know how that plays into the state bar suspension. I figured you could help navigate that part of things." The look on Melinda's face said she knew Cory was holding something back. She felt bad for fudging the truth, but that was as much as she felt comfortable saying at this point.

"Sure, but you're going to owe me a really good bottle of wine when this is over." She stood. "Let's go take this meeting."

Frank Alvarez was an extremely tall hulk of a man. His imposing physical presence contrasted sharply with his kinder, gentler approach to prosecution. Cory had only met him in passing, which wasn't surprising considering the large number of employees in the office, but she was generally impressed with his knowledge of the law and his apparent willingness to make changes in an environment that many viewed as stagnant. His first step as the newly-elected DA had been to set up a new unit within the office to handle writs claiming prosecutorial misconduct and actual innocence claims. Julie bitched about him behind his back about what she called his soft on crime approach, but in public, she sang his praises. She'd do whatever she needed to do to climb up the ladder, but Cory had never considered that Julie's ambition extended to stepping on her back on the way up.

"Cory, it's good to see you. Thanks for coming by on such short notice."

She shook Frank's outstretched hand and returned the firm grip. "Thanks for the opportunity, sir." She introduced Melinda as her attorney, and added, "She's assisting me with the proceeding at the state bar. I brought her along in case there are any issues that overlap."

He motioned for both of them to have a seat. "Good idea. Frankly, I don't know what's involved with regard to this probationary period they have you on, but I'm ready to discuss having you back here. Julie has described the work you've been doing, and I'm impressed that you've taken it upon yourself to get some perspective."

Julie sat in a chair close to Frank's desk and beamed as if Cory's work at the clinic had been her brainchild. Cory wanted to smack her, but she had to admit, Julie was keeping her end of the bargain. Still, she couldn't resist a slight jab. "I can't take the credit for the clinic work since it was Melinda's idea. She negotiated the deal with the state bar and convinced Paul Guthrie to take me on."

Melinda chimed in. "Mr. Alvarez, I can assure you that your word would go a long way with the bar examiner assigned to Cory's case. Her probation is almost over anyway."

"Then I'm prepared to call whoever I need to. We're shorthanded around here, and it's been a real hardship being without one of our more experienced prosecutors."

Cory breathed a sigh of relief. When she'd entered the doors of the courthouse, she hadn't been entirely sure she wanted to return, but now it seemed the decision had been made. Julie had kept her promise; the new boss was willing to intercede with the state bar to get her back, and judging by Melinda's big smile, she considered Cory's reinstatement a win. Who was she to argue differently? Besides, what else would she do? She worked her whole life to have this career. She had a second chance to make it work and she wasn't going to squander it.

"Julie has drafted a formal apology for you to sign. We'll need your signature before you can return. I assume you and Ms. Stone will want to review the language, but I'll tell you right now, I've already approved it and there's not a lot of flexibility." He handed her a sheet a paper. "There's an empty office down the hall if you need a moment to talk it over."

Cory read the first few lines:

I, Cory Lance, acted on my own and improperly withheld evidence from the defense in a pending case. No one else at the district attorney's office was either aware of my actions or instructed me to act in this manner. I sincerely apologize for my actions...

Seeing the words on paper stung. Especially since she knew she hadn't done anything wrong. Knowing that Julie had penned the apology, formally shoving the blame solely onto her shoulders was another blow. But she'd made the bargain, and no way was she going to back out now. She pulled a pen from her suit jacket, but before she could uncap it, she felt a hand on hers. She looked up to see Melinda with a firmly fixed "we need to talk" expression. She shot back an "I know what I'm doing" look, but Melinda was not dissuaded. She stood and yanked the paper from her hand and, after skimming the lines, announced. "We'll take a look at this and get back to you tomorrow."

Cory followed her out of the office, fuming. She contained her growing anger through the long, crowded elevator ride, but once they reached the steps in front of the courthouse, she let loose. "What was that all about?"

"I don't know, pal. Why don't you tell me? Why are you so anxious to take all the blame for that case while your trial partner stands there sucking up to the new boss? You realize you're going to have a reputation as an unethical prosecutor that will never go away?"

"None of your business. It's my job, my decision."

"Is that so? Then why did you have me tag along if you aren't interested in an objective opinion? You're a lawyer. Maybe you should represent yourself from now on."

Melinda's frustration was palpable, and Cory bit back an angry retort. After all, Melinda was right. She was the one who'd reached out for help. She'd known what she was going to do when she'd gotten Julie's call. Why had she felt the need to drag Melinda along to witness her sacrifice her pride one more time? Why was she having mixed feelings when her career was back within her reach? Why now?

"Look, Cory, I'm sorry I barked, but I get the impression there's something you're not telling me. That's fine. I'm not trying to invade your privacy. You want your job back, and I get that. Obviously, they need you back. Sleeping on it isn't going to kill you, and my advice is that you do just that."

She was right. Tomorrow she could quit the clinic and march into Alvarez's office and sign the apology. In the meantime, maybe she could figure out why the excitement of returning to work carried a sour tinge.

This morning, Serena had been in her bed and her future seemed bright and hopeful. Now, she faced the reality that her career as a prosecutor would never be the same. She wondered what else wasn't as it seemed. Was the writ she filed on Eric's behalf good enough to give him a second chance? Was the passion she felt for Serena strong enough to sustain a relationship? Part of her wanted to run to Serena's arms, relive the ecstasy of their lovemaking. For a few hours, they'd managed to block out the painful reality of their tenuous real lives. Would they be as successful in the light of day? Was what she felt for Serena really love, or was it only escape?

She didn't know the answers, but she did know that she had begun to question her instincts in a way she never had before.

CHAPTER TWENTY

Serena grabbed her ringing cell phone and fixed on the caller ID. Skye. Disappointed, she considered letting it go to voice mail where it could sit with the message she'd gotten from Cory an hour earlier. Cory's message had been simple, yet vague. Something had come up and she'd have to miss lunch. She'd call later. Serena had imagined many variations of the conversation, but since they all ended with Cory returning to her job, leaving the clinic and Eric's case, she assumed every version of their talk would end in some form of good-bye. Probably inevitable. She felt foolish for letting herself assume any other conclusion, but after last night, she couldn't help fantasizing a future between them. Time for the walls to go up again.

In the meantime, she didn't feel like talking to anyone about anything. If Skye had information about Eric's case, she should call Cory. Actually, no, she should call Paul. Did Skye know Cory had probably already left her work at the clinic? Had she known all along that Cory's first allegiance would be her old job, her old boss? The phone continued to ring, and she answered, angry she'd have to be the one to tell Skye what Cory should have.

"Hello," she barked.

"Hi, Serena, thought you weren't going to answer. Are you okay?"

Whatever was going on between her and Cory wasn't Skye's fault. She adjusted to a neutral tone. "I'm fine. What's up?"

"I have some news for you."

"You should probably call Paul. I think Cory's already left the clinic to go back to the DA's office and Paul is going to handle Eric's writ from here on out."

"Sorry, what?"

"Cory filed the writ this morning, but then she was headed to a meeting with her old boss. I haven't heard from her, but I got the impression from Paul that her work at the clinic is done and she's going back to her old job."

"Well, that's odd, but I'm not calling about Eric's case. I have information on that other matter you asked me to look into. I think you're going to be very interested in what I found out."

Serena spent a moment reflecting until she finally remembered what Skye was talking about. The Nelson case. Did she still care about what had happened with that case? If Cory was going back to work at the DA's office, the furor must have blown over. Whatever Skye had learned about the Nelson case wouldn't matter, at least as far as Cory's future was concerned. But it still mattered to her. She'd sensed all along, whenever Cory talked about the case she'd held something back. And now, even after they'd shared such closeness the night before, Cory was still holding back. She'd blown off their lunch, wiped her hands of Eric's case, and was headed back to her former employer. And Cory hadn't felt the need to discuss any of her decisions with Serena.

Why should she? A night of torrid sex was not a new event in Cory's life, definitely not something she would treat like a major milestone. Serena wished she could feel the same way, affecting nonchalance instead of deep-seated desire. Sleeping with Cory had changed everything, including how she felt about her past and her future. She'd come to think her past limited the future. But if it weren't for her past, she never would have met Cory, faced her fears, and taken the plunge. What had been the ultimate test of fate for her, had apparently been nothing more than a night of fun for Cory. If Cory didn't care for anything more than a fling, why should she?

But she did. She never would have gone to bed with Cory had she not trusted her, had she not had deep feelings for her. And she knew what those feelings were, even though she was feeling them for the very first time. She loved Cory, and no matter what happened between them, no matter whether Cory returned the emotion, she knew she always would.

"Serena, you still there?"

Skye. Waiting to tell her a secret. Cory's secret. Would knowing make a difference? Would it change how she felt? She knew it wouldn't, but she wanted to know anyway. She wanted to know everything about Cory—what she liked to read, her favorite color, who she most admired. But most of all, she wanted to know what motivated her, and she knew that whatever Skye had learned would give her a glimpse. Maybe a glimpse was the start of something more, or maybe it was all she would ever have.

She'd take that chance. "I'm here. Tell me what you found out."

Cory had picked up the phone to call Serena four times, but she didn't have a clue what she would say so she'd disconnected each time before the call could go through.

She had to figure out a way to ignore the feelings she'd allowed to slip in over the course of the last several weeks. Her initial attraction to Serena's outer beauty had quickly deepened, and she knew she was in love, for real, for the first time in her life. But what she felt didn't— couldn't—matter. It was time to get her life back in order, and cutting ties to anything, anyone connected to the detour of the past couple of months was the best way to get back on track. She never should have slept with Serena. She'd taken advantage of her vulnerability, and she had to find a way to draw back, as gently and as quickly as she could.

She took a deep breath and punched in the numbers. Serena answered on the first ring and Cory winced at her anxious, "Hello."

"Serena, we need to talk." Why had she started with the calling card of bad breakups? That may be what this was, but she didn't have to be so damn obvious. She scrambled to cover. "I'm sorry I missed lunch today. A lot's happened."

"I know. Paul told me you got a call from the DA's office."

There it was. The perfect opening to tell Serena she was headed back to her old life, a life Serena didn't understand, wouldn't want to be a part of. She knew moving on would be more painful if she drew it out, but she wasn't ready to let go. Not just yet. "I'm taking a day to consider their offer, but basically, they're ready for me to come back. I have the work on Eric's case to thank for that. Alvarez, the new DA, is a big supporter of programs like the Justice Clinic. He thinks my work there will help smooth over any flack he'll get over bringing me back on board." Cory cringed as she listened to the playback in her head, and she rushed to assure Serena the work had meant more to her than a simple PR stunt. "Working on Eric's case gave me a fresh perspective. I think I'll be a better prosecutor for it." That didn't sound so great either. She needed to end this conversation before she said anymore truly stupid things.

Serena spoke up. "Cory, before you make any big decisions, I think there's something you should know. I asked Skye to look into the Nelson case, and you're not going to believe what she found out."

"You asked Skye to do what?" She was pretty sure she'd heard Serena correctly, but she couldn't quite process the words. Why would Serena have asked Skye to look at anything that wasn't related to her brother's case, let alone a closed case? Why would she have Skye look into *her* closed case?

"I'm sorry. I should've told you. It's just I felt you were holding something back. I was wrong. I think there's something you don't know, but you should, before you make any decisions about your future."

Serena's words were a blur, and all Cory could see was betrayal. Serena hadn't trusted her. She'd gotten Skye to dig into her past. Had Skye discovered she had taken the fall for Julie? Old news now, and it didn't matter anyway. She'd done the right thing by taking the blame. Julie had stayed in Alvarez's good graces, and she was getting her job back because of it. It had all worked out for the best, but the fact Serena hadn't accepted her version of what had happened stung. And the sting was the perfect catalyst to end what she never should have started in the first place.

"I don't want to hear whatever it is you have to say. I'm going back to work at the DA's office tomorrow. I wish you and your brother the best of luck."

"Hold on a minute. After what we shared last night, that's all you have to say?"

"I had a great time with you, but…" Cory knew the right words, but she wouldn't speak them. Instead, she stuck with safety. "But what happened between us was the result of circumstance, and nothing else. I don't regret what we shared, but it's time for both of us to go back to our respective worlds."

"Our respective worlds? You mean where you're the white knight prosecutor and I'm the sister of a convict? Damn you, Cory Lance. Last night meant something to me. No, that's not right. It meant everything to me. I knew you'd do anything, say anything to get what you wanted. I just made the mistake of thinking you wanted me. You want me gone? Consider it done."

"Serena, wait!" Cory shouted into the silence, but there was no response. Serena had disconnected the call, disconnected completely the connection they'd shared. She told herself it was what she wanted, but she knew it wasn't true.

❖

Cory strode through Sue Ellen's. She wanted a drink, but she'd wait until she'd finished what she came for. She needed to be sober for this little chat. She made a lap around the downstairs floor, and then headed upstairs. Skye was waiting on the upper balcony.

"Hey, Cory, what's up?"

"Don't play with me, Keaton."

"You're the one who wanted to meet at a bar in the middle of the day."

"If you had a real office, we could've met there."

"What the hell are you so pissed off about?"

Should've been an easy question to answer, but it stopped Cory cold. She was mad, for sure, but she hadn't paused to consider exactly why. Serena had hired Skye to look into how she'd handled a case. She loved Serena. Serena didn't trust her. She loved Serena. She'd sent Serena packing. Serena had barely protested. She loved Serena and Serena didn't love her. End of story.

So why had she stalked across town to take out her anger on Skye? She gave the most honest answer she could. "I don't know."

"I don't blame you for being pissed. If it was me, I'd want to strangle that bitch."

"Holy shit! You better back off."

"I can't believe you're defending her, even now. She never had your best interests at heart."

"Maybe not at first, but she tried to tell me what was going on and I didn't listen. I was just so mad that she'd asked you to look into it."

Skye's expression morphed from indignant to puzzled. "Wait a minute. I'm not sure we're talking about the same thing. Serena told you about Julie, right?"

"Julie?" It was Cory's turn to be puzzled. "What about her?"

"The Nelson case? Julie hid evidence. I told Serena I didn't think you knew anything about it. She agreed and insisted on telling you what I'd found out."

Cory slid into a seat as her confusion spun out of control. "She didn't tell me anything other than she asked you to look into the Nelson case. I didn't give her a chance to say anything else. Julie did what?"

Skye pulled a piece of paper from her jacket and handed it to Cory. "Read for yourself."

She skimmed the lines of the sworn affidavit signed by retired Dallas police detective, Russell McCoy. He was on the team that had investigated Nelson and had retired a few months after Nelson's conviction. She didn't need to read it all to get the gist. He'd personally handed over all the evidence the police had amassed in the Nelson case to the district attorney's office, including the taped statements and supplemental report that had never been turned over to the defense counsel.

"Maybe he just said all this to protect the police department."

"What's his motivation? You already took the fall. Besides, he has proof. He kept copies of his files. He has a copy of the signed receipt from the day he brought the evidence, and the missing items are clearly listed. Guess which assistant DA signed for the evidence?"

She didn't have to guess. She knew. She should've known it all along. "Doesn't matter anymore."

"What do you mean it doesn't matter? Julie Dalmar has her job while you work pro bono cases. Doesn't seem quite fair to me."

"Actually, I've been offered my job back."

"Well, that was sudden."

"Not really. My suspension is almost over. Julie promised she'd keep my job open."

"Of course she did. You kept quiet for her. She'd likely do anything for you."

"Wait a minute. I didn't know anything about this." Cory waved her hand at the affidavit. "I just thought one of us was likely to go down, and I'd suffer the least if I took the blame." Hadn't seemed like such a bad decision when she thought Julie had clean hands. Now, the events of the morning—the apology Julie had crafted for her to sign, Julie's clear attempts to suck up to the boss—hammered home the extent of Julie's betrayal.

And Serena. Serena had tried to tell her about Julie, and she'd accused her of betrayal. Serena, who'd been nothing but honest since they'd met. She'd shared her deepest secrets, trusted Cory with her most tender feelings. Yet, she'd chosen to place her loyalty, her future with Julie, who didn't deserve her, rather than Serena, whom she wasn't sure she deserved.

Time to right the wrongs.

"Skye, you willing to share what you found out, on a wider scale?" Skye may have left the force, but the force was strong. Detective Russell may have given a fellow former cop this info, but that didn't mean he or Skye was willing to go public.

"Russell doesn't care what we do with it. He's got proof he didn't do anything wrong. He's pretty pissed that Nelson got to walk because the DA's office fucked up. I made it clear to him you didn't know. You didn't know, right?"

Of course she had to ask. In her attempts to protect Julie, Cory had compromised her own reputation, personally and professionally. For once in her life, personal mattered most. She had to find Serena.

CHAPTER TWENTY-ONE

Y ou plan on working all night?"
Serena looked up from the files she'd spread all over the conference table. She'd been poring through the Rinson County DA's files on Eric's case for the last few hours, but so far, hadn't found anything helpful. Paul's eyes were kind, and she detected a hint of concern. "I keep thinking there must be something here. Otherwise, all the effort you've put into his case isn't worth it."

"Everything we've done was worth it. The truth is always worth fighting for, even if it isn't what you expect or want it to be."

"You really believe that, don't you?"

"Have to or I wouldn't be able to do this kind of work." He sat across from her. "Besides, we already know the police mishandled the investigation, or at the very least, did a slipshod job. At the risk of sounding cliché, where there's smoke, there's fire. All we have to do is find it."

Serena had been trying to do just that all evening. Paul had called to let her know that, thanks to Judge Fowler's sternly delivered discovery order, they'd been able to copy the files late that afternoon and could use some help sorting through the materials. He'd given her a quick lesson on what to look for, and she dove into the project, relieved to have something to take her mind off Cory.

But it didn't. Every page reminded her of Cory, and how she'd fought so hard to get this information, yet seemed so disinterested in seeing the case to conclusion. Instead, Cory seemed to prefer to ignore the fact she'd been betrayed by her lover, choosing to return to the office that had hung her out to dry.

Her lover. Julie. How could Cory choose Julie over her? Was it experience? She knew her own advances had been awkward, but she'd been convinced Cory had been aroused and satisfied.

Cory had left several messages in the last hour. All of them imploring her to call. *We need to talk. I need to explain.* She'd thought she might be falling in love, and after last night, she'd been convinced it was true. But if she called Cory back now and let her smooth over the rejection she'd delivered, she'd be just like her, accepting less when she knew she needed more. Cory may be able to settle, but now that she'd experienced what she could have when her heart and mind were open to the possibilities, she wasn't willing to do the same.

She'd call Cory back. Eventually. When her plans were set, when she was strong enough to resist the pull of attraction and resolute enough to wait for real love from someone who would love her back. She'd been convinced Cory was that person, and the realization that she wasn't was a hurt that would take time to heal.

In the meantime, Eric's looming execution date demanded all her attention. Paul was under the impression they could get a stay if they could find something in the boxes of evidence that raised an issue about Eric's innocence. "I figure if I keep looking, something will pop up. I've started an index of all the materials we received this afternoon." She handed him the detailed list she'd prepared. "I plan to compare it to the files we have to see what, if anything, was missing."

"Perfect. We can go over it in the morning. I'd stay and work with you, but today's my anniversary and I promised I'd be home at some point, while it's still today." He glanced at the clock on the wall, which had just ticked past eight p.m.

"I didn't know you were married." Serena felt silly at her own surprise. Of course, the people at the clinic had lives that didn't include working on cases.

"Indeed I am. Fourteen years. She's an attorney too. She works for a non-profit environmental organization, so she's more understanding than most. But on special occasions, we always make time for each other. I managed to send flowers today, which should keep me out of trouble, at least as long as I get home pretty quickly." He delivered the last comment with a grin and he handed her a key. "Stay as long as you want. Just lock up when you leave." He paused with his hand on the doorknob. "You know, you really can stay as long as you want. You're really good at this work. If you ever decide you want a job, let me know. I'm sure I can find a grant to keep you on."

Serena didn't have time to respond before he rushed out the door. Home to his wife. Home to celebration. Eventually, she'd go home too. To her steady, boring job. To her lonely apartment. To her solitary, passionless life. To hoping each day would bring distance so she could forget her feelings for Cory.

Paul's words echoed in her mind. *You're really good at this work. Stay as long as you want.* An idea began to form, but she couldn't focus on it right now. She picked up a file folder and spent the next hour meticulously reviewing the reports contained inside. The forensic lab had listed all the evidence it had received from both the police and the medical examiner. After she'd finished her list, she set the folder aside, but a nagging feeling caused her to pick it up again.

She combed through the pages several times. She'd seen these pages before. They were part of the chain of custody documents introduced at trial, but something was different about this set. Still grasping the lab documents in her hand, she walked down the hall to what used to be Cory's makeshift office, and located the boxes that contained the trial record.

She'd practically memorized the transcript of the trial, so it only took a moment to find what she was looking for. The lab technician who had testified for the state had been on the stand for the better part of a morning, as the prosecutor introduced evidence of the testing that had been done on the evidence in the case. Eric's fingerprints on Nancy's car, at her house. The blood spatter evidence at Nancy's house. Analysis of the weapon used in the crime. As she ticked off the items he'd testified about, she matched the reports offered into evidence against the ones in the folder they'd obtained from the DA's office.

Her hunch was right. The file from the DA's office contained a document that hadn't been introduced at trial. The medical examiner had done a rape kit complete with a vaginal swab and smear, pubic hair cuttings and combings. Based on the research she'd done, they'd had everything necessary to test for DNA, but nothing in either the trial record or in the DA's file suggested DNA testing had been done.

She could barely breathe. She'd struck gold. Hadn't she? In this day and age, there was absolutely no reason for the state not to test DNA evidence, especially when they planned to put a man to death. At the very least, the fact that these samples had been collected was information that should have been shared with the defense.

She picked up the phone, anxious to share her find, but put it back down again when she realized she had no one to share it with. She didn't have Paul's cell or home phone. Besides, he'd barely made it home in time to celebrate his anniversary. It was almost ten o'clock. There was nothing he could do with this information tonight. Still, she wanted, needed to tell someone, and she knew who that someone was.

She scrolled through the missed calls on her cell phone. Cory had called six times. The way their last conversation ended, Serena hadn't expected to hear from her again. She'd imagined they would both go back to their—what was it Cory had said? Respective worlds.

But Cory had called six times. And every time the phone had rung, she had been tempted to answer. More than tempted. She longed to answer. To tell Cory that she knew last night had been special for both of them and that she didn't understand why Cory wouldn't admit it. Only pride held her back.

Sitting alone, at the clinic, bursting with news, she craved a partner. Someone to share good times and bad. Someone she could trust, like she'd trusted Cory last night. Someone she loved and who made her feel loved in return. That Cory could evoke such strong emotions from her told her all she needed to know.

Pride wasn't going to get her what she wanted. She picked up the phone and dialed Cory's number.

❖

Cory peered over Serena's shoulder, distracted by the faint smell of her perfume. She'd rolled out of bed to answer her cell out of habit. She'd never expected Serena would call her this late, or even at all, after their earlier, harsh exchange. She hadn't asked any questions, only obeyed Serena's plea for her to come to the clinic. She arrived close to midnight, excited about the prospect of seeing Serena again and hoping for a chance to start over. Serena had met her at the door, bursting with news.

"See what I mean? They had DNA evidence, but they didn't even bother testing it."

Cory gently eased the papers from Serena's hand and studied them. When she was done, she set them down and motioned for Serena to take a seat. "You're right. This could be huge."

"Could be? Seems like it is huge."

"Most big rewards come from taking big risks. If we get the judge to order DNA testing and it comes back as Eric's, he will have absolutely no chance of winning his freedom."

"He said he didn't do it. I believe him. I thought you did too."

"I do. I really do. But what if he slept with Nancy, but didn't rape her? Maybe he didn't want anyone to know, so he omitted that information. No one will believe that he didn't kill her if his DNA shows up in a rape kit."

"He didn't do it. He said he didn't sleep with her, and I believe him." Serena's voice rose. "I never should've called you. I don't know what I was thinking."

Cory moved her chair closer and slid an arm over Serena's shoulders. "Hey, I'm only telling you what Paul or Greg would tell you. I wouldn't be a good advocate for your brother if I didn't think about all the angles.

"If you want to know what I really think, I'll tell you. I think Rick Smith knew he could win a conviction against Eric with the flimsy circumstantial evidence he had. He didn't want to risk testing the DNA, because if it didn't come back as Eric's, then he'd have a more complicated case. If the lab had tested the DNA, he wouldn't have been able to keep it out of evidence, and if the DNA belonged to someone else, the defense would've pointed to that person as the suspect the police should've arrested. Rick figured what he didn't know wouldn't hurt his case.

"That's what I think. But as Eric's lawyer, I have a duty to look at the overall strategy. The majority of DNA tests confirm guilt. I want to talk to Eric before we go any further with this because ultimately, it's his decision. My advice to him will be to have the material tested. I'm sure the clinic has a contact for an independent lab that can do the testing pro bono, or at least at a reduced charge. I'll call Paul right now. We should get a DNA testing motion ready to file first thing—"

Serena placed her fingers across her lips.

"What?" she mumbled.

"You sound like a defense lawyer. 'As Eric's lawyer,' 'My advice to him,' 'I'll call Paul.' Did you forget that you're going back to work at the DA's office tomorrow?"

She had. Totally and completely slipped her mind. When Serena called, she hadn't hesitated. She'd left her bed and driven to the clinic for two reasons. She was Eric's lawyer, and she wanted to see what Serena had found with her own eyes. But the primary reason she'd come running was because Serena had called, and it hadn't really mattered why. Serena had wanted her to be the one who shared the excitement of her find, hear what she'd discovered, offer advice. She cherished the role, but she wanted more.

"I don't really know what my future holds. At least not as far as my career goes. What Skye found out about Julie, really rocked my world. I don't know if I can go back to the job I had, knowing what I know now.

"But here's what I do know. Whatever my future holds, I want you to be a part of it. Do you think you could ever trust a prosecutor enough to give a relationship with one a go?" Cory held her breath while she waited for Serena's response.

A playful smile danced across Serena's face. "I don't really know any prosecutors. At least none who are currently employed. But I think I could definitely explore a relationship with a pro bono attorney who's currently between jobs.

"How about you? Do you think you could fall in love with a woman who quit her job and moved to another state to start over?"

"What? You quit your job?"

"Well, not yet, but I'm thinking about it. I need to start over too. I've spent my life never taking a chance on anything because I thought risks would always lead me down the wrong path. If I stuck to what was safe, I'd be happy. But I was never happy. Not until I took a chance with you. I love you, Cory Lance, and I want to give us a chance. You with me?"

Cory pulled Serena into her arms. "Like I said, big rewards come from taking big risks. I love you too. Let's be risky, together."

Chapter Twenty-two

One month later

Serena sat in the chair between Cory and Paul and leaned over to whisper in Cory's ear. "Are you sure it's okay for me to be up here?"

"Sure. I told the judge you're working as a paralegal for the clinic. He's fine with you sitting at counsel table."

"My official start date isn't until tomorrow."

"You know us lawyers. We're always putting a spin on the facts." Cory grinned and Serena smiled back. "Cut me some slack. This is my last official duty before I retire as a defense lawyer."

As Cory reviewed the papers in front of her, Serena leaned back in her chair and let the reality of her new life wash over her. She'd spent the last few weeks wrapping up her old job, her old apartment, and she was once again a resident of Texas. Her heart-to-heart with Don and Marion had included the revelation not only was she quitting her job and moving across the country, but she was in love. She still wasn't sure they'd adjusted to any of her announcements, but they were sitting in the courtroom to support her today, and she was confident they'd come around.

Cory had returned to the clinic to finish her work on Eric's case, but when today's hearing was over, she would go back to the Dallas County DA's office to head up the Conviction Integrity Unit. After Frank Alvarez learned what had really happened with the Nelson case, he'd fired Julie and convinced Cory she could do her best work as a prosecutor making sure zealous advocacy didn't mean cheating the other side. Cory relished the idea of getting another chance at her chosen career, but she'd been cautious when she'd broached the plan with Serena.

Cory had relayed the offer, then stated the obvious. "We'll be on opposite sides."

"If we're both looking for the truth, we'll always be on the same side."

"I think you know it's not always that simple."

"I do, but nothing worth having ever is. Do what you love. It'll make you happy and I want you to be happy."

"What did I ever do to deserve you?"

"You took a risk. We both did. And boy, did it sure pay off."

Whatever their future held, she was grateful Cory was sitting at the defense table today, even though Cory had assured her this hearing had been choreographed in advance and promised there would be no surprises. In a few minutes, the bailiffs would bring Eric to their table, dressed in the new suit Serena had purchased the day before. Then Judge Fowler would take the bench and make a show of reviewing the motions that had been filed in the case.

When the DNA results had confirmed that Dale Bolton, the witness who pointed the finger at Eric, had been the one who'd raped Nancy McGowan, the case against Eric fell apart. Bolton's jailhouse bragging, Wilkins's revised testimony, and the DNA were enough to grant Eric a new trial, but the Rinson County DA had already admitted defeat. Rick Smith had been suspended for failing to turn over the evidence about the rape kit, and Cory and Paul had persuaded the DA to join them in a motion to set aside Eric's conviction. The hearing that was about to take place was all for the cameras.

And there were a lot of them. Serena counted six news outlets among the crowd in the courtroom. She could understand all the media attention, but who were all the other folks filling the seats? Don and Marion sat in the first row, but she didn't recognize any of the other faces in the crowd. She asked Cory who grinned again.

"Paul wanted to pack the house since it's great PR for the clinic. I got Melinda to make all the first year associates at her firm come watch. The rest are students from the law school. It's good for them to see real justice in action."

Serena realized these events were usually populated by friends and family of the wrongfully convicted, not a room full of strangers. She'd told herself she wouldn't cry today, no matter what, but she felt tears begin to well and she was too choked up to talk.

Cory leaned close and asked, "You don't mind the crowd do you?"

She had to get a grip. The hearing hadn't even started. She cleared her throat. "Mind? No, I don't mind at all. Especially since no matter what you say about why these people are here, I know you wanted there to be a crowd for Eric's sake, not just so the clinic could get new donors." She dropped her voice to a soft whisper. "I love you more every day."

Before Cory could respond, the bailiff shouted, "All rise!" and the crowd lumbered to its feet. Judge Fowler took the bench. The rest was a blur. Moments later, Eric wrapped her up in a big bear hug and then everyone was hugging—lawyers, court personnel, students, strangers. The crowd flowed into the hall and posed for pictures in front of a hungry press corps before they adjourned to the clinic to celebrate with a catered barbeque dinner. A few hours passed before the crowd finally began to thin out, and Serena wandered through the halls looking for Cory.

She found her sitting at the folding table she'd used as a desk during her term at the clinic. "Hey, lover, what're you doing in here all by yourself?"

"I just wanted to clean up this space before I left. Did I miss anything?"

"Nope. All the food and beer are gone and most everyone's headed out. Paul arranged for Eric to have a hotel room. I invited him to come with us, but Paul suggested he might want to be by himself for the first few nights, to adjust. You about done?"

Cory pointed at the neat stack of documents on the edge of the table. "That's my final report on the case. I guess this chapter is closed. You ready to go home?"

"With you? Absolutely. There's no place I'd rather be."

THE END

About the Author

Carsen Taite works by day (and sometimes night) as a criminal defense attorney in Dallas, Texas. Her goal as an author is to spin plot lines as interesting as the cases she encounters in her practice. She is the author of six previously released novels, *truelesbianlove.com*, *It Should be a Crime* (a Lambda Literary Award finalist), *Do Not Disturb*, *Nothing but the Truth*, *The Best Defense*, and *Slingshot*. She is currently working on her eighth novel, *Battle Axe*, the second book in the Luca Bennett bounty hunter series. Learn more at www.carsentaite.com.

Books Available from Bold Strokes Books

Crossroads by Radclyffe. Dr. Hollis Monroe specializes in short-term relationships but when she meets pregnant mother-to-be Annie Colfax, fate brings them together at a crossroads that will change their lives forever. (978-1-60282-756-1)

Beyond Innocence by Carsen Taite. When a life is on the line, love has to wait. Doesn't it? (978-1-60282-757-8)

Heart Block by Melissa Brayden. Socialite Emory Owen and struggling single mom Sarah Matamoros are perfectly suited for each other but face a difficult time when trying to merge their contrasting worlds and the people in them. If love truly exists, can it find a way? (978-1-60282-758-5)

Pride and Joy by M.L. Rice. Perfect Bryce Montgomery is her parents' pride and joy, but when they discover that their daughter is a lesbian her world changes forever. (978-1-60282-759-2)

Timothy by Greg Herren. *Timothy* is a romantic suspense thriller from award-winning mystery writer Greg Herren set in the fabulous Hamptons. (978-1-60282-760-8)

In Stone: A Grotesque Faerie Tale by Jeremy Jordan King. A young New Yorker is rescued from a hate crime by a mysterious someone who turns out to be more of a *something*. (978-1-60282-761-5)

The Jesus Injection by Eric Andrews-Katz. Murderous statues, demented drag queens, political bombings, ex-gay ministries, espionage, and romance are all in a day's work for a top-secret agent. But the gloves are off when Agent Buck 98 comes up against The Jesus Injection. (978-1-60282-762-2)

Combustion by Daniel W. Kelly. Bearish detective Deck Waxer comes to the city of Kremfort Cove to investigate why the hottest men in town are bursting into flames in broad daylight. (978-1-60282-763-9)

Ladyfish by Andrea Bramhill. Finn's escape to the Florida Keys leads her straight into the arms of scuba diving instructor Oz as she fights for her freedom, their blossoming love…and her life! (978-1-60282-747-9)

Spanish Heart by Rachel Spangler. While on a mission to find herself in Spain, Ren Molson runs the risk of losing her heart to her tour guide, Lina Montero. (978-1-60282-748-6)

Love Match by Ali Vali. When Parker "Kong" King, the number one tennis player in the world, meets commercial pilot Captain Sydney Parish, sparks fly but not from attraction. They have the summer to see if they have a love match. (978-1-60282-749-3)

One Touch by L.T. Marie. A romance writer and a travel agent come together at their high school reunion, only to find out that the memory of that one touch never fades. (978-1-60282-750-9)

Night Shadows: Queer Horror edited by Greg Herren and J.M. Redmann. *Night Shadows* features delightfully wicked stories by some of the biggest names in queer publishing. (978-1-60282-751-6)

Secret Societies by William Holden. An outcast hustler, his unlikely "mother," his faithless lovers, and his religious persecutors—all in 1726. (978-1-60282-752-3)

The Raid by Lee Lynch. Before Stonewall, having a drink with friends or your girl could mean jail. Would these women and men still have family, a job, a place to live after…The Raid? (978-1-60282-753-0)

The You Know Who Girls: Freshman Year by Annameekee Hesik. As they begin freshman year, Abbey Brooks and her best friend, Kate, pinky swear they'll keep away from the lesbians in Gila High, but Abbey already suspects she's one of those you-know-who girls herself and slowly learns who her true friends really are. (978-1-60282-754-7)

Wyatt: Doc Holliday's Account of an Intimate Friendship by Dale Chase. Erotica writer Dale Chase takes the remarkable friendship between Wyatt Earp, upright lawman, and Doc Holliday, southern gentlemen turned gambler and killer, to an entirely new level: hot! (978-1-60282-755-4)

Month of Sundays by Yolanda Wallace. Love doesn't always happen overnight; sometimes it takes a month of Sundays. (978-1-60282-739-4)

Jacob's War by C.P. Rowlands. ATF Special Agent Allison Jacob's task force is in the middle of an all-out war, from the streets to the boardrooms of America. Small business owner Katie Blackburn is the latest victim who accidentally breaks it wide open but may break AJ's heart at the same time. (978-1-60282-740-0)

The Pyramid Waltz by Barbara Ann Wright. Princess Katya Nar Umbriel wants a perfect romance, but her Fiendish nature and duties to the crown mean she can never tell the truth—until she meets Starbride, a woman who gets to the heart of every secret, even if it will be the death of her. (978-1-60282-741-7)

The Secret of Othello by Sam Cameron. Florida teen detectives Steven and Denny risk their lives to search for a sunken NASA satellite—but under the waves, no one can hear you scream . . . (978-1-60282-742-4)

Dreaming of Her by Maggie Morton. Isa has begun to dream of the most amazing woman—a woman named Lilith with a gorgeous face, an amazing body, and the ability to turn Isa on like no other. But Lilith is just a dream...isn't she? (978-1-60282-847-6)

Andy Squared by Jennifer Lavoie. Andrew never thought anyone could come between him and his twin sister, Andrea...until Ryder rode into town. (978-1-60282-743-1)

Finding Bluefield by Elan Barnehama. Set in the backdrop of Virginia and New York and spanning the years 1960-1982, Finding Bluefield chronicles the lives of Nicky Stewart, Barbara Philips, and their son, Paul, as they struggle to define themselves as a family. (978-1-60282-744-8)

The Jetsetters by David-Matthew Barnes. As rock band The Jetsetters skyrocket from obscurity to super stardom, Justin Holt, a lonely barista, and Diego Delgado, the band's guitarist, fight with everything they have to stay together, despite the chaos and fame. (978-1-60282-745-5)

Strange Bedfellows by Rob Byrnes. Partners in life and crime, Grant Lambert and Chase LaMarca, are hired to make a politician's compromising photo disappear, but what should be an easy job quickly spins out of control. (978-1-60282-746-2)

Speed Demons by Gun Brooke. When NASCAR star Evangeline Marshall returns to the race track after a close brush with death, will famous photographer Blythe Pierce document her triumph and reciprocate her love—or will they succumb to their respective demons and fail? (978-1-60282-678-6)

Summoning Shadows: A Rosso Lussuria Vampire Novel by Winter Pennington. The Rosso Lussuria vampires face enemies both old and new, and to prevail they must call on even more strange alliances, unite as a clan, and draw on every weapon within their reach—but with a clan of vampires, that's easier said than done. (978-1-60282-679-3)

Sometime Yesterday by Yvonne Heidt. When Natalie Chambers learns her Victorian house is haunted by a pair of lovers and a Dark Man, can she and her lover Van Easton solve the mystery that will set the ghosts free and banish the evil presence in the house? Or will they have to run to survive as well? (978-1-60282-680-9)

Into the Flames by Mel Bossa. In order to save one of his patients, psychiatrist Jamie Scarborough will have to confront his own monsters—including those he unknowingly helped create. (978-1-60282-681-6)

Coming Attractions: Author's Edition by Bobbi Marolt. For Helen Townsend, chasing turns to caring, and caring turns to loving, but will love take five steps back and turn to leaving? (978-1-60282-732-5)

OMGqueer, edited by Radclyffe and Katherine E. Lynch. Through stories imagined and told by youth across America, this anthology provides a snapshot of queerness at the dawn of the new millennium. (978-1-60282-682-3)

Oath of Honor by Radclyffe. A First Responders novel. First do no harm…First Physician of the United States Wes Masters discovers that being the president's doctor demands more than brains and personal sacrifice—especially when politics is the order of the day. (978-1-60282-671-7)

A Question of Ghosts by Cate Culpepper. Becca Healy hopes Dr. Joanne Call can help her learn if her mother really committed suicide—but she's not sure she can handle her mother's ghost, a decades-old mystery, and lusting after the difficult Dr. Call without some serious chocolate consumption. (978-1-60282-672-4)